KASTERA & KLAU

Part I:
The Beginning of Future Hope

PAUL W. GIBBS

SonWright Books

Kastera & Klau
Part 1: The Beginning of Future Hope

v4.0

This is a work of fiction. Names, characters, businesses, places, events, locales, and incidents are either the products of the author's imagination or used in a fictitious manner. Any resemblance to actual persons, living or dead, or actual events is purely coincidental.

The opinions expressed in this manuscript are solely the opinions of the author and do not represent the opinions or thoughts of the publisher. The author has represented and warranted full ownership and/or legal right to publish all the materials in this book.

SonWright Books

ISBN: 979-8-218-94771-2

Library of Congress Control Number: 2026909494

Cover Illustration by Victor Guiza © 2026 Paul W. Gibbs.

PRINTED IN THE UNITED STATES OF AMERICA

Books by Paul W. Gibbs

Nyght & Daie

Part 1:
The Girl and Hanna

Part 2:
Nyght Tyme

Part 3:
When Nyght and Daie Collide

Visit paul-w-gibbs.com

GLOSSARY

Sun-cycle: One day

Moon-cycle: One month

Sun-mark/mark: One hour

Moon-mark: One week

Season: One year

Land-mark: One mile

Blessed Day: Birthday

Handbreadth: Three inches

Kingdom-land: Country

NAME PRONUNCIATION/DERIVATION

Eirene- Ai-reen (Greek word for Peace. Pronounced as *Irene, eye-reen*)

Kastera- Kas-tehr-uh (Derived from the Icelandic word Kastara for Caster)

Keia- Kay-uh (English name. First part is pronounced like *Say*)

KhoraThraks- Kor-uh-Thraxs (Khora ancient Greek word for land. Thraks is derived from Thrakon/ Thrakena Greek forms for dragon. Khora is pronounced like *ora* beginning with a *K*. *Thraks* is pronounced like *Sack* except with a *THR* instead of an *S* and ending in *ax, Kora-Thrax)*

Klau- Claw (Frisian/German/Dutch word for Claw)

Kord- Cord (Derived from English name Cord)

MiteraThrakena- My-tehr-uh-Thrak-ee-nah (Derived from Mitera-Greek for mother/Thrakena-ancient Greek for dragon, feminine. The first part of Thrakena, *Thrak,* is pronounced like *Sack* except with a *THR* instead of an *S.* The second part is pronounced like *Key.* The third part is pronounced as *nah, Thrak-ee-nah*)

NovoVida- Noh-voh-Vee-duh (Derived from the words New Life-Spanish/Portuguese)

PateraThrakon- Pah-tehr-uh-Thrak-aan (Derived from Patera-Greek for father/Thrakon-ancient Greek for dragon, masculine. The first part of Thrakon, *Thrak,* is pronounced like *Sack* except with a *THR* instead of an *S.* The second part is pronounced as *aan, Thrak-aan*)

X'Jahan- Sha-hahn (Origin Unknown)

ONE

A better life. So many hope for it. So many pray for it. So many work for it. So few ever find it. Yet even those who may fail never give up trying. Why? Why is it that so many people seek a better life, and before they find it, their life is taken away?

Is it because of how they saw their parents live and decided that they wanted their own life to be something more? Maybe they are not happy with the life they are living and decide that the only way to be happy is to seek a better one. So, is happiness a factor?

Maybe it is the parents who seek a better life so their children will not have a life as difficult as their own. Perhaps that is a way parents show their love for their children. So the question is, what will a parent do to make a better life for their children? That answer is quite simple. Almost anything.

The opportunity for Lieutenant Ackers to provide a better life for his son was presented to him by the king of NovoVida. A kingdom-land that is only a little over three hundred seasons old and has much land that has not been settled. Out of the vast amount, not even half of the land has been established to make way for new villages, towns, or cities.

Over the many seasons, since settlers began to arrive from the other side of Eirene, the current king, along with the previous ones, began claiming the land where the settlers first arrived by ship, and since then, they have continued to develop the kingdom-land. Farther and farther into the territory, they would establish a new village. Once that village grew to a certain population, it would be considered a town. When the population increased to a certain level, it would be considered a city. This has been the way for over three hundred seasons, and it has worked. The kingdom-land of NovoVida was growing.

Some decided to make their own way in the world, and a few villages or towns were established because people wanted a better life and did not wait for the king to provide it for them. Groups of families would set out on their own, and when they believed they had found the place that was right for them to settle down, they would begin a new life, hoping for a better one. Some of those groups were successful, and over time, they became a village, and some became towns, and even some became cities. However, some never succeeded in finding a better life.

Those who chose to go off on their own did so without the king's protection. They were on their own, and in seeking a better life, they ended up losing theirs. One reason for their demise was because of Mountain Raiders; men and women who live in the mountains, and for some reason, unknown to anyone, have become savages. They would raid villages that did not have the protection of the king's military and take what they needed to survive. One of those items was children under the age of ten seasons. They needed them to increase their numbers. Everyone knew that those children would never see a better life.

With growth, there is always a risk.

It was time for the king to establish a new region, and like the kings before him, he started with a scouting party. They would seek out a suitable location for development. Once an area was decided upon, the king would send military troops to build an outpost. Once that was complete, he would send what was needed to make a village, families.

It was the possibility of a better life that many would accept the king's offer. When a soldier agreed to be part of the kingdom's expansion, they would be promoted by one rank. With that promotion would come an increase in wages. With the increase in wages, the possibility of a better life would be available. The king's offer only applied to those who had families, and that was how the new villages would begin. The soldier would take their family to the outpost, where they would establish a village. Soldiers do not make a village; families do.

Lieutenant Ackers had been traveling with his caravan for over two moon-cycles. As the highest-ranking officer, he was the one in charge, and it was his responsibility to ensure the safety of everyone. His family was part of the caravan; his wife of ten seasons and his son who was seven seasons. Along with them, seven other families had joined in the venture, hoping to find a better life.

There was a total of fifty-nine people. Thirty of those were low-ranking soldiers who would be stationed at the outpost temporarily. They would assist those who would be remaining and calling the new place their home. Once dwellings were built for the newcomers and the outpost was made more secure, those thirty soldiers would return to the military outpost they came from. These soldiers accepted the assignment because when they returned to where they were originally stationed, they would be promoted by one rank, and with that came an increase in wages. With that came a better life.

Twenty-nine people were part of the seven different families. Like Lieutenant Ackers, five other soldiers brought their wives and children. Among those families, one soldier, along with his wife, brought all his children who totaled five. The other members of the party would joke about how that soldier had brought his own army.

Another soldier had his wife with him but did not have any children. He did bring his parents along in hopes that in the last few seasons they had remaining, they would have a better life. With that, the soldier was hoping that not long after they arrived at the outpost, his parents would be able to see their first grandchild. Any parent would feel that their life was complete when they saw the child they brought into the world and raised, have a child of their own.

Lieutenant Ackers rode on his horse next to the lead wagon. A soldier drove the wagon, and in it were two other soldiers who were all part of the thirty. Along with the lead wagon, five other wagons had four soldiers in them as well. All six of these wagons carried supplies that the outpost would need. The other seven wagons were for the families that were part of the convoy and their belongings. These wagons were driven by one of the thirty soldiers as well. That freed up the soldiers who brought their families to ride their own horses beside the caravan.

The journey had been an uneventful one. The only entry, which was somewhat unusual, Lieutenant Ackers had written in his daily journal, was that on one day, just as the caravan started traveling, a strange event happened concerning the sun.

The caravan had broken camp before the first rays of the sun had crossed the treetops. As the wagons began to start their daily trek, the sun rose suddenly into the sky to the point where it would have been if it were midday. The incident did not last long, and after a few moments, the sun had returned to the point in the sky where it was supposed to be. Lieutenant Ackers knew that it was a peculiar event, and he made sure that he immediately documented it in his journal so that it would be part of his report on the journey of the caravan.

Afterward, he did not think any more about what had happened that morning. It had no direct effect on his responsibility of overseeing the safety of the caravan, which was his main concern.

Now and then, Lieutenant Ackers would ride a circuit around the caravan to ensure that there were no problems. He had done this every day since they had begun their journey, and fortunately, he never had a problem to deal with. The worst thing that had happened was that one of the children kept getting sick from riding in the back of the wagon. After a couple of sun-cycles, the child became used to the moving wagon, and he finally stopped vomiting.

During his inspection of the caravan, Lieutenant Ackers would always make sure that he stopped by the wagon where his wife and son were riding inside. It was not just to check up on them; he did that with all the families, but when it came to his own, seeing them brought him joy, knowing that they were going to be making a better life together. They did not deceive themselves, and neither did any of the other families. Everyone knew that starting a new village would not be easy, and there would be times when they would wonder if they had made the right decision, but there were risks in life, no matter where you lived.

Lieutenant Ackers had taken over the driving of the wagon that his wife and son were riding in. He did occasionally, so that he could spend time with them, as well as taking a break from being on his horse the whole time they were traveling. He also allowed the other soldiers on horseback to do the same. He knew that for them, as it was for him, family was the most important thing they had.

He loved his wife. They had been married for ten seasons, and it was just over seven seasons that his wife had given birth to his son. One of the things that brought a smile to his face was seeing how much his son was enjoying the journey they were on. His son would ask him questions about what it would be like to live in a new village. Most of the answers his father gave him would be whatever Lieutenant Ackers believed in his own mind. He believed that even though there may be some challenging times, he, along with his wife and son, would always find a way to ensure that the better life they were hoping for would be there waiting for them.

As much as Lieutenant Ackers wanted to spend the entire journey with his wife and son, he had a job to do. After he had given them both just some of the attention that he wanted to give them, he had to return to his duties as the leader of the caravan. He would give his wife a kiss and pat his son on his head, then once again take his place on his horse and be the one responsible for everyone in the caravan.

He loved his wife and son, but he knew that others were depending on him as well.

Two sun-cycles had passed since the incident with the sun rising into the sky, faster than it normally would. The caravan had started traveling at its usual time and pace, knowing that in a few sun-cycles, they would reach the outpost that they would be calling home.

Lieutenant Ackers was riding at the head of the caravan; it had been about two sun-marks since they had been on the road, so he decided to make a circuit to make sure that everything and everyone were okay.

He passed the wagon his wife and son were riding in, and even though he wanted to stop and talk with them, he had a job to do. As he was passing it, he saw that his son had taken up his usual spot next to the soldier who was driving the wagon. When they had begun the journey, his son decided that sitting next to the soldier was where he was going to be. Most of the time, talking to the soldier and asking him questions. Lieutenant Ackers had told his son not to be a bother to the soldier and allow him to concentrate on his duties. The soldier said that his son was making sure that the soldier did not get lost and was keeping an eye out for any dips in the road that would jolt the wagon and make the ride for his mother uncomfortable. They all laughed, and afterward, the lieutenant just allowed the soldier and his son to do as they pleased, thinking that if his son spent time with the soldier, maybe one day, he would take after his father and join the military as well. That thought alone brought a smile to Lieutenant Ackers' face.

The day was no different, and as he passed the wagon with his wife and son, Lieutenant Ackers nodded to the soldier driving the wagon, who nodded back to let him know that everything was well with his family.

The lieutenant continued with his rounds, and when he was almost at the end of the caravan, he heard a noise, and at first, he did not know what to make of it. It was only when he heard the screams of the people in the wagons that he realized what was happening.

More than one of the soldiers on horseback yelled out the words that brought fear to the hearts of anyone who heard them, "Mountain Raiders!"

It is difficult being a soldier, especially one who is responsible, not just for the soldiers under your command, but for civilians as well, and when two of those civilians are your own family, the question of responsibility can weigh heavily on a person's thoughts.

For a moment, he was not Lieutenant Ackers, he was only Taron Ackers. He had a wife and a son who were in danger, and their safety was the only thing he was responsible for. The thought did not last long, and Lieutenant Ackers knew that he was responsible for every man, woman, and child that was part of the caravan.

"Soldiers, draw your weapons and protect the civilians!" Lieutenant Ackers yelled as he drew his own sword and circled to the other side of the caravan. When he made it there, he saw that the soldiers were already out of the wagons and had set upon the Mountain Raiders.

TWO

The lieutenant had joined the king's military when he was eighteen seasons old, and he had been trained in combat. The reason he was a lieutenant was because he came from a noble family. When he accepted the assignment to be the leader of the caravan, he went from being a second lieutenant to a first lieutenant. With the promotion came more wages and more responsibility. No one told him that it would come with more regret.

There was a total of fifty-nine people in the caravan. Thirty-seven were part of the military. The remaining twenty-two were the family members of the seven military men who volunteered for the journey. Out of the twenty-two, there were the seven wives of the seven men; that left a remaining fifteen civilians. Out of those fifteen, two of them were the parents of one of the seven soldiers. That meant that the last thirteen individuals were the children of the seven military men and their wives.

Lieutenant Ackers did not intentionally calculate all those numbers the moment he saw the horde of Mountain Raiders. In fact, if it were up to him, he would never have even thought about the number of people, but he could not stop himself since one of those individuals was his son.

Mountain Raiders came to take what they needed to survive. Very seldom would they attack a caravan, seldom, but there were exceptions. Caravans, far into the unsettled wilderness, were not common, so the Raiders would search for a village or a small town that had no military protection. Even if the village had walls surrounding it, the Raiders would be able to lay siege to it and take what they wanted. Any village with a military presence would more than likely be able to fight off the Raiders, so they would not take the risk of losing some or all their male fighters. They needed them to survive in the harsh environment of the mountains.

On this day, fortune was with the Raiders, not with the caravan. Lieutenant Ackers knew they were at a disadvantage when he saw that the numbers of the Raiders were greater than not only the numbers of the soldiers, but the number of all the people in the caravan combined. There were fifty-nine who started the journey, but there were fewer now since the Raiders began their attack, and even though the soldiers were able to kill some of the Raiders, their numbers were too great for what little damage the soldiers were doing.

Lieutenant Ackers stayed on his horse and rode into the fight, swinging his sword at any Raider that came within his reach. He was able to take down five of them before his horse fell from an attack. The lieutenant had enough awareness to jump away from his horse as it was falling so that he would not be trapped under it. As soon as he hit the ground, he was back on his feet and ready to fight, not just for his life, but for all the lives he was responsible for, including his wife and son.

He was a soldier. He had the responsibility to protect all those under his charge. He did the best he could, but no matter how much of a soldier a person is, when they are a parent, the instincts of a parent to protect their child will take over. Maybe that is why he was able to kill every Mountain Raider that he brought his sword upon. He was trained in combat, yet he was not the best with the sword, but on this day, at this moment, no one in the entire world would have been able to stop Lieutenant Ackers from doing what his instincts were telling him to do, and that was to make his way to his wife and son.

He did not stop fighting, but as he continued to move, he saw glimpses of the surrounding conflict. Some of his soldiers were still on their feet, fighting to stay alive and fighting to protect the civilians. Some of the soldiers were lying on the ground, never to stand again. He saw one soldier, or at first, he saw the body of the soldier. It was not until he slightly looked to the left that he saw the head of the soldier lying an arm's length away from the body.

Lieutenant Ackers continued to fight, continued to move toward the front of the caravan. When he reached the sixth wagon from the back of the caravan, he saw two more bodies who were civilians. They were the parents of one of the soldiers. They had accompanied their son and his wife to make a new life for all of them. They were hoping to see the birth of their first grandchild; that was no longer a possibility.

The next wagon in line belonged to the soldier and his wife who had five children. Lieutenant Ackers continued to fight, but still looked around to see if any of the children were alive. What he saw was the two eldest children, a boy and a girl, lying on the ground. Both of their eyes were open. The looks on their faces were a mixture of fear and unbelief, as if the last thoughts they had were how something like this could happen to them. As hurtful as seeing those two children lying in the dirt made him feel, it was not seeing the other three children that hurt him even more, and in doing so, he increased his ferocity in fighting the Mountain Raiders.

Once again, he calculated without even knowing what he was doing. Two more wagons to go before he reached the one with his wife and son. He was a soldier, and he continued to act as one. He fought as hard as he could to protect the ones under his charge, while at the same time, he fought as a parent wanting to reach his family, to make sure they are safe.

When he finally reached the wagon with his wife and son, he fought off two more of the Raiders. Now, his rage was so great that he killed one with a single slice to the throat, and the other he stabbed straight in the heart. Before the second body hit the ground, he spun around and looked at the wagon. Someone, more than likely the Mountain Raiders, had released the horses. That was either to make sure that no one could use the wagon to escape or so that the horses could be taken back with them when the Raiders finished what they started.

He did not call out for his wife and son; he did not have to. From where he was standing, he could see them both, taking cover under the wagon. Neither one of them was moving. His son was short enough so that he could sit under the wagon, which was the position he was in, holding his mother. If it were any normal day, someone would think that she was sleeping and just lying her head on her son's lap. That was not the circumstance that was occurring. Lieutenant Ackers knew that his wife was no longer with him or his son. His son, however, was still alive, and what was even more important was that he was still there.

Mountain Raiders will attack a village to take what they need to survive. Food, cattle, horses, wood, and anything that they can carry back with them. That included children ten seasons or younger. The fate of any child that was taken by the Raiders was worse than any horror a parent would dread to see their child go through. The children's past life was beaten out of them, and that was one of the ways the Raiders increased their numbers. No parent would want their child to suffer in such a manner, and many parents would rather see their child dead before they would be so harshly treated.

When Lieutenant Ackers saw two of the five children, belonging to the soldier, dead on the ground, he thanked the Creator that the children had not been taken by the Raiders, and had died where they were. Most would think that was an awful prayer, but the three children the lieutenant did not see would be suffering a worse fate. A fate he did not want his son to go through.

The battle was lost. Lieutenant Ackers knew what the outcome would be the moment he saw how many Raiders had attacked the caravan. He did everything he could, but it was not possible to save everyone. He saw his wife dead, not even having the chance to say goodbye to her. That was one of the reasons he fought so hard to reach the wagon with his family.

He now had his son to deal with, the son he loved with all his heart. The son, whom he thought would have a better life once they reached their destination. The son, whom he thought would one day follow in his father's footsteps and join the military. The son, whom he could not let the Mountain Raiders take alive, because no parent would want their child to suffer.

He pulled out the dagger that he had sheathed on his left hip. He had not used it throughout the fight with the Raiders because he wanted to make sure he did not lose it if he was able to make it to the wagon and his family. Now, he was going to put the dagger to use. Was he a coward? Many would think so, but this was his son, and he loved him more than life itself. A coward would not have the courage to do what he was about to do. The Raiders would not just destroy the body of his son, they would destroy his mind and his spirit, and once they were done, his son, the son that he knows and loves, would no longer exist.

He walked over and knelt so that he could see under the wagon. This was the perfect time for one of the Raiders to come up behind him and kill him. They could take his life before he finished what he was planning to do. Part of him wanted just that, but he knew that if he did not go through with his intention, his son would suffer an even worse fate. Not a single Raider attacked him. Was this the Creator's way of letting him know that what he was planning was the right thing to do? It would free his son, and in a moment afterward, he knew that a Raider would take his life as well. Then he, his wife, and his son would all be together.

That was his plan. To take the life of his son so that he would not have to suffer. He had his dagger in his right hand, so all he had to do was take hold of his son and either slice the dagger across his throat or force the dagger into his heart. Afterward, he could use the same dagger and take his own life.

That would be the more honorable thing to do. If he had to kill his son, he would kill himself as well.

He positioned himself so that he was under the wagon and closer to his son. Lieutenant Ackers could see in his mind everything he had to do to free his son and himself. It was at the last moment, before he reached for his son to force the dagger into his chest, that instead, he grabbed the right hand of his son. He then placed the dagger in his hand and said his last words to him, "I love you. Run." He then turned, crawled out from under the wagon, picked up his sword, and once again fought the Mountain Raiders.

He could not do it. He loved his son and did not want to see him suffer at the hands of the Raiders, but there was nothing in the world that could make him take the life of his own son. Maybe he was a coward. If he were not, maybe he would have been able to go through with what he had planned. He did not, and his thought was that his son's life was now in the hands of the Creator. All he knew was that he would fight to his last breath to give his son a chance to escape, and he continued to fight even harder when he got a glimpse of the view under the wagon, and all he saw was the body of his wife.

Would his son escape and live? He would never know. All he knew was that he had given his son a chance, and maybe that was all he needed. That was the last thought Lieutenant Ackers had before he fell to the ground from being struck in the head by a

Mountain Raider's weapon. He saw the body of his wife, and he smiled because he did not see his son.

Generations had passed, and X'Jahan was doing the task his father had given him. What his grandfather had given to his father, and what had been passed to every son in his family.

"My liege, we have made our way to the inner chamber," a man of no significance spoke.

X'Jahan nodded to the man for him to lead the way.

They continued to walk down the tunnel that had taken generations to dig out. Now, during his lifetime, X'Jahan was the one who would finish what so many of his forefathers had started and worked toward their entire lives.

X'Jahan knew that it was his destiny and was even given a sign that his lifelong dream, the same dream as his ancestors, would be seen in his lifetime. A few sun-cycles ago, the sun rose into the sky to the midpoint as soon as it had entered the morning sky. It lasted only a short while, but X'Jahan took it as a sign that what he had waited so long for would soon be achieved. Now, his followers had not only found the great hall, located deep underground, but had cleared the way to enter it.

It took them over four sun-cycles to reach the entrance to the great hall once the passageway had been discovered. There were many standing at it, yet no one would dare be the first to enter the sacred chamber; that honor was for their master. He would be the first to set his eyes on what was buried so long ago.

X'Jahan did not pay any attention to those who were waiting for what was to happen next. They were nothing more than followers of their calling, and like him, they were mere tools. Yes, X'Jahan did not deny the fact that he was nothing but a tool to be used for the one purpose for which all those present lived.

When he reached the opening, X'Jahan grabbed a torch out of the hands of one of the workers and entered the chamber alone. The light from the torch was enough to see that the chamber was not empty. In fact, what was inside was exactly what X'Jahan had expected to be there.

They would need more torches to provide enough light for the workers to continue with their task. It was not because he was concerned about the workers, which brought him to the conclusion about needing more light; it was the fact that the workers had a task to do, and for them to be more efficient, more light would be needed.

"Taskmaster," X'Jahan yelled without taking his eyes off the contents of the chamber. He did not even look away when the taskmaster came up behind him three steps away and to the right.

"Yes, my liege," the taskmaster said with his head bowed and eyes on the floor to show respect for the one he followed.

X'Jahan continued to gaze at what was before him, "You know what needs to be done. Make it so."

"Yes, my liege."

X'Jahan heard the taskmaster's response and knew that the man would continue to succeed in what was required of him. If he did not, there was always someone else ready to become the next taskmaster. Since X'Jahan had taken over the task given to him by his father, just before he passed away, there had been five other taskmasters. With every new one, they knew the fate if they failed in performing their task to the expectations of their master.

X'Jahan took one last look at the sight before him, then turned and walked out of the chamber. His job was to ensure that the task given to him and his father before him was completed. Others would do the menial labor. That was what they were for.

X'Jahan knew that there was still much to be done, but he would wait and be patient. Generations of his family have passed since the work began, but he would be the one to complete the task, and when it was finished, there would be greater rewards for him.

THREE

When Kord heard the words, he opened his eyes and looked around. All he saw were the same trees he saw before he fell asleep last night. He looked around one more time, but only with his eyes; he was too frightened to move, just in case there were still Mountain Raiders in the forest searching for him.

"I love you. Run." Those words he would never forget, because they were the last words his father had spoken to him. With that thought, he slowly lowered his head back onto his knees, which he had pulled up to his chest. He did not know when he had stopped running, but it was well into the night. At some point, he had just stopped, sat down on the ground, and taken up the position he was now in, trying to make his body seem as small as possible to avoid being seen.

He closed his eyes, and he thought that he would try to get some more sleep. He was tired, worn out, and the weight in his heart made him want to stay where he was for the rest of his life, never to move. *"I love you. Run."* Even though the thoughts were in his head again, to him it seemed as if he heard them in his ears; the voice of his father telling him what to do. "I can't, Father. I can't run anymore," he said, not to himself but to his father. Even though he was not there, Kord talked to his father as if he were, but kept his voice to a whisper, just in case there were others in the woods.

He was only seven seasons old, but he knew all about Mountain Raiders. Both his mother and father had told him about the humans who lived in the mountains that would come down and attack villages and pillage everything they could to take back with them. His parents even explained to him about what the Raiders did with the children they would capture. Yes, they did this to frighten Kord, but all parents who lived in or near the wilderness told their children about the dangers of the Mountain Raiders; they needed to be prepared for what might happen.

Kord's mother would tell him the stories, but she would always finish them with the same ending. "We don't have to worry about the Mountain Raiders, because your father will always be there to protect us." After what had happened, he realized that, as much as his mother believed what she had said, she was wrong.

When the Mountain Raiders first attacked, Kord was sitting with the soldier on the driving bench. As soon as they heard the roar of the Raiders and the call from Kord's father to draw their weapons, the soldier jumped down off the wagon and took his position to defend Kord and his mother. Kord thought that what he was seeing was the bravery of what a soldier in the King's Army should be. Unfortunately, the soldier was young and inexperienced when it came to fighting, and the Mountain Raider who was coming for the soldier was a warrior, and even though he did not seem any older than the soldier, he was trained to do what the Mountain Raiders did best, which is to fight and kill.

The soldier fell to the ground, only able to block two of the Raider's attacks. The third struck the soldier on the head. The weapon appeared to Kord to be a stone attached to a wooden stick held together by rope. The weapon was crude, but with it being wielded by the warrior, it was more effective than the fancy sword the soldier carried. Once the soldier was on the ground, possibly already dead from the attack, the Raider hit him once more on the head with the crude weapon. Kord knew at that point that the soldier would not be getting back up.

When a child is scared, their first response is to seek out their parents. Kord was no different, and after he saw the death of the soldier, he jumped into the back of the wagon where his mother was. "Mother!" he yelled to her and was about to tell her what he saw, but she reached out and placed her hand over his mouth. He took this to mean that he was to remain quiet, and he was going to, but his mother still did not remove her hand.

"Listen to me, Kord. You must do exactly what I tell you to do." His mother removed her hand and frantically began looking around in the back of the wagon. When she had found what she was looking for, Kord saw that she had one of her cooking knives in her hand. She then moved inside the wagon to the side that was opposite to the direction the Mountain Raiders had come from. She then pushed the knife into the canvas of the cover that was over the wagon and began to cut a hole in it. When she was finished, she had a hole made just big enough for them to slip through.

She turned around and took hold of Kord by his shoulders, then told him what they were going to do. "I will go first, and I want you to follow me. Once outside, we are going to run for the woods and hide there until your father comes for us. Do you understand?"

Kord nodded his head to let his mother know that he knew what she wanted him to do. The look on her face told him that even she did not believe that his father was going to arrive in time to save them.

"I will climb down first, then I will help you down, and then we will run to the woods. Are you ready?" she asked, and Kord nodded again to let her know that he was.

His mother looked to her right and grabbed one of the waterskins they kept in the back of the wagon. It had a leather strap attached to it, and she placed it over his head. "You keep hold of that; we are going to need it." Even Kord knew that water is the most important thing a person needs to survive, and since his mother took the time to make sure they had some, Kord knew that survival was what his mother was trying to do.

Once she had placed the waterskin over his shoulder, she gave him a kiss on the top of his head, then leaned back to look directly into his eyes, "Are you ready?" Kord nodded again to let her know that he was. Somehow, maybe it was his mother's way of trying to comfort him, but she smiled at him and said, "I love you," then turned away to face the opening in the wagon cover. Kord did not see her face, but he had a feeling that the smile was no longer there.

Kord's mother slowly stuck her head through the opening and looked to the left and right. The Mountain Raiders had attacked the caravan from the other side of the wagon. The fighting was taking place there, so she decided to make their escape in the opposite direction. She did not see any of the Raiders, so she looked straight in front of her and saw the woods. If they could make it into the trees, they would be able to hide from the Raiders. She had no plans as to what to do afterward; the first part was going to be difficult enough, so she concentrated on the task at hand and not the future.

Her thoughts were to keep her son safe. She knew that her husband was going to do everything he could to save her and their son. She only had to find a way to keep them alive until he came for them. Even though she knew that was more than likely not going to happen. She was the wife of a military soldier, and she knew that the ones who attacked them were vicious humans whose only desire was to kill and pillage. She also knew that since her son was only seven seasons old, they would take him back with them and make him just like them. That thought frightened her even more than her own death.

When she was sure that none of the fighting was taking place on her side of the wagon, she climbed through the opening and stood outside. She took one more look around and still did not see any of the attackers. She then turned around and stretched her arms into the opening to help Kord through and lower him to the ground. She had hold of his hands, but suddenly she was struck on the side of her head with something. She did not know what had hit her, nor did she even think about it. She was still holding onto her son's hands, and that was the only reason she did not fall to the ground immediately. He had such a tight grip on her hands that he was the one who was supporting her to remain standing.

In the wagon, Kord had barely seen what had happened. The opening was not big, and his mother was standing in front of him. When she had reached into the wagon to help him to the ground, he had taken hold of her hands, and just when he was about to go through the opening, he saw, just for a brief moment, something striking the side of his mother's head. He then saw blood running down the side of her face from the wound she had received.

Neither of them knew it, but at some point, a Raider had taken one of the horses from a soldier, after the Raider had removed the soldier from the saddle and chopped off his head. The Raider climbed onto the horse and rode up and down the caravan, killing as many of the people as he could. When he reached the front of the caravan, he circled around to the other side, and to his delight, he saw a woman had climbed out of one of the wagons and was facing it. The Raider provoked the horse into a run, and since her focus was on what was in front of her, she did not see him.

As he rode up to her and as he passed, he struck her on the side of her head with the wooden club that he used as a weapon. The Raider did not stop to see if she was dead or alive. He knew from past attacks that the force from the blow was powerful enough that if she did not die when he had struck her, she would be dead at any moment. She was just one dead body; she just did not know it yet, so the Raider did not want to waste his time with her. The main fight was on the other side of the wagon, and that is where he raced toward.

The weight of his mother's dead body was too much for Kord. As much as he wanted to hold onto her, he lost his grip on her hands, and she fell to the ground. Kord did not hesitate to jump through the opening, and when he saw his mother lying there, he bent down to call her, but somehow, he knew that she would not answer him.

He did not cry. He lost his mother and knew that he would never hear her call his name again. He would never hear her laugh; he would never see her smile. He would never have his mother in his life ever again.

Kord climbed under the wagon and pulled his mother's body along with him. He was now sitting on his knees with his legs under him and had his mother's head in his lap. The view in front of him was nothing but the legs of the people who were still fighting and the bodies of those who had died. A couple of those were the bodies of the Mountain Raiders, but the majority of them belonged to the ones who traveled with the caravan; soldiers and civilians.

When they had started their journey, Kord thought that it was going to be the most exciting thing that he had ever done in his life. What more could a boy of seven seasons ask for than to go on an adventure? He would be with his mother and father, and they would travel to a new place and start a new life.

When he was old enough, Kord had already decided to join the King's Army, just like his father. He would become a soldier and protect those who needed protection. When he was five, Kord asked his father why he did what he did. His father told him, "There will always be people who need protecting. You must decide if you are going to be one that needs protecting, or will you be the one who protects them." Kord knew at that moment which one he was going to be.

Sitting under the wagon and remembering what his father had said, he could not see how he could protect anyone. He could not even protect his mother. With that thought, he looked down and saw her lying on his lap. Her eyes were closed, and she looked as if she was sleeping, but Kord knew better. She would never open her eyes again.

Kord looked back up and saw the fighting from under the wagon. He waited there. Not for his father to come and save him, he waited for the moment when one of the Raiders would notice him and come and take his life. Then he remembered what his parents had told him.

He was seven seasons old. Any child of ten seasons or younger, the Mountain Raiders would take back with them and make them as they were. Kord had heard the stories, and now he had seen the brutality with his own eyes. The Raiders had killed his mother, and if they found him, they were going to do something worse to him. They would make him the same as they were, and if they succeeded, then one day he would do the same. He would kill a woman who had a child of her own, and then if that child was ten seasons or younger, he would take that child away and do the same. Kord was only seven seasons old, but at that moment, he knew that he would rather die than become like the Mountain Raiders. To him, they were not even human.

Kord did not know what to do. He did not want to leave his mother's body, but he knew that he could not stay where he was. He then thought that his dad would know what to do, and that was who he had to find.

He looked around and decided that he would try to sneak out from under the wagon on the opposite side, away from the fighting. So far, no one had taken notice of him, so he had to make his move before they did, but then he looked down and saw his mother's body. How could he leave her there all by herself? He could not leave, nor could he stay. Kord needed someone to tell him what to do.

At that moment, he saw his father kneeling under the wagon, looking at him. He had a dagger in his hand, and Kord thought that he had used it to fight his way to him and his mother. He had no idea that his father had only just pulled his dagger, intent on taking the life of his own son. To save him from a fate worse than death.

Kord saw the look in his father's eyes, yet he did not know what he was seeing. If he had, he would have known that it was love. His love for his son was so deep that even though he wanted to take the life of his son, he did not have the strength to do so.

His father took hold of his right hand and placed the dagger in it.

Kord had been waiting for someone to tell him what to do. He was only seven seasons old, and he needed guidance from his parents; it was his father who gave him his instructions. “I love you. Run.”

He knew what to do. His father had arrived, so he would not have to leave his mother alone. His father told him to run, and he always obeyed his parents. Not once in his short life had he ever disobeyed either of them when they instructed him on what to do. He was a good son, and a good son always obeys his parents.

Kord turned around under the wagon and crawled out on the opposite side of the fighting. When he stood up, he did not look to either side to see if anyone had spotted him. His father told him to run, and that is what he did. He ran, and in just a few strides, he made it into the woods, but he did not stop. His father told him to run, and he continued to do so.

He still held onto the dagger that his father had given him. He had no sheath for it, and the blade was too long for him to stick it in the waistband of his trousers, so he held it in his hand.

He ran, and at some point, he stopped running. The sun had set, and even though he wanted to keep on running, his body would not allow it, so he sat down on the ground with his back to a tree, pulled his knees up to his chest, and placed his head on them. He did not want to fall asleep, but he could not stop himself and only woke when he heard in his sleep the last words his father had said to him, *"I love you. Run."*

FOUR

When he woke, the sun had just begun to enter the sky. With the trees surrounding him, it blocked out the majority of the first light, but Kord was still able to see. Although it was not what he saw that startled him, it was what he heard.

Behind him and the tree which he had his back against, he heard footsteps coming closer. Someone was stepping on sticks and leaves that had fallen to the ground. Whoever it was, they were making enough noise that Kord had no trouble hearing them moving toward him.

Mountain Raiders had found him and were coming to take him away. That was the only thought he had in his mind. He knew that he did not have the strength to run anymore. He had run so much that his legs burned and was not even sure if he was able to stand. When he had stopped during the night, and since he had remained in the position that he was currently in, his legs were stiff and felt as if they weighed more than his entire body.

He raised his right arm and saw the dagger he

had in his hand and realized that his only option was to fight. He knew that he was no match for the Mountain Raiders, but he had no choice. He would stay hidden, and when his pursuers were just on the opposite side of the tree where he was hiding, he would jump out and stab them. With any luck, he would be able to make a killing strike, or maybe he could scare them enough that they would strike him down. At least if that happened, he would not be taken back and become just like them.

Since he was sitting, he knew that he was not in the best position to put his plan into action. He forced his legs to move, pushing himself upward so that he was now standing. With the running and the crouching position he had been in all night, it seemed as if his legs were as solid as the tree he was hiding behind, but with effort and determination, he was standing with his back against the tree, which was giving him the support to remain upright.

He could hear the footsteps coming closer. He then started to think about when he should jump out and strike. How would he know when the right time was? Where should he aim, the stomach or the chest? How hard would it be to stab the dagger into the body? How long would it take for his attacker to die? How much blood would there be? After he stabs his attacker, would he have time to remove the dagger and run? All these questions and more ran through Kord's mind and continued to do so all the way up to the point where he finally heard the footsteps close enough to him that he was sure he should make his attack.

He took one final breath, then, with all his might, he forced himself to move to his left and to the other side of the tree where he knew his attacker was. As soon as he was around the tree, his legs gave out and he fell to the ground, lying face down in the wet leaves.

He waited for the strike from his attacker that would take his life. When it did not come, his mind took him to an even worse ending for his future. They did not kill him because they wanted him alive. To take him back with them so they could make him into a Mountain Raider.

He was on the ground face down for what seemed like an eternity to him. He thought that maybe there never was anyone after him and that he had just worked himself up into a frenzy from being tired and alone. That was until he heard someone shuffling in the leaves, only three steps away from him.

Kord knew that he could not stay on the ground forever and finally decided to lift his head to see the one who was going to end his life. As he raised his head, he first saw the feet, which seemed a little too small to belong to a Mountain Raider. When he glanced up a little higher, he saw the lower parts of the legs of the one that had made their way to him. Once again, he thought that they did not look like the legs belonging to one of the Raiders. He did not waste any more time, and even though he was still lying on the ground, he lifted his head as high as he could and saw the one who had forced him into the current position he was in.

"I'm thirsty," the little girl said. Kord continued to look at her, not knowing what to say. "I'm thirsty," the girl said again when Kord did not reply to the first time she spoke.

He finally came to his senses and realized that he was still lying on the ground. He knew he did not have the strength to stand, so he forced himself into a position where he was sitting on his knees and legs. He let his head fall to his chest, thankful that the one who had come upon him was only a little girl. He did not think that he had anything to worry about from her. She was definitely not one of the Mountain Raiders.

When he had gained some of his pride back from making a very embarrassing attempt at defending himself, he looked up at the little girl. "You shouldn't be sneaking up on me like that. You could have gotten yourself killed." He thought that would prove to the girl that he had not been frightened just a few moments ago, before he saw who he was up against.

"You fell down," the girl said to him. "I'm thirsty," she repeated for a third time.

Kord looked at the girl, then at the waterskin he had hanging on his left side. He pulled it over his head, removed the stopper, and stretched out his arm and the waterskin so the girl could take it. She moved over to him, took the waterskin, and began to drink.

"Don't drink too much of it, that is all I have until I can find a stream or something to get more," Kord said when he thought she had drunk enough to last her for the moment.

The little girl stopped drinking, and even though she wanted more, she handed the waterskin back to Kord, who then replaced the stopper to make sure that no water would spill out. It was the only water he had, and he had to make it last.

Kord placed the strap of the waterskin over his head and let it hang down at his side. He then looked at the girl, "What is your name?" he asked.

"Keia," the girl replied. Kord looked at the girl and realized that he had seen her before. She was one of the children who was with the caravan. Somehow, she had escaped as well.

"Have you seen anyone else? Any of the adults?" Kord asked. The girl shook her head to let him know that she had not.

He wanted to ask her if she knew where her parents were, but he did not because he knew that more than likely, they were just like his parents. He did not want to think about them, so the girl probably felt the same. It was a topic that, for the moment, was best left unspoken.

"Why did you fall down?" Keia asked.

Kord may have been only seven seasons old, but he was still a male, and he did not want to admit that the first time he tried to be brave, it ended with him lying face down on the ground. “I had to, or I would have probably killed you. I thought that you were one of those Raiders, so I was going to attack you. When I saw that you were just a kid, I had to stop myself. You’re lucky, I could have really hurt you.” Kord thought the girl would believe his explanation, but as Keia continued to look at him, he was not sure if he had succeeded in making her believe his story.

“I’m still thirsty,” Keia said again.

Kord did not give her the waterskin. He knew that he had to be careful not to run out before he could find more for himself. Then he realized that it was not just him any longer. Keia was with him, and that made it even more important to save the water. Two people require twice as much as one.

“What are we going to do, Kord?” Keia asked, and he realized that he had never told her who he was.

“How did you know my name?”

Keia took a moment but finally answered. “My father told me who you were. I saw you one day and asked him. Your father was the one who was in charge. My dad is a soldier too.” She stopped speaking, realizing what she had just said. Her dad was no longer a soldier, because she knew that her dad, just like her mother, was dead.

It was her father who had saved her. As soon as the Mountain Raiders attacked, her father picked her up and rushed her into the woods in the opposite direction the Raiders had come from. He told her to remain there until he came for her. He never did.

The memory of what she saw in the first few moments of the attack, and the last time she saw her father as he rushed away from her, was too much for her, and she could not stop herself from crying. Even though she had cried throughout the night, she still had enough tears to cry even more.

Kord forced himself up so that he was standing. He took a step closer to Keia, and even that felt as if he was walking in mud because his legs were stiff from everything he had been through. When he reached her, he placed his left hand on her shoulder. Since she was shorter, she looked up. When he had her attention, he said, “I lost my parents too, and it’s ok to cry.”

Keia did not know why, but for some reason, his words helped her to stop her tears, at least for the moment. Kord realized that even though he believed what he had just told Keia, he had not cried for his parents. He had seen his mother killed in front of him, and he knew that his dad had not survived the attack, so why had he not cried for them?

“We have to keep moving. I don’t think that the Mountain Raiders are coming after us. They probably went in the other direction, back to where they came from.” Kord was not sure if he was trying to convince Keia or himself, but either way, he wanted to believe what he had just told her.

Kord looked around and all he could see were

trees. He had run for so long and during the night that he was not sure where he was. The caravan had been traveling for a while, for over two moon-cycles, and Kord had no idea if there were any settlements around or where to even begin to look for one.

He thought that if they could make it back to the road the caravan was on and follow it, then eventually they would be able to find someone who could help them, but he did not even know which direction to go to make their way back to the road. To him, any direction would be just as right or wrong as any other choice.

"We have to find someone to help us," he said when he stopped looking at the different directions he had for options. "If we can make our way back to the road, then maybe someone will come along that can help us, or maybe we can find a village or something." Kord looked around again, then back at Keia. "While we're walking, we need to keep a lookout for any water that we can find, and maybe something we can eat." The last part only came to him when he heard his stomach announce that it had not been fed in a while.

He took one more look around, then one last look at Keia, "Ok, follow me." He then turned and started walking in the direction he had chosen. He had only taken a few steps when he realized that Keia was not following him. He stopped and turned to face her. "We have to get moving, before it gets too dark to see." He then turned and began walking again but stopped when he once again realized that Keia was still standing in the same place she had been. He turned once more to face her. "I know you are thirsty and tired, so am I, but we can't stay here, so we have to keep moving." Kord waited for her to start walking, but she did not move.

Keia slightly turned her body and pointed in the direction behind her, while still looking at Kord, "We have to go that way," she said, without a single bit of doubt in her voice. "In one sun-cycle we will find a stream where we can get more water. Near the stream we will be able to find some wild berries that we can eat so your stomach will stop making that noise."

Kord looked down at his stomach and realized that the noise it was making was louder than it had been a moment ago. His thoughts did not stay on his hunger for long because he suddenly heard Keia walking off in the direction she had pointed to just a moment ago.

He was not sure which direction to go, but if he had no idea, then how did the little girl, who was younger than him, know? "What makes you so sure we will find water and food in that direction, and in just one sun-cycle?"

Keia stopped and turned to look at Kord, "Because the voice told me that we will." She then turned and continued to walk in the direction she had started in.

Kord thought that maybe the strain of everything

she had gone through had taken its toll on Keia's mind, but he would play along. "What voice told you?"

She did not stop walking, nor did she turn to face Kord, but she did give him an answer. "The same voice that told me how to find you," Keia said, and continued to walk away.

Kord was not sure about the little girl. Maybe she was not right in the head somehow. He looked around and saw that there was no way to know which direction he would be able to find water, food, or help. He then saw Keia, who was getting farther away from him. She seemed to know where she was going, and since he did not, following the little crazy girl was just as good as anything else he could come up with. "Hey, wait for me!" he yelled and began following Keia to wherever she was leading them.

FIVE

In one sun-cycle, just as Keia had said, they came upon a small stream where they were able to drink as much water as they wanted, as well as refill the waterskin Kord carried. Not only was there plenty of water, but there were bushes of wild berries that they could fill their stomachs with. Kord did not know which berries were good to eat and which were poisonous, nor did Keia, but the voice that she was able to hear knew, and that saved Kord from becoming sick when he almost ate a handful of berries that were not the good kind. Keia told him that the voice told her that the ones he had picked would make him sick, and even though he had doubts about the voice Keia continued to mention, he thought that since she did lead them to water, or at least the voice did, he would listen to her about the berries.

Kord wanted to continue to keep moving in hopes of finding someone who could help them. Once again, Keia told him that the voice told her that they should rest by the stream for three sun-cycles to regain their strength. Even though he could not hear the voice nor was he even sure that Keia was actually hearing one, he thought that maybe it would be a good idea for them to stay a while. It had been two sun-cycles since the attack on the caravan, and neither of them had an opportunity to rest for a long period of time, not wanting to stay in one place for too long, in case there were Mountain Raiders still about. Keia told him that the Raiders were no longer around and that they would be safe. Kord had to take her word for it because he was too worn out to continue to go any further without some much-needed rest.

When night came, and even though the moon provided some light, Kord was able to get a small fire going using his dagger. He had seen his father start one, so he thought that he would be able to as well, which he did, with some help from Keia and the voice.

He first gathered some leaves and twigs that had fallen on the ground. He piled them up correctly with the twigs on top of the leaves. He then took a stone he found and struck it against his dagger. He did not see what he was hoping for, which was a spark that would ignite the leaves. He continued for a few more attempts without success.

"You're not doing it right," Keia said as she was squatting down across from him, looking at the pile of leaves waiting to see what would happen.

"I am too," Kord replied, not wanting a girl to tell him that he was wrong. "I just have to keep hitting the stone against the dagger until it makes a spark," which he continued to do, but no sparks had appeared so far.

Keia stood up and walked over to the stream. When she found what she was looking for, she went back over to Kord. "Here, use this one," she said, stretching her hand out to Kord.

He looked from what he was doing to see what she was holding, "It's just another stone."

"The one you're using isn't the right kind. It has to have some flint in it," she told him.

"How do you know?" he said and went back to trying to start the fire.

"The voice said so."

As much as he wanted to tell her that there was no voice, he could not deny the fact that whenever Keia said the voice said so, Keia was right. So even though he did not want to take the stone from her, he did. "Wait," Keia said, then turned and walked over to a tree. When she came back, she handed Kord something else.

"What's that?" he asked.

"Um, it's fugus," she took a moment, then changed the word, "I mean fungus." She had mispronounced it the first time. "It will catch on fire faster than the leaves."

Kord took the fungus without saying anything to her. He decided that wherever she had learned the things she was telling him, she was probably right, and he did not want to hear that the voice had told her what to do.

He placed the fungus on top of the leaves and under the twigs. He then pressed his dagger against the fungus and struck it with the stone Keia had brought to him. With his first strike, there came a spark. Kord looked up at Keia and saw that she was smiling. Kord was sure that it was because she knew that she was right about what to do, but more importantly, that Kord was wrong.

He went back to focusing on getting the fire started. Keia, after seeing the first spark, went back to her spot across from Kord, kneeling down to get a better view. After three more strikes on the dagger, the fungus caught fire. No one was more surprised than Kord.

"You have to blow on it to get it going," Keia said.

"I know," Kord told her, which he did; he was just taking a moment to enjoy the small accomplishment of being able to get the small fire started.

He bent down and started blowing on the lit fungus, and soon the leaves underneath caught fire as well. He then started placing more leaves on top of the fungus, but just enough to feed it. Kord knew that if he placed too many, the fire would not be able to breathe and might go out.

Once the small twigs were burning, Kord reached over and grabbed some bigger ones that he had collected and placed them on the fire. He used those to keep the fire going since they would burn longer. Once he was sure that the fire would not go out, he smiled, looked across the fire, and saw

Keia, who was also smiling; and when she saw that he was looking at her, she nodded, letting him know that he had done a good job. For some reason, that gesture made him feel very proud of what he had accomplished.

"We need to gather some more branches to keep by the fire for when it gets low," Kord said, and they both stood up and started gathering up all the sticks they could that were around them. Neither one of them strayed too far away from the light the fire provided.

The first night they were together, they had stopped traveling when the sun had gone out of the sky. That night, they did not try to get a fire started. One reason was because they had walked all day in the woods, and by the time they settled down for the night, they were too tired to do anything. Another reason was that Kord thought it was still too dangerous. If the Mountain Raiders were still in the area, then a fire, even a small one, could lead them to the two, and neither of them wanted that to happen.

When Keia told Kord that the voice told her that they would be safe and that they could start a fire, Kord did not question it. The season was warm, and they did not need the fire to keep the cold off them, nor did they need the fire to cook any food, since all they had to eat were wild berries, but after the first night they spent in the woods, Kord did not hesitate to get a fire going.

Kord had grown up in one of the cities, so he had never slept outside in the wilderness until his father had brought him and his mother on the journey that led them to where they were now. During their travels, the caravan stopped just before the sun went out of the sky, and the soldiers always made sure that there was more than one fire in the camp that they had set up for the night. With the fire came light, and with the light came some sense of safety.

After the first night in the woods with just the two of them, Kord wanted to feel some safety, even if it was not much. Not just for him but for Keia as well. When they had stopped the first night that they were alone in the woods together, both Kord and Keia fell asleep. Not that they had wanted to, because they both felt that it would be better to stay awake and make sure that nothing happened to them. Unfortunately, their bodies decided that they were too worn out to remain awake.

While they were sleeping, Kord woke up in the middle of the night when he heard a noise. It was not the sound of anyone coming near them nor the sound of some animal. He heard whimpering. He knew that some animals whimpered, but he realized that it was Keia making the noise in her sleep.

It did not take him long to figure out what she was dreaming of. He was sure that her dreams had something to do with what had happened to her parents, the same thing that had happened to his own.

At first, he thought that maybe he should wake her up, but he decided that was not the right thing to do. Instead, the idea that came to him bothered him at first, but the more he thought about it, the more he believed it was the best choice.

They had fallen asleep, Kord on one side of a tree and Keia on the opposite side from where he was. He quietly and gently moved over to where Keia was and positioned himself so that his back was toward hers, enough to be touching. After a few moments, he no longer heard any noise from her, and with that, he believed she would be able to sleep peacefully. He let out a sigh to himself, to assure him that the only reason he moved to lie next to her was so that she would stop making any type of noise and he would be able to get some sleep. It had nothing to do with making her feel better, at least that is what he thought to himself.

He was the first to wake up in the morning and he remembered how he had fallen asleep. He was sure, without a doubt, that he was lying next to Keia with their backs together. When he woke, he slowly lifted his head, looked over his left shoulder, and saw that at some point during the night Keia had changed her position and was now lying facing him, against his back, very, very close. So close that Kord thought that there was no space between them at all, which there was not.

Kord at least had enough self-control not to jump up and startle Keia, but he did adjust his position so that he was sitting up and not in contact with her. “Hey, we need to start moving,” he said to her as he gently shook her with his hand on her shoulder.

Hearing Kord’s voice, Keia opened her eyes and sat up. When she looked at him, all she did was nod her head, took a moment to fully wake, then stood and started walking in the same direction they had been going in from the day before. Kord was still watching her from the same position, sitting on the ground. Watching her, wondering when in the night she had moved so close to him, and why it bothered him the way it did. He finally got his mind back on what was important, stood up, and started following Keia, who, for some reason, unknown to him, knew where she wanted to go, which she did.

They had spent three sun-cycles by the stream, and no more. Keia told Kord that it was time for them to start walking again, so she did, and Kord, without any objections, followed her.

Kord had filled his waterskin, and Keia had picked as many berries as she could and wrapped them in the smock she had wrapped around her waist. She carried the bundle in her arms while Kord carried the waterskin and the dagger. They did not have much, but what they had they held onto, because they needed those items to survive.

As they traveled, just before the sun went out of the sky, they stopped and made camp. The first thing they did was gather what they needed to make a fire, and after the first time Kord had made one, after Keia told him what to do, he had no problem getting one started. By the seventh suncycle in the wilderness, Kord thought that he was probably the fastest person in the world who could start a fire.

Once they had the fire going, they would sit around it and eat their evening meal of berries. At first, Kord wanted to ration out the berries to make sure that they would not run out of food, but Keia told him that there were plenty of them in the area, and the voice would lead them to where they were, so they did not have to worry about going without. Once again, Kord was not sure if he believed Keia or not. She had not been wrong yet, but the thought that she was hearing a voice did not sit well with him.

While they were walking, Kord decided to find out more about the voice and asked her why he did not hear it. Keia stopped walking, turned to him, and said, "The voice said that males are too stubborn to listen when they need to." She then turned and continued walking.

Kord stood where he was for a moment. Under his breath, he said to himself, "I'm not stubborn." He then thought to himself, *"What does stubborn mean anyway?"* He decided not to ask Keia any more questions concerning the voice, which he thought did not exist.

During one of the nights, after they had settled

down to get some sleep, Kord sat with his back against a tree staring at the fire. He did not fall asleep as fast as Keia, so he would watch the fire and let the crackling of it lull him to sleep. Only this night it seemed that it was taking longer to do so.

While watching the flames, he heard Keia begin to whimper in her sleep, which she did every night. Usually, that was when Kord would move closer to her and position himself so that his back was against hers. Once he settled, she would sleep without making any noise. This night was no different, only this time, he did not move closer to her, at least not right away.

He could not help himself; he just watched her lying there in a restless sleep. He knew that she was dreaming of that day the Mountain Raiders attacked, and even though he was sure about it, when they were awake, he never asked her about her dreams. It was bad enough that she had to deal with them in her sleep; he did not want her to have to think about them while she was awake as well.

While watching her, what his father had told him came to his mind, *"There will always be people who need protecting. You must decide if you are going to be one that needs protecting, or will you be the one who protects them."*

It was not difficult for Kord to make up his mind, and as he sat there watching Keia, he told himself that he would protect her no matter what. He then settled down next to her with their backs against one another, and it was not long before Keia was sleeping peacefully again, as was Kord.

They continued their journey, walking by day, resting by night. When they found berries, they would eat what they wanted to and gather some to take with them. Keia, or as she said, the voice led them to another small stream so they could fill the waterskin, and Keia told Kord that they should follow the stream for four more sun-cycles. Since Kord did not have any better ideas, he agreed with her.

On the fourth sun-cycle, Keia started walking in a direction that led them away from the stream. Kord did not say anything because he had become used to her leading the way. Whichever way she went, Kord would follow.

One more sun-cycle passed, and they came upon the entrance of a cave. Before Keia even said anything, Kord knew that was where she wanted to go. It was not as if he was scared, but the cave did give off an eerie feeling, and Kord did not think it would be the best decision to make.

"We have to go inside," she said, then turned to face Kord, who had the look as if he knew that was exactly what she was going to say.

"There might be a bear in there." Kord was just pointing out the obvious since everyone knows that bears like to make their dens in caves. Just like the one he was staring at.

"It's empty," she said, with a bit of mockery in her tone to let him know that she was not worried about anything in the cave. "The voice said that we have to go in, and that we will be safe." She turned, looked at the entrance, then turned back to look at Kord, "I'm going in." That was all she said, then started walking toward the cave. When she was standing just inside the entrance, she turned once again to face Kord, "What's the matter? Are you scared?" She then continued to walk deeper into the cave.

It was the last thing she had said to him that swayed him to start making his way to the cave. He might be only seven seasons old, but he did not want anyone to think that he was scared.

When he reached the entrance, he stopped for just a moment to prepare himself to enter. "I'm not scared," he told himself, and for the most part, he believed it. He then walked inside the cave, hurrying to catch up to Keia. After all, she was probably scared, and he would have to protect her. At least that was what he told himself, and for the most part, he believed it.

SIX

They had not traveled far into the cave before Kord was ready to turn back. It was not because he was scared, at least that was not the main reason. He realized that neither he nor Keia had thought about lighting a torch before they began their little adventure into the dark cave. Keia had slowed her pace as well, and even though their eyes had adjusted somewhat to the dark, they both were more cautious about making their way into the unknown.

Just as Keia was about to suggest that they go back to the entrance and make a torch, the cave began to glow with light. She was just as surprised as Kord, which she could tell by the look on his face when she turned around and looked at him. Both of them nodded their heads to the other to let them know that they should continue. Even though the light, coming from some type of rock embedded in the walls of the cave provided what they needed to be able to see better, the sudden appearance of that light made them both a little more nervous.

At first, Keia had no problems with entering the

cave. The voice had instructed her to do so, and she had trusted the voice from the moment it had spoken to her. She did not know whose voice she was listening to, but it had begun to speak to her after the Mountain Raiders had attacked the caravan, and Keia had been hiding in the woods.

The first words it relayed to her were simple and precise. *"Child, you must run into the forest. I will guide you to safety."*

When she first heard the voice speak to her, Keia thought that it was that of her mother. She did not know why, but the way the voice sounded was soft and soothing; the way only a mother could speak to a child. When she heard it, Keia listened and obeyed. Her father had told her to wait, and he would come for her. She may have only been six seasons old, but she saw what happened with the attack on her family and on the rest of the caravan, and she knew that if the Mountain Raiders found her, they would take her back with them. Even at her age, she knew what that meant.

She did what the voice had instructed her to do. She ran into the woods, and even though she was crying while doing so, she did not stop. There were times when she stumbled over a branch or even her own feet and fell to the ground, and every time she did, she heard the voice speak to her, *"Child, you must get up. You must keep moving."* Once she heard the voice, she did not hesitate to do as it instructed.

For some reason, hearing the voice gave her the strength to continue.

She did not know how long she had run, but even she realized that over time her pace had become slower. The voice said nothing to her about how fast she was moving, maybe because it knew that she would only be able to keep up a fast pace for so long. Eventually, the voice spoke to her again, "*Child, you are safe for now. Stop and rest for a moment.*"

Keia did not need to be told again to do as the voice instructed her. She immediately fell to the ground, face down, lying in the fallen leaves, crying. She had so much to cry about, and she was not even sure what specific reason she was letting the tears fall. Was it for her mother and father? Was it for the fact that she was in the woods alone and scared, or because she had no idea what to do? She stayed on the ground where she was and cried. The voice did not tell her to stop or do anything else because the voice knew that, at the moment, crying was what the child needed.

At some point, Keia had cried herself to sleep. Even though the sun was only midway in the sky, she had been through so much that sleep came to her and she was not able to fight it off. The voice thought that maybe that was for the best. The child was going to have to travel during the night, and she would not have time to rest. She would not have to go very far, but she would have to travel while it was dark, to where the voice would lead her.

The sun had left the sky long before Keia woke. The full moon was already past its midpoint. *"Child, it is time that you begin again. I will guide you,"* the voice said, once Keia had fully awakened.

"I'm thirsty," Keia spoke. She heard the voice in her head but spoke aloud when replying to it.

"I will lead you to where you can find water and someone to help you." Upon hearing that, Keia stood up and looked around her thinking that whoever was going to help her would be close. The voice could not read her thoughts, but by the way she had reacted, the voice knew that she would have to say more. *"You will have to travel during the night, but by the time the sun rises in the sky, you will find someone to be with."*

Keia wanted to ask the voice if it was her mother or father, but she knew that was not likely. Somehow, she knew that her parents were no longer with her in the world. She felt an emptiness in the world and in her own life, as if she had lost what was most precious to her. She did not mention her family. She had cried herself to sleep thinking about them and she did not have any more tears to cry. At least not at the moment.

The voice gave Keia her first instruction. *"Turn around, from where you are."*

Keia did, and was now facing in the opposite direction, but she did not move. "What do I do now?" Keia asked.

The voice could not help but be amused. It

thought that the child would have known to start walking, but Keia was an obedient child and waited for the voice to tell her what to do next. *"Begin walking. I will tell you when you need to adjust your course."* Keia did as the voice instructed. She began walking, taking her first step on her new journey.

As Keia continued to walk through the cave, when she thought about the first time she saw Kord, she could not help but smile. In fact, she could not stop herself from turning around to look at him, who was following her. The thought of him jumping out from behind the tree and falling on his face almost made her burst out in laughter, but when she had turned and looked at him behind her, she held it back.

"Why did you stop, and what are you smiling for?" Kord asked when he saw that she had stopped moving, and he had only just noticed the moment before he bumped into her.

"I'm not smiling," she told him.

"Yes, you are, and stop it and keep walking," he told her.

She took one more look at him, then turned and continued making her way through the cave.

Kord waited a moment to let her get a few steps ahead of him so that they would not bump into one another. In the past few sun-cycles, since he had found Keia, or by her viewpoint, she found him, Kord was beginning to believe that maybe Keia's mind was not right, and that she was a little bit crazy, especially since she kept on telling him about the voice that she continued to listen to. On the other hand, Keia was guiding them more than he was, and his male pride was not too happy about that, even though he was only seven seasons old.

They did not know how long they had been in the cave traveling. They could not see the sun, which would let them know how much time had passed, but eventually Keia told him that the voice had told her that they should stop and rest for the night. Kord was tired and did not even say anything when she told him what to do. Whether it was Keia or the voice, Kord was ready to take a break, and from the way Keia flopped to the floor of the cave, she felt the same way.

They had traveled for some time, moving more with the purpose of getting out of the cave than to get somewhere specifically. Even though there was light coming from the rocks embedded in the walls of the cave, just being surrounded by stone made them both feel a little uncomfortable. However, the voice knew that they were only children, and they were not strong enough to make it through the cave without taking a break.

They sat on the floor and ate some of the berries they had and drank some of the water. Kord told Keia that since they did not know how long it would take to get through the cave then they had to be careful with their food and water. Keia told him that they would find the exit sometime tomorrow. Of course, she told him that the voice had told her, which did not make Kord feel any more comfortable, even though the voice had not been wrong so far.

There was no need to build a fire, and Kord was thankful for that because they did not have any sticks or leaves to do so. The light from the rocks in the walls gave them enough to see their surroundings, and the temperature of the cave was comfortable enough that they would not feel a chill. When Kord thought about it, he decided that the cave would make an excellent place to live in, if he had to. The next thought he had was how maybe a bear would have the same idea. He looked around and listened for any noise. Thankfully, the cave seemed to be quiet and quite safe.

He was not sure when he had fallen asleep, but when he woke, he was sitting on the floor of the cave with his back up against one of the walls. It was not the noise of a bear that had woken him but the sound of Keia whimpering in her sleep. It is what she had done every night since they had met each other, and every night, Kord would do the same thing to help her have a restful sleep. He quietly took his place next to Keia with his back to hers. It was not long before she had stopped whimpering and rested peacefully. As usual, Kord would wake up first and find that she had positioned herself facing him, lying against his back as close as she could. He would make sure not to wake her and adjust his position so that when she woke, she would not see that she had adjusted her position to sleep so close to him. He did not want to embarrass her.

When Keia rose from her sleep, and after they had eaten some berries and drank some water, they began to make their way through the cave. They were not sure how long they had been traveling when Kord felt something on his face. Even though it was slight, it was a breeze. "We're almost to the exit," he told Keia when he was certain that he was not mistaken.

"Are you sure?" she asked as she turned around to look at him.

"Yes, I'm sure. Can't you feel the breeze? It is cooler than the air in the cave," he said to let her know that he knew what he was talking about.

Not that she did not believe him, but Keia had her own way of finding out, "Are we almost to the exit?" she asked into the air. Once she received her reply, she relayed it to Kord. "The voice said that you are right and that..." She left off what the rest of the message was.

Kord realized that there was more to what the voice had said, even if he was not sure if the voice really did exist or if it was all in Keia's mind. "And that what?" he asked, wanting to know what she was going to say.

"Nothing," Keia said, turned, and continued to walk on.

"You were going to say something else, or that

voice told you more than what you told me, so what was it?" Kord asked, now definitely wanting to know what she was going to say.

Keia knew that Kord did not believe that there was a voice speaking to her, and since he was so eager to hear what the voice had said, she stopped walking, turned, and faced him, then told him. "The voice said that you are right and that maybe you weren't so dimwitted after all." She then turned around, with a smile on her face, and continued walking.

Kord stood there, not knowing what to say. He was not sure if Keia, or the voice she said that she heard, had called him dimwitted. The point was that he was not so dimwitted that he did not know what dimwitted meant. He then remembered the time when Keia told him that the voice said that he was stubborn. Whether the voice existed or not, Kord was sure that it did not like him very much, and he decided that he felt the same way about it.

As they traveled closer to the exit of the cave, the breeze they were feeling on their faces grew stronger, and the air became fresher. With each step they took, their spirits lifted.

When they finally saw light coming from the exit, they both stopped and looked at one another. They smiled, and without saying a word, they took off running. Not just because they were happy to be out of the cave, but the thought of what was beyond the exit excited them more than they could imagine.

As soon as she was out of the cave, Keia took only four more steps before she came to a complete and sudden halt. She could not stop herself, for what she saw made her stare in awe. Her eyes opened as wide as they could. She could not stop her mouth from doing the same. She was sure she wanted to say something, but she did not know what it was. The one thing she was certain about was that she was sure that she knew the voice she had been hearing was coming from the one standing in front of her.

They were legends, that was all that was left of them, at least that was what most believed. Many stories were told about how at one time, their kind could be seen in many different areas, but those were just stories passed down from one generation to another. The stories were told to amuse children or to pass the time around a campfire. Only now, Keia was staring at what no one had seen in many, many seasons.

The dragon was standing in front of Keia, waiting for her. Silver scales covered its body and glimmered with the light of the sun. Its head rose to a height of at least two wagons high, and yet Keia knew that the dragon could raise its head higher if it decided to do so.

Keia was able to see its long tail stretched out behind it, yet still long enough that it curled back beside its body to lie at its side.

Even though the shining scales, its long neck and

tail were impressive, nothing amazed her more than seeing the wings of the dragon folded at its sides. As if the dragon knew what she was thinking, it stretched out its wings so that Keia was able to see the full splendor of the sight before her. Keia thought that she had never seen anything so beautiful.

She came to her senses, and even though she was still awestruck by the sight before her, she wanted to know what Kord thought of the dragon. She turned to her left to look at him, and she did, only she had to look down at the ground because that was where he was. Lying on his back, having fainted at the sight of the dragon.

Keia did not know what to say so she turned to look at the dragon, who was staring at the boy lying on the ground. When the dragon decided that he could lie there for a moment, she put her focus again on the little girl whom she had led to her. They both just shook their heads, thinking that males were not the brightest creatures in the world.

X'Jahan stood looking at what had been added to the large statue, which had been found in the cavern. A scaffold had been built to allow the workers to commence with the next stage in what had to be done. "Taskmaster!" X'Jahan called, and a man came up and stood behind him and two paces to the right. It was not the same man whom X'Jahan had called taskmaster when they had first entered the cavern. He had given the old taskmaster seven risings of the sun to have the scaffold completed. When the time had passed, so did the old taskmaster. Failure was dealt with immediately.

The new taskmaster was given only four risings of the sun to complete the scaffold. It was finished in three. His reward for being obedient was his life; there was nothing more.

X'Jahan wanted to be present for what was about to take place. His dream, the dream of his forefathers, was closer than ever to being completed, and X'Jahan would make sure that it would be finished without failure. He also knew that it would still take time. Many seasons would pass before everything that his forefathers had worked for would take place. He had time; he was only twenty-five seasons old. If it took another ten seasons, he would only be thirty-five. If it took another twenty, he would only be in his forties. Plenty of time for him to continue with what his forefathers had started.

X'Jahan was dedicated to the cause. He had no thoughts that he was greater than it. He had no plans that would make him more important than the task he was given by his father, and he knew that in life, nothing was set in stone.

It was time for him to make preparations. If something were to happen to him, the task would have to fall to his kin. He decided that it was time for him to find wives. It was time for him to bear children, and from those he sired, he would choose the one he felt would be able to take over the task of his lineage if something were to happen to him. His children who were not worthy would end up working for the task as well, only they would be doing so in the cavern where X'Jahan was standing, gazing at the wonder before him.

He brought his mind back to the moment, "You may begin now," he said to the man behind him.

"Yes, my liege," was all the taskmaster said, then nodded to his own servant behind him.

That servant raised the horn he was holding and blew into it, sending the message to the ones at the top of the scaffold to begin. As soon as the note from the horn ceased, they did.

Their hammers made contact with the structure in front of them. When they struck, the sound echoed through the cavern, making a loud ringing noise. To X'Jahan, it was the most beautiful sound he had ever heard. As if with each strike of the hammers, the workers were creating a song that would ignite the world on fire.

He stood there listening to the workers continue with their task, and with each strike, X'Jahan savored every note. He had other preparations to oversee, and although he could have remained in the cavern until the task was complete, other duties required his attention as well. He turned and walked through the cavern to make his way to where the slaves were kept. He would choose five or six of the women slaves and hoped that out of the ones he chose, at least one of them would bear him a child he could raise to take over the task assigned to him if something were to happen to his life. His life was not important; the task was.

As he walked, he could not stop thinking of how beautiful the sound of the hammers was, like music to his ears.

The sound came to them as if lightning had crashed through the sky. They had no warning, but the moment they heard it, they knew what it signaled. The ringing continued with every strike, and they both knew that it would be many seasons before it came to an end. They did not know how many times the sun would rise and set before they would not have to listen to the unbearable noise that broke their hearts with every strike. They also knew that when the agonizing ringing stopped, what came forth would break their hearts even more.

SEVEN

Kord sat straight up. He did not look around; he stared directly in front of him. All he saw was that he was inside some type of small dwelling; he just did not know where. What he did not see was what he thought he had imagined before, and that was the dragon. "You're awake," Keia said to him, and he turned his head to the left and saw her sitting next to the straw mat he was on. Since he did not say anything, possibly still from the shock of what he saw, she continued. "You fainted." It was those words that jarred him out of his silence.

"I did not faint," he said in a manner to make sure that she knew that was not what had happened to him.

"You did," she said with a smile.

"I did not. I was just tired from walking so much." So that he did not have to continue the conversation they were having, Kord turned to his right, away from Keia, and stood up from the mat. He looked around but did not recognize anything. "Where are we?" he asked and turned around to face Keia.

She stood up as well, "This is an old hut where

MiteraThrakena brought us to rest." She wanted to say, *and wait until he woke from fainting*, but kept that thought to herself. "She said that once you are awake, she would come and speak with us again."

"Who is Mitera..." He stopped before he finished asking his question because he could not remember the word Keia had just spoken.

"MiteraThrakena, that is her name," Keia said to let him know the name of the dragon.

Kord looked at her. He could not understand how she remained so calm after seeing a dragon. He was sure that was what he had seen, and he was also sure that he remembered some of the legends that he had heard as he was growing up about dragons.

They were only legends and stories. No one had ever seen a dragon, and no one was even sure that they ever existed. If they had, it was many, many seasons ago. Some parts of the stories were how dragons would fly through the sky, and as they passed over villages, they would breathe fire down on them and then eat the burning bodies, bones and all.

At that thought, Kord felt as if he might just fall asleep again, which was his way of thinking he was going to faint.

It was at that moment that they both heard someone outside the hut. Keia smiled, ready to once again talk to the dragon. She grabbed Kord's hand and started pulling him toward the small door of the hut. Knowing what she was planning to do, he held his feet firmly against the floor, not moving at all, which caused Keia to stop as well. While still holding onto his hand, she turned and faced him, "What are you doing? We have to go and talk to her."

Kord was not sure what he wanted to do, and he let go of Keia's hand. A part of him really did want to go and talk to a dragon, but there was a part of him that wanted to make sure that they were both safe, and even though the small hut did not offer much protection, it was more than what they had outside with the dragon.

Keia moved closer to him to speak, "I know that she will not hurt us. She led us here."

"To eat us," Kord said to voice his opinion.

Keia was growing annoyed with the way he was talking about the dragon. It was her voice that led her to Kord and then led them both to where they were. She had no problem in trusting the dragon, unlike Kord, who still seemed afraid. "I trust MiteraThrakena, so please trust me."

It was not the words she spoke that helped to persuade Kord to ease his suspicion, but the smile on her face. Even though it was not the first time he had seen her smile, since he had met her, it was the first time he had felt something in his heart. He just did not know what it was.

"Are you ready?" she asked, and before he could give his answer, she took hold of Kord's right hand with her left, turned, and started pulling him along with her. Just before she reached the door, she turned once again to say something to him, and this time she was not smiling. “Do not embarrass me.” She turned again to face the door but turned back one more time to face Kord and now she had a finger on her right hand pointing at him. “And do not faint.” From the look she was giving him, Kord was more than ready to face the dragon. He thought that it might be safer than staying inside with Keia.

When they exited the small hut, it was not the sight of the one dragon that made him think that he was ready to go back inside and faint; it was seeing two of the legendary creatures.

The one on the right was the one he had first seen when he had exited the cave. Its scales were silver; its long neck was elegant and reminded him of a swan. Its slender head was high off the ground, and unfortunately, its eyes were fixed on him.

He continued to look down the body of the dragon and saw the wings of it folded at its sides and its long tail stretching out behind it. It stood on all four of its legs, and when his eyes lowered, he saw clearly the sharp claws at the end of its paws. Claws that he was sure could tear him apart with a single swipe.

Even though it was a dragon, he could not help but think of how beautiful it was. He could not say the same about the one standing next to it.

The larger dragon’s scales were gold and glistened in the light of the sun. Its neck was just as long as the silver dragon’s neck, but at least two times the size in girth. Where the head of the silver dragon was slender, this one was more square and broader than the one next to it. Its body was broader as well, and even though it also had its wings folded at its sides, it was easy for Kord to tell that if it were to stretch them out completely, they would stretch farther than those of the silver dragon. They would have to, since its body was bulkier, and it would need powerful wings to fly. Even though he had not seen the dragon actually fly, he was sure it would be able to, not just because it had wings, but because the old stories said that dragons would fly through the sky, destroying villages.

As Kord continued to inspect the gold dragon, he noticed that like its body, its powerful legs were wider than the silver dragon's legs, as well as its claws, which were twice the size.

He took his eyes off the claws and looked back at its head, especially its maw. He was not sure what the dragon was doing. The dragon had opened its mouth so that its teeth were now showing, and Kord was certain that it had done so to show him that it would have no problem in eating him whole.

Keia decided that it was time for introductions, or else Kord would stand there gawking at the two dragons until he fainted again. "Kord, this is MiteraThrakena, she said, pointing to the silver female dragon, then pointing over to the gold one. "And this is PateraThrakon." She lowered her arm and looked at Kord, "Say something," she whispered to him.

Kord decided that it was best to get the most

important question out of the way. "You're not going to eat us, are you?"

Keia was the first to reply by shoving her elbow into his side. Kord paid no attention to her and kept his eyes on the gold dragon. Even though Kord's focus was not on it, the silver dragon could not hold back the smile she had from hearing such a straightforward question. It was the response from the male dragon that caused everyone to take note of the situation.

"I might," PateraThrakon said, and snarled just a little to emphasize his point.

Kord could not stop the gulp that came from his throat. Keia was no longer smiling, and the surprise look on her face showed that she thought that maybe Kord had been right. It was MiteraThrakena who decided that it was time to move the greetings along in a more positive manner.

First, she took her tail and adjusted it to the right side of her body, and with a firm, but loving tap, touched PateraThrakon on the hind quarter of his left leg, to let him know that he had gone far enough with his mean and vicious act. He looked at her, and the expression he gave told her that he understood. He may be a fierce male dragon, but when it came to his queen, he would back down easily to please her.

She then smiled at Keia, and even though when she did, her sharp pointed teeth were visible, the smile conveyed to the girl that she had nothing to fear from either of the dragons. Keia did not hesitate to return the smile.

As for the boy, she was going to have to do more than smile to convince him; in fact, a smile from a dragon might just make him faint again, although MiteraThrakena did not say that to Kord. "We will not eat either of you," she said in a calm voice. Where PateraThrakon's voice was rough when he spoke, hers was gentle.

"You might not," Kord said, looking at the female dragon, then placed his eyes back on the one at her side, "But what about him?"

The meeting was not going the way that MiteraThrakena wanted it to, and unfortunately, it was her king who had made the situation more tense than it needed to be. She turned her head to her mate, "Tell him that you will not eat him," she said to PateraThrakon. He did not reply immediately, but when his queen made a low growling noise, he knew that he had taken his intimidation too far.

"I will not eat you as well," PateraThrakon said, and even though it might not have sounded as if he was sincere, he did mean it. He would no sooner eat a human than he would any animal. No matter what the legends say about his kind.

Now that the tensions were less than hostile, for the most part, MiteraThrakena felt that she could continue with the greetings. "As Keia said, I am MiteraThrakena, and I welcome both of you to KhoraThraks."

"Khora...what?" Kord asked.

"KhoraThraks. That is the name of the land that you entered when you stepped out of the cave. Translated into your language, it simply means Land of the Dragons," MiteraThrakena replied.

"Where are we really? How far away is the King's Court?" Kord asked, wanting to know exactly where he was, in relation to a place that he knew of, already planning on what he needed to do to escape. Especially from the male dragon.

MiteraThrakena was not unwilling to answer his question, but there would be enough time to discuss the entire story on where they were. "We can speak later about where you are, but do not worry, you both are safe here." To emphasize her point, she looked over at her king, and since he knew what she wanted, he nodded his great head to let the two children know that he agreed with his queen. She turned her attention back to the two children. "For now, I am sure that you are hungry. Many different types of trees grow throughout the land, and you will be able to pick their fruit and fill your stomachs."

Kord decided that it was time to speak his thoughts on the matter of filling their stomachs. "Why, so you can fatten us up before you eat us?"

It was not MiteraThrakena who replied to his comment but Keia, who shoved her elbow into his side, and this time she used enough force so that it jolted Kord a bit, which PateraThrakon found quite amusing and let out a noise which, for a dragon, would be considered a snicker. However, MiteraThrakena was not going to allow her mate to unravel the small success she had with convincing the children that no harm would come to them, and that he should refrain from any form of bad manners, so she struck him on the side of his neck with the end of her tail, letting him know that she had had enough of his rudeness.

He gave her a look and wanted to say something, but her eyes told him that he had taken his little jest too far, and she would not allow him to take it any further. He was almost twice her size, but he knew that when it came to backing down, he would be the first between the two, so he looked once again at the two children and behaved himself.

Now that the situation was resolved, she continued, "I will lead you to where you will be able to pick some fruit, and there is also a stream with fresh water for you to drink."

"Thank you," Keia said and curtsied to the female dragon to show that she was grateful. She looked over at Kord, and when he did not respond promptly, Keia once again elbowed his side.

"Ouch! Stop hitting me!" he said to her as he rubbed his side. When he made eye contact with her, the expression on her face told him that he should thank the dragons for what they had done. Since he did not feel like being hit again, he faced the dragons and bowed. "Thank you," he added just to make sure that he was doing what he thought Keia wanted him to.

"Follow me then," the female dragon turned her long body and began to walk away. Keia took Kord by the hand and started following her.

As he was being led, Kord turned his head so that he could see the male dragon behind him. PateraThrakon was now facing the three, and to show him that he was still not sure if he trusted the dragon or not, Kord gave him a sneer.

For his reply, PateraThrakon yelled to them. "After they have finished filling their bellies, perhaps they should have a bath as well. The boy especially reeks as if he has been rolling around in a mudhole for a moon-mark!"

The sneer left Kord's face as soon as he heard the word *bath*. It had been a while since he had one, and he was not looking forward to one now. He decided that the gold dragon had won their first round.

They ate a variety of fruits: apples, peaches, persimmons, and more. There were also bushes that had wild berries on them, but both Kord and Keia had had their fill of those, so they stuck to the fruit that they could gather from the trees. Since they were only seven and six seasons old, they were not tall enough to pick the fruits themselves, so MiteraThrakena helped them by shaking the branches and allowing the fruits to fall, which gave the children the thrill of trying to catch the fruit before it hit the ground.

Once they were done with their meal, MiteraThrakena led them to a stream where they could drink their fill of water. It was fresh, and the female dragon told them that it came from high in the mountains when the snow melted. It was when she mentioned the mountains that the demeanor of Keia and Kord had suddenly changed. MiteraThrakena knew how the two children had come to be in their situation, and only by accident did she mention the mountains, which would remind the two of the Mountain Raiders who had attacked their caravan and killed their parents.

"Do not worry. You are safe here. I will not let any harm come to either of you," MiteraThrakena said in a soothing voice to comfort the children. She decided that they should move on to take their minds off unpleasant thoughts. "Come now, it has been a while since you both have bathed, and in this, PateraThrakon is correct." She began to turn but stopped and placed her focus on Kord, "Especially you, child." She then turned and led them to where they would be able to wash themselves clean.

Kord could not help but think to himself that just a moment ago, she told them they would be safe, but in his opinion, taking a bath was close to falling into the category of unsafe.

If what they were doing was considered a bath, then there would have been many more children willing to take one.

MiteraThrakena had led them to a spot where the stream had run off its course and formed a small pond. Once she had commanded all the fish and wildlife that had made it their home to leave, she breathed fire onto the water to heat it so it would be more appropriate for the children to bathe in. If she had not instructed the inhabitants to temporarily evacuate, she would have boiled them alive, and no matter what the legends may say, MiteraThrakena considered all life precious.

The children played more than they bathed. They had taken off their outer clothes and were now jumping around in the pond in their undergarments. MiteraThrakena used her tail and forced their clothes under the water in hopes that it would help remove some of the stench that was on them.

Their playing eventually led to them splashing each other with water. Kord had the advantage since he was stronger, faster, and taller than Keia, so to even the odds, when she thought that Keia had taken enough punishment from Kord, MiteraThrakena slammed her tail into the pond so that she forced a wave of water to completely cover Kord. When he realized that he had been bested, he could not stop laughing. Keia joined in, and even MiteraThrakena gave a slight chuckle for what she had done. She also thought that Kord could use the extra rinse of water to take away the stench. Although she did not tell him so. She allowed the children to play and bathe, which allowed them to feel comfortable but also safe. They had been through quite the ordeal.

When they had finished bathing and when their clothes had finished drying in the sun, MiteraThrakena led them back to the trees where they could pick more fruit. She told them that they should gather some to take back to the hut with them so that they would have something to eat for their evening meal. They both picked enough fruit to last them for their evening meal as well as for the morning when they woke.

Once they had made their way back to the little hut, they went inside. Since MiteraThrakena was too big to enter, she remained outside but watched through the opening as the two children placed the fruit on the small shelf that was in the hut.

The sun was almost out of the sky when MiteraThrakena informed the two children that it was time for them to go to sleep. Like all children, hearing that phrase made them want to stay awake even more, but with all that they had been through in just the short amount of time, with the attack on their caravan, their trek through the forest and cave, and the meeting of not one but two dragons, as well as their full stomachs, and the playful bath time, it did not take them long before they were lying down on the straw mat inside the hut, both with their eyes closed for the night.

MiteraThrakena had waited until both children had fallen asleep before she left them. She had not gone fifty paces when she met up with PateraThrakon.

"Did the boy bathe?" the male dragon asked. The only response she gave was her dragon smile. "What do you make of the two?" he asked her, and the seriousness of the question was greater than the first he had asked.

She turned her neck and head to look at the small hut behind her, off in the distance, then looked back at PateraThrakon. "They have been through a great ordeal, but they have survived."

The answer she gave did not comfort the gold dragon. He knew that many humans had survived troubling and even horrific trials. It is how they deal with those trials that form the path they choose to walk in their life.

"You are not sure if they are the ones." She did not speak as if asking a question; she only stated what she knew. That he had doubts, because she did as well.

Yes, he had doubts. He would not rush into making a decision; he would wait, watch, and see if the children would be the ones whom they had been waiting for.

The two dragons looked up into the sky and to the lands far away from KhoraThraks. It was not what they saw that bothered them, but what they heard. The sound that had started such a brief time ago, and had not ceased since it began. The ringing brought pain to both the dragons' hearts.

The children had been through a lot, and with the time they spent with the silver dragon and the full bellies, they had fallen asleep in no time at all. In the middle of the night, Kord woke to the sound that he had heard every night since the two had found each other. Keia was whimpering in her sleep. Kord adjusted his position so that once again, his back was to Keia. He then moved closer to her so that their backs were touching. As soon as she settled down, Kord closed his eyes and went to sleep himself, knowing that when he woke in the morning, Keia would have adjusted her own position so that she was snuggled up against his back. This was their nightly routine, and Kord did not mind it at all. In fact, he welcomed it.

EIGHT

There was much for the two children to do. MiteraThrakena made sure that they had chores to take care of every day. Keia thought that the tasks were fun and always went about them in high spirits. Kord on the other hand thought that it was work, and even though he was not lazy, he believed that there were better ways to spend his time.

The first chore MiteraThrakena gave them to do was to clean the hut from top to bottom. It had not been used in some time, and never used by the two dragons, so over the span of seasons, a great deal of dust had collected, and it needed to be removed.

Keia took to the task with a smile on her face. She was quick to find the broom in the corner and began sweeping the floor. Kord, since he had no choice in the matter, found an old cloth and began wiping the walls in a half-hearted manner.

They eventually realized that they had to open the small wooden door to the hut, because all the dust that they were moving was going nowhere and was hanging in the air inside. They only realized that when they both began to cough, and their eyes began to water. It took them some time, but they eventually removed the majority of the dust, with Keia putting in more of an effort than Kord.

The next chore was given to Kord, which of course, he was not happy with. MiteraThrakena showed him where there was a wooden bucket behind the hut, and next to the bucket was a clay water jar that was about the same height as himself. It was easy to tell just by looking at it, but when he walked over to it, he was just tall enough to tilt his head over the edge to see inside, which he quickly realized was empty.

He was your average child, and even though some might not think he had much intelligence, it was easy for him to understand just what MiteraThrakena wanted him to do.

He stopped looking into the jar and looked up at the silver dragon who was watching him. "How much do I have to fill it?" he asked, knowing what she wanted him to do.

Her answer was simple, even for Kord to understand, "The brim of the jar is there for a reason; it is to let one know when they have reached it." Without another word, she turned and left him to his task. Kord gave her a sneer to let her know that he was not happy with what she wanted him to do. "I saw that," she said, even though she had not even turned to look at him. Kord decided that it was probably best to do the chore without any further disagreements, verbal or silent ones.

He took the bucket and began his trek to the stream. He remembered where it was from when MiteraThrakena had led them to get a drink after they ate the fruit from the trees. He would not have to go to the grove where the trees were; he could head straight to the stream, which would save him some time.

When the sun was midway in the sky, Kord had made about ten trips to the stream and back. The jar was almost halfway full when MiteraThrakena called to him and told him it was time for the midday meal. He left the bucket next to the water jar and went to the front side of the hut, where he saw the silver dragon. "Your meal is inside," she told him, and he went directly in, not wanting to speak to the mean dragon, for that is the way he felt.

Once inside, he saw Keia sitting on the mat, where they had slept, eating the fruit which she had picked as one of her chores for the day. Kord sat down in front of her and began to eat one of the apples in front of him.

"Are you still filling the water jar?" she asked as she took a bite of a peach.

He stopped chewing for a moment to give her his answer, in a not too pleasant tone, "Yes." He then went back to eating his meal.

Keia bit down on the peach she had and held it in her mouth. She then stretched over to her left and grabbed a basket that was next to the mat. When she sat back up, she took the peach out of her mouth and held it in one hand while she kept the basket in the other. "Look what MiteraThrakena showed me how to make." She thought that maybe what she said was not the entire truth, so she changed her story a little. "Well, she told me how to fix it. It had some holes in it, so she showed me how to weave some long grass into it to make it better. I used it to gather fruit for us. Isn't it pretty?"

Pretty was not the word Kord was thinking of. "I've been hauling water all morning, and all you have been doing is making a basket."

Keia, not thinking that she had done anything wrong, wanted to make sure that Kord understood what she had done. "I told you; I didn't make it; I just fixed it." She did not understand what Kord was trying to say. To her, fixing the basket was just as important as fetching the water. She placed the basket down next to her and went back to eating her peach. Kord took a long sigh, then went back to eating his apple.

When they had finished their meal, Kord stood up and went back outside, where MiteraThrakena was waiting for him. "Have you finished filling the water jar?" she asked. Kord did not even reply. Since she asked the question, and with him knowing the answer, he knew what he was supposed to do. That was to continue to fetch water to fill the water jar.

Kord went to the back of the hut and picked up the bucket he had been using to carry the water from the stream to the water jar. When he turned around, he was startled by the sight of PateraThrakon. Who, for a dragon of his size, was able to come up behind him without making the slightest sound. Something that came to Kord's thoughts immediately followed by it would benefit the dragon if he decided to eat the child.

Kord's eyes focused upward to the dragon's head when he had turned around, more specifically, the dragon's maw, which was what he was looking at when the dragon spoke, "This should help," the dragon said, then looked down at what he had placed in front of him on the ground. The gold dragon turned and walked out of Kord's sight, having finished with what he had to say to the human child.

Kord waited until the dragon had disappeared from his sight completely before he looked down at the item the dragon had been referring to. When he noticed the second bucket, Kord had mixed feelings toward it. Yes, he could carry two buckets at the same time, which would reduce the trips he would have to make to fill the water jar, but on the downside, he would have to carry two buckets at the same time.

He looked at the bucket he was holding, then at the one on the ground a few steps away. He repeated the act a couple of times, then a smile grew on his face, and he was happy with himself for coming up with what he had planned. Instead of heading directly back to the stream, he would make his way to the forest first, where they had picked fruit.

Keia was sitting on the ground outside the hut, while MiteraThrakena was not too far from her, lying on her underbelly with her tail wrapped around her, and her front legs crossed over one another while she guided Keia in making a basket from the beginning.

When Kord had returned from his latest trip to the stream, when he reached where they were, and just before he went to the back of the hut, he stopped and turned his head to look at Keia and the silver dragon. He stood there only long enough for them to see what he had come up with all on his own. He then made his way to the back of the hut where the water jar was kept.

He carefully lifted the wooden stick off his shoulders and placed it and the buckets on the ground. He took a moment to look at what he had accomplished. He had gone to the woods and found the best solid branch he could. When he saw the second bucket, he noticed that it had a piece of rope tied to the handle and then realized that the bucket he had been using at first had one as well. He had seen many people, including his father, use a stick to carry two buckets across their shoulders to make the task easier and allow them to carry more water at one time.

Kord emptied the buckets of water into the water jar and looked inside. With the addition of the two buckets, the level rose quite a bit more than when he was only filling the water jar with one bucket. He knew that he would only have to make about four more trips to the stream before the level of water would reach the top of the jar. He did not even mind the number of trips it would take, happy with what he had accomplished.

Once the buckets were empty, he placed the ends of the stick back in the rope loops on the buckets, then positioned the stick across his shoulders and behind his neck. To emphasize the fact that he was smarter than anyone else, he decided that he would whistle himself a tune while he worked, and so he did. He continued with his whistling when he went around to the front of the hut, without even looking at Keia or MiteraThrakena. His thoughts were that he had a job to do, and the females could stay at the hut and weave baskets. His job required someone with smarts and strength, and in his mind, he was perfect for the task.

Some distance away from the hut, PateraThrakon had been watching the boy return from his trip to the stream. Even though he thought that Kord was strutting just a little too much for what he had accomplished, the gold dragon could not help but smile a bit at what he was seeing.

He had given the second bucket to Kord to see if he would be able to figure out how to best use the two. He did not make any suggestions or even give the boy a hint. He wanted Kord to figure it out on his own. It was not much of a test, PateraThrakon knew that, but it showed him that the boy had some intelligence and that maybe he was not as brainless as the male dragon had first thought when he saw that the boy had fainted just from seeing one dragon.

PateraThrakon watched the boy as he continued on his way back to the stream. The dragon noticed that the boy was thinking more about what he had achieved than where he was walking because he stumbled over a rock and lost his balance, just barely stopping himself from falling to the ground. That was when PateraThrakon decided that maybe his first impression of the boy was accurate.

After two moon-marks, the children had taken up a routine for their lives. They would wake up in the morning, eat their early meal, take care of some chores, eat their midday meal, finish up their chores, and then they were allowed to wander around and do what they wanted until it was time for their evening meal. Afterward, MiteraThrakena would sit with them and talk, mostly about what they would be doing the next day.

Every three sun-cycles, she would lead the children to the small pond where they would take their baths. Kord tried to convince her that he would not be that dirty in such a short amount of time; however, PateraThrakon told him that if he did not do as he was told concerning his bath time, he would be going every two sun-cycles and the gold dragon himself would be the one to take him to the pond.

Kord quickly agreed that every three sun-cycles was fine with him. He knew that if the male dragon took them, they would be doing a lot more bathing than playing in the pond, which MiteraThrakena allowed them to do.

At the end of a moon-cycle, just as the children were about to settle in for the night, PateraThrakon made his way to the small hut and was about to call for Kord, calling to him by the name he had been using since the child had arrived, and that was *boy*. Because he was there for a very important reason, he called the child by his name. “Kord, come out,” the gold dragon said, and when Kord had exited the hut, he told him what to do next. “Follow me.” He did not give any explanation as to where they were going, and Kord was sure that the time had come for the male dragon to find out what a little boy was going to taste like.

“It is alright, child,” Kord heard MiteraThrakena speak from off to his right, and he had not even noticed that she had been there, since he was so focused on the male dragon. “Go with him. I will stay with Keia until you return.”

At that moment, Kord realized what was more important to him. That Keia was not left alone when it was so close to being dark outside, and she would be falling asleep. He needed to be there in case she had trouble sleeping peacefully.

“Go with him, child,” MiteraThrakena said again.

Kord looked at her, then looked behind him where Keia was standing. When he looked back at the female dragon, she nodded to him to let him know that he should go with the male dragon, and that Keia would be alright. He nodded back to her, then started following PateraThrakon to wherever he was leading him.

They walked for a while, and the gold dragon came to a stop on top of a hill. Since the dragon's steps were greater than Kord's, it took him a little longer to reach the top of the hill, and when he did, he kept some distance between himself and the dragon.

"Come closer," PateraThrakon said, and even though he took a big gulp, Kord moved to stand next to the left front leg of the dragon, which was way bigger than the boy was. "You have never cried over the loss of your parents," the dragon said and waited for Kord to answer, but he did not. PateraThrakon then turned his neck and head and looked down at the boy. "You are holding in the pain that you have from your grief." Kord still did not reply, not sure what to even say. The dragon then adjusted his neck and head so that he was looking up at the sky and let out a deep sigh, which came with a grumbling sound that Kord could hear coming from the dragon's throat.

"It does you no good to hold those feelings in." The dragon then looked back down at Kord. "Although you are not aware that you are doing so. Since the time that your parents were killed, you have been too occupied with just staying alive." The dragon looked behind both of them in the direction of the hut, then put his focus back on Kord, "You have been focused on making sure that Keia is well."

Kord still did not speak. He was not sure if he even understood what the dragon was saying. He never even thought about what he was doing; he just lived one day at a time and dealt with whatever needed to be dealt with at the moment.

When he decided that Kord had thought about what he had said, PateraThrakon continued, "You need to mourn for your loss; if you do not, the pain from it will settle in your heart, and eventually tear away at you, allowing a dark spot to grow on your soul. You will not notice it, but you will change to mirror what is in your heart." The dragon gave him a moment, then said the last thing he had to tell the child. "Your mother and father would not want you to become someone with a darkness inside." The dragon then turned and started making his way down the hill. It was only a brief moment before Kord asked his question, and PateraThrakon was pleased to hear it.

"How do I mourn for them?" Kord did not know what he was supposed to do, but what the dragon had said moved him to not want to become something his parents would not like.

PateraThrakon stopped and answered Kord's question, "Think of your parents. Think of the smiles they would give you. Think of the love that they showed you. Think of the happiness you shared with them. Then think of how you will never have those things again." The dragon, having said what the boy needed to hear, continued on his way.

It was not long before he first heard sniffling coming from the child at the top of the hill. Not long after, he heard the mournful cries that came deep from the heart of the boy. PateraThrakon did not bring the child out into the night to hurt him. He only wanted the child to be able to move on from the death of his parents, so that his life would be more than just sorrow and grief. Two things even a dragon could suffer through.

When he had run out of tears and his heart felt lighter from what he had done, Kord made his way back to the hut where he would be able to rest, and for some reason, he thought he would sleep better.

Before he even reached the hut, he saw MiteraThrakena outside, right where she had been lying down on the ground when he went off with the gold dragon. Kord was thankful that she had stayed with Keia while he was away. He did not know that the female dragon had not only remained for the sake of Keia, but for his as well.

As he reached the hut, she asked him, "Do you feel better?" He answered her with a smile and the last sniffle he had from crying. He looked at the door to the hut and knew that Keia was inside. "She deals with her grief in a different way." He turned to look at the silver dragon. "She mourns for the loss of her family in her sleep; that way, she can keep her spirits up when she is awake."

Kord looked at the hut and now knew why Keia would whimper in her sleep. He had known that she was probably dreaming of her family, but with what MiteraThrakena had said, Keia was mourning in her own way. "Will she ever get over them?" Kord asked.

"She is young, and eventually the loss in her heart will lessen, and when she has finished grieving, it will be but a memory." She stopped speaking and waited for Kord to look at her. When he placed his eyes on her, she continued, "Until that day, be there for her while she sleeps. Continue to let her lean on you for support." Kord was surprised at what the dragon had said. "You forget that I have been watching both of you since the time after that dreadful moment, so I have seen how you make sure that when she sleeps, you always have your back to her so that she can rest against you for comfort."

Kord did not confirm or deny what the dragon had said. He decided that it was time for him to turn in, so he walked over to the door of the hut, opened it, then stepped in, closing the door behind him.

He saw that Keia had already fallen asleep on the mat, so he took up his nightly position next to her with his back toward her. It was not long before Keia moved closer to him, so that their backs were touching one another, even though she never woke up to do so.

Kord closed his eyes and went to sleep. His heart was lighter than it had been for some time.

NINE

Kord and Keia spent the next moon-cycle keeping their thoughts on everyday life and not the past. They were young, and even though the tragedy that fell upon them changed their lives forever, they had plenty of time to place those memories in the recesses of their minds and build new memories over the old ones. It was not easy, but they continued to live.

MiteraThrakena watched the two children play outside the little hut where they dwelt. She was some distance away, but with her dragon eyes, the children were as if they were right in front of her.

She was the one who made sure the children finished their chores, took their baths, ate their meals, and went to bed on time. To them, she was the mother they no longer had. To her, they filled a part of the emptiness she had in her heart. Not completely, for nothing would be able to achieve such a task, but at least there was something.

The two children, especially Kord, learned that if they hurried and finished their chores, they would have more time to play. So as soon as they woke, they went about doing their assigned duties. The tasks they had to perform were not many; however, to children of six and seven seasons, anything that did not have to do with fun was a chore, and it seemed as if it took forever to complete.

The sun was now at the midpoint of the sky. Kord and Keia, having finished their midday meal, were playing tag around the hut. As usual, Kord had quickly tagged Keia and was now running from her, and since she was not as fast, she was having trouble trying to catch him.

MiteraThrakena could not stop herself from smiling because she knew that once he thought that Keia was going to give up, he would either slow down or trip over something, even his own two feet, to allow her to finally catch him, and then it would be her turn to run away from him again. He would fake being too slow and would allow Keia to stay just out of reach so she would think that she was getting the better of him. Kord enjoyed the game, and he made sure that Keia had fun playing it as well.

While she rested in the meadow, watching the children run around and making the type of noise that only children can make when they are having fun, PateraThrakon walked up beside her and lay down next to her. Their bodies were in contact with each other, which was a way that all of nature's creatures show love to one another.

"Do they have to make so much noise?" PateraThrakon asked. Even though the two children were a few land-marks away, his dragon ears had no problem hearing the growling noise Kord was making as he chased Keia, who was making a high-pitched shrieking noise as if he was actually going to harm her when he finally caught her.

"They are human children, and human children are noisy," MiteraThrakena answered him, turning her head to see him staring at the two.

"They could be quieter. Before they arrived, this land was more peaceful, and a dragon could get some sleep," he said.

MiteraThrakena turned her head to look back at the children. She did not even reply to her mate's comment because she knew that he had just woken up and had been asleep from the time the moon was at its midpoint until now. The male dragon had no problem sleeping, no matter how much noise the two humans made. He just wanted to have something to complain about, and as usual, the two children were an easy target.

She knew why, and his ramblings concerning the children had increased lately, and since his mood was not going to change for the better anytime soon, it was the perfect time to discuss what they both knew had to be talked about. "To this day, they have been with us for two moon-cycles," she said while still watching the children. His only reply to her statement was a growl deep in his throat. "It is time that we decide what we are going to do with the two humans."

He waited a moment, then gave her his decision, "I will eat the boy, and you can feast on the girl." For her answer to his statement, she whipped the back of his head with the end of her tail to let him know that he should not say such things, even though they both knew that neither of them would ever eat a human being. "I was only thinking about it," he said to apologize to his queen. He then watched the children, this time with the seriousness that was required of him and of the situation.

"They are our only hope," MiteraThrakena spoke when the silence had gone on long enough between them. PateraThrakon could only take a deep breath and let out a sigh. Hope was not something he was used to, and hope had failed them both before. "We have to trust that they will grow into the humans that can fulfill what is needed of them."

"Human hearts change," he said, knowing that she could not disagree with him. Both dragons have been around long before any human ever walked on the world of Eirene. They had watched the humans turn not only against other races but their own as well. Humans were unpredictable, and that caused the male dragon to be wary of them, even if they were children.

He was deep in thought, but she knew that the two of them were running out of time. "Keia has a pure soul. She has never once been angry or shown a sign of hatred in her heart. As for Kord..."

PateraThrakon had his own opinion of Kord and

broke into the conversation to let it be known. "His tongue is going to get him in trouble. He shows no respect for us dragons."

Not to be outspoken by her mate, MiteraThrakena looked at PateraThrakon and spoke her mind, "Maybe because you show him none as well."

He turned his head to look at her and saw her staring at him. "He is a human. We are dragons. The child cannot even begin to understand what that means."

She turned back to watch the children. They had run themselves ragged from playing tag. Now they were lying on the ground looking up at the sky. "As you said, he is a child. He needs to mature; in that, I agree with you, and he will. What he needs is something he can focus on, something that will allow him to see a better way." She turned and looked at him. "The dragon way." She went back to watching the children.

He knew she was right, but that did not make him feel any more comfortable in making the decision. "Do you trust the boy enough to take the risk?" he asked and was surprised by her answer.

"No," she turned and looked at him, seeing the shock in his eyes. "But I trust the girl." She put her focus back on the children. "She has seen death at such a young age, and yet her heart is still full of goodness. She fights the memories while she sleeps, but while she is awake, she has joy in her eyes and in her laugh."

"What does that have to do with the human boy?" he asked.

For her it was simple. "It is the human girl who will ensure that the human boy never strays. He will watch over her and protect her, and she will simply be who she is. If he should even think of stepping out of line, she will chastise him and put him in his place."

"And how would you know that?" he asked.

She did not even take her eyes off the children when she replied, "Because that is what I do with you, and the girl looks at the boy, the same as I look at you." She turned and looked at her mate sitting beside her and said, "With love." She gave him a dragon smile, then turned back to watch the children who were now rolling on the ground. She then thought that even though the two had a bath yesterday, another one today would not hurt them. She was always watching them as a mother would her own children.

PateraThrakon was still thinking about what his queen had just said. He knew that she was the one who kept him from making unwise decisions. Not that she was any wiser, but she knew his heart and that sometimes, just like most males, their ego and pride tried to grow bigger than what their heart was. It was the female's responsibility to make sure that the male they loved stayed true to their heart.

MiteraThrakena stood up and began walking toward the hut to gather the children to take them to the pond to bathe. Of course, Kord would complain about how he just had a bath in the past sun-cycle, but she knew that Keia would tell him to stop complaining and do as he was told. Just as any female should.

"We will speak with them tonight," PateraThrakon said to her as she was walking away. "We will see if they will be the ones that we can entrust our hopes to."

She did not say anything to him; she simply spread her wings and took to the air to fly to the children. Of course, she was smiling to herself, because she knew that no matter how ferocious he wanted to be, he always listened to her advice.

"Come on, Kord," Keia was shaking him to try to get him to wake up. After they had their bath, Kord decided that he had time to take a nap before it was time to eat their evening meal. "Kord, her Lady wants us." They had taken to calling MiteraThrakena *Lady* and PateraThrakon *Lord*. This was because Keia thought it only proper since the two dragons were the King and Queen of Dragons, and Keia thought their names were too long to say anyway. Even though Kord called them Lady and Lord as well, he did not understand how they could be the King and Queen of Dragons when there were only the two of them. "Wake up," Keia said more irritably and shook Kord even harder.

"If she wants us, then she can come here," Kord

said, not wanting to cease his napping or show any obedience to the dragons; he still wanted to let both dragons know that he was going to do what he wanted to do. At least that is what he thought.

Keia decided that she had shaken him enough and stood up to leave. “She told me that we are to go to them.” MiteraThrakena would still speak to her in the same way when the female dragon had led them through the woods and to KhoraThraks. Keia could hear her in her thoughts, and she could speak to the female dragon in the same manner, something that Kord was a little jealous about, but never said anything. “The Lord and Lady want us to go to their den.”

The words piqued Kord’s interest, and he sat up to continue the conversation, “What den?” he asked, because since they had been in KhoraThraks, they had never seen the den of the dragons, and they certainly had not been to it.

“It’s where they live. It is a ways off, and it is going to take a couple of marks to get there.”

Now Kord was really interested. To him, going to a new place, especially a dragon’s den, would be an adventure. He could also see through the cracks in the door’s planks that it was almost dark out. If it was going to take them a couple of marks to even reach the den, then it would be night before they would even make it there and back, and a night adventure was greater than a regular adventure in the day.

It had been two moon-cycles since Kord and Keia had arrived, and even though Kord was thankful that he had a place to sleep at night, food to eat, and water to drink, he would never say that to the two dragons. Especially his Lordship, who always seemed as if the male dragon was talking down to Kord simply because he was a human, but Kord was growing restless. Every day was the same routine. Wake up, eat; do chores, eat; finish chores, eat, go to bed. There had to be something more, and an adventure was something that he could look forward to.

"Wait for me," he yelled to Keia. She had already left, while Kord was still thinking about going on an adventure. He jumped up and ran out of the hut to catch up to Keia. When he reached her, he fell in step to walk at her side. "What do they want with us?" Kord asked.

"I don't know. My Lady only said to come to them, and that she would lead us."

Kord decided that there was no need to ask any more questions. Keia would not have the answers anyway, so he would just have to go along with her to find out what the dragons wanted. He remembered that he had heard stories that dragons would keep all the treasure they collected in the caves where they slept. Maybe he would be able to see gold coins and jewels, or better yet, maybe the dragons would give him some of it so that he could leave and have a comfortable life.

He was spending the gold just as quickly as his mind could convince him that the dragons were going to give them not just some of the gold but all of it. His take on his own thoughts was simple. What do dragons need with gold anyway?

He took a glance over at Keia, who was walking to his right. As usual, she did not speak much when she was doing as her Lady had commanded her to do. Kord would not even bother her with any questions because he knew that she was listening for her next instructions. His thoughts drifted toward where they would be able to find a place for them to live once they left KhoraThraks. Of course, he was thinking about Keia as well; they would find a place together, and for some reason, that thought alone made him seem a little nervous.

He decided that he would have to buy himself some new clothes too. Something that he would be able to wear when he goes on more adventures, and he would have to buy a sword as well, he would have to protect Keia while they were out in the world, there are always a lot of dangers, and he had to make sure that Keia was safe. He glanced at her again and got a funny feeling in his heart.

He decided that he was just getting too excited about going to the dragon's den and seeing all the treasures that they would have. He might be able to find a sword among all the riches that they were hoarding, then he thought that *might,* was not the right word. He *would* find a sword he could use.

He then glanced back at Keia. She would need some new clothes as well. The dragons had provided both children with different sets of clothing, but they were nothing fancy. The dragons had said that they belonged to some humans and had come into their possession. Since they had clothes, Kord had not thought much about obtaining more, but with all the gold he was going to have, both he and Keia would be able to buy all the clothes they wanted.

The next item on his list was food. He would no longer have to eat fruit. He could have meat. Chicken, fish, beef, oh, how he missed the taste of beef. "Kord!" He came out of his daze and looked to his right, thinking that he would see Keia. He quickly noticed that she was no longer at his side. "Over here." He looked to his left and saw that at some point, Keia had begun to walk in a different direction. "Listen when I am talking to you," she said, irritated that Kord was holding her up from reaching the dragons.

"When did you say something?" he asked because he was sure that she had not spoken a single word since they had left the hut.

"I said that we have to go this way." She had her arm stretched out, pointing behind her to show the way they needed to be heading, which was not the same direction Kord had continued in. Since he seemed confused, she decided that she would have to take charge. She walked over to Kord, grabbed his right hand with her left, then started walking again to get them both moving in the correct direction. "Come on and stay with me or you are going to get lost."

"No, I'm not," he said to let her know that he was sure that he knew where he was going, but held on to her hand anyway, just to make sure she did not get lost herself. That is what he told himself. He was sure that he did not need her to get to where he needed to be.

They continued to walk, and Keia adjusted their heading when MiteraThrakena instructed her to do so. If she had not been holding onto Kord's hand, there was no telling where he would have ended up, because his mind kept returning to the gold and to how he was going to spend it all.

They finally reached the entrance of a cave. They could see light coming from inside, but beyond the entrance, it was too deep to see the dragons.

"You may enter," MiteraThrakena relayed to Keia.

"Come on," Keia said to Kord without looking at him, but still holding onto his hand as she started moving forward into the dragons' lair.

Kord now remembered some of the stories he had heard about when someone entered the den of a dragon. How those who did, never came out. He tried to get his mind off the despairing thoughts and tried to think about all the gold that he was going to find, but for some reason, instead of piles and piles of gold lying deep within the cave, there was nothing but piles and piles of bones, belonging to all the brave but foolish people who tried to get their hands on the dragons' gold. Still, he held on to Keia's hand because she needed his support, not because it was the other way around.

They continued through the cave and eventually came to the part of the den occupied by the dragons. There were torches on the wall that were lit, so there was plenty of light for the two humans to see. Normally, the dragons did not ignite the torches since they had no problem seeing in the dark, but since the humans would be present, MiteraThrakena made sure that there would be enough light for the children to see.

When they reached the two dragons, Keia and Kord saw that they were each lying on a raised dais. PateraThrakon's was a little higher than MiteraThrakena's, which was to his left. To his right, there was another dais, which was lower than the one MiteraThrakena rested on; however, it was empty.

"You called for us, My Lady," Keia said and curtsied to the dragons. In the time she had been with the dragons, she thought that it was fun to treat the two dragons like any king and queen. Just because they were dragons meant no difference to her.

"Yes, child, and thank you for being swift in your arrival." It pleased MiteraThrakena to play along with Keia's manner, because with the way she responded to the child, it had brought a smile to the little girl's face, and that in turn brought a smile to hers.

Kord looked around and was torn at what he saw. He was sure that his eyes were not playing tricks on him, and he was thankful and sad at the same time. Thankful that he did not see any piles of bones lying on the floor in front of the dragons, that brought a smile to his face; however, it did not last long. To make sure that everyone else present understood his disappointment, he asked the most important question that he had ever thought of, “So where is all the gold that dragons are supposed to hoard in their dens?”

In response to his question, MiteraThrakena could not help but smile. Keia hit him in his side with her elbow, and PateraThrakon was wondering if eating the boy was still not the right thing to do.

TEN

After MiteraThrakena had finally convinced Kord that the legends about dragons hoarding gold were just that, legends, they were able to move on to the reason the dragons had brought the two children to meet with them. Although Kord still believed that the dragons would want to keep the gold for themselves, so of course they were going to tell him that it was only a legend, but he kept quiet about it, for the moment.

MiteraThrakena gave PateraThrakon a nod with her head to let him know that he could proceed with the gathering. "The two of you have been in KhoraThraks for two moon-cycles." He saw that Kord was about ready to say something, probably something amusing to the boy but irritating to the male dragon, so PateraThrakon gave him a look to let the boy know that if he opened his mouth, the dragon would open his and swallow the boy whole; he then went back to the reason they summoned the two children.

"You both have shown that you are strong. You have suffered a great loss, yet you have not succumbed to your hardships." PateraThrakon stopped for a moment to let the memory of their parents pass through their thoughts before he continued. "Because we believe that you both have a caring heart, we would like to offer you a gift."

"A gift!" Kord said with way too much excitement, since the first thing that popped into his mind was gold. To make sure that he did not ruin the moment, Keia poked him at his side with her elbow, the usual warning for him to keep his mouth shut.

"Thank you, My Lord," Keia said and bowed to show her respect for the two dragons. "We are grateful for all that you both have done, and a gift is appreciated, but we do not need anything else from you." Even PateraThrakon could not help but be pleased by her response. He was starting to believe that his queen was correct about the child.

"This gift is not something material that we can hand to you, my dear," MiteraThrakena said, "It is a blessing that we would like to bestow upon the two of you."

The two children turned their heads and looked at each other. They both understood what a gift was, but as for a blessing, they were completely at a loss. They placed their focus back on the two dragons.

"If you choose to accept, we will bestow upon each of you a dragon trait," the male dragon said to further explain what they had planned. "You would be able to use these gifts to help others."

"What do you mean by others?" Kord asked in

the most serious tone he had spoken in since he had entered the den of the dragons.

"Humans," PateraThrakon replied and waited to see the child's response. He could see that Kord was very interested in what the dragon had said, yet he was not sure if the young boy would accept the blessing in the way the dragon wanted him to.

Thoughts ran through Kord's mind; he did not even know what the specific details to what the dragon was offering yet he could not hesitate if what he was thinking was possible, so he looked directly at the male dragon and asked his question, "You said we would help others, humans; does that mean that we would be able to protect them?"

PateraThrakon did not show it, but at that moment, the thoughts he had about the boy altered. Protecting humans was the boy's first thought; it was more than what the dragon had hoped for. "Yes, you would protect them." The dragon still had one question to see if the boy's heart was truly right for the blessing. "Do you have a problem with protecting humans?"

Kord instantly took a step forward and bowed to the male dragon. When he rose, he gave his answer, "My father said that there will always be people who need protecting and those who need to protect them. I will be the one who protects those people."

"And so will I," Keia said, stepping forward to stand next to Kord and bowing to the two dragons. Both were very proud of the two children who had come to their land and into their lives, to give the dragons one last chance at hope.

"What do we need to do?" Kord asked.

The two dragons looked at each other and nodded to let their mate know that they agreed it was time to place their blessings on the children.

"Keia, come and stand before me," MiteraThrakena said, "Kord, you shall stand before His Majesty." Keia did not hesitate to walk over so that she was standing in front of the dais on which the Queen of Dragons was positioned. Now seeing Keia, Kord knew where he needed to move to; however, his thought was that standing directly in front of the male dragon was not a good idea. He would be in the perfect spot for the dragon to chomp down on him and swallow him whole.

"What are you waiting for?" Keia said to Kord, trying to get him to move because he was the one who was holding her up from the blessing she was going to receive from the dragon in front of her.

Kord took one more look at Keia, then at the male dragon, which, for some reason to Kord, looked a lot larger than usual, especially its maw. He had mixed feelings of dread and excitement, but eventually his curiosity got the better of him, and he walked over to stand in front of the dais where the male dragon was.

When the two children were in place, both dragons began reciting the blessing:

We are Dragons of Eirene,
Created to protect the living,
We give our lives, so others may live,
We give our breath, so others may breathe.

When they stopped speaking, the two dragons extended their necks and heads, positioning them to be directly in front of the two children. Then they exhaled and allowed their breath to pass over them. Kord prepared himself for what he believed was coming. He thought that he was going to get a whiff of stinky dragon breath, but the scent coming from the male dragon's breath was that of the morning breeze. Keia thought the same. The dragons continued:

We give our blood, so others need not bleed.

Kord did not like the sound of the last statement. He was not sure who was going to do the bleeding.

The two children watched as the dragons raised their right front paw to their maws and bit down on one of their digits. They then lowered their paw, positioning the cut over the children's heads. The dragons then allowed a single drop of their blood to fall onto the children. Before Kord could say anything about what had just happened, the blood disappeared, absorbed into their bodies. The dragons continued with the blessing:

We give our honor, so others will be honored,
We give you, The Dragon's Rite.

Since the two dragons had stopped speaking, the children thought that whatever the dragons were doing was now complete, and they looked at each other. Keia was not sure what to do next, but Kord thought that he should check to see if there was any dragon blood in his hair, so he reached up and rubbed his hand over his head, then brought it down and looked at it. He did not see any blood, and a part of him was disappointed that he did not. He then looked up at the male dragon and gave his opinion about what he had just experienced. "Is that it? You breathe on us and put blood on us. Hey, while we're here, do you want to spit on us too?"

PateraThrakon lowered his head so that he was a handbreadth away from Kord's head, "Do not tempt me," he said, then raised his head and remembered that he was more mature than the boy, so he had to restrain himself. "Raise your right hand," he said to Kord. The boy did, positioning it so that it was at the height of his face. "Focus on your finger," the dragon said to give the boy his next instructions.

"Which one?" Kord asked since he had four to choose from, as well as his thumb.

PateraThrakon decided to make it easy for the boy to know which finger to use. "The one you use to pick your nose with." Kord curled all his fingers in except for the one next to his thumb. He was about to pick his nose with it, to show the dragon that he did not care what the dragon thought about his less-than-decent habits, but decided he did not want to test the male dragon's patience.

PateraThrakon raised his front right leg and closed three of his four digits so that he was showing only one, just like Kord. "Now focus on mine, and picture it in your mind."

Kord raised his head and looked at the dragon. The digit it was holding up was long and gold. It had scales on it, and it ended with a claw. Kord could see it clearly, but he still did not know what to do. "What is supposed to happen?" he asked.

"Are you picturing what you see in your mind?" the male dragon asked.

"Yes," Kord said, a little frustrated that he was not seeing anything amazing happening. PateraThrakon was also not thrilled at witnessing the failure of the boy, though he was not surprised.

"Try closing your eyes," MiteraThrakena spoke up before the two males began to bicker at one another.

Kord did as the female dragon suggested and focused on making an image of the dragon's digit appear in his mind. He did not know how long he stayed that way, but he eventually heard Keia speak to him, "Open your eyes, Kord." Her tone was that of surprise.

Kord opened his eyes and looked at his finger that was in front of him. Although it was no longer his finger he was looking at. He thought it was, but it was not at the same time. His finger no longer looked human; it was now covered with scales and was the color of copper. At the end of his finger, he did not have the fingernail of a human, but the claw of a dragon. It was not as long as the claw of PateraThrakon, but it was longer than his normal human fingernail.

He tried to bend his finger, and it moved just as his human finger would. He then turned his hand around to look at his finger from different angles, and no matter how he saw it, it was definitely a dragon's finger.

"In time, once you have trained, you will be able to alter your entire body, just as you see before you," PateraThrakon said.

"You mean I'll be able to become a dragon?" Kord asked excitedly. The thought of becoming a dragon was better than anything he could imagine, and then the best part of that thought came to him. "Will I be able to grow wings and fly in the sky like you? That will be wonderful!"

PateraThrakon saw how happy the boy was, and that only added to the dragon's own happiness when he decided to tell the boy the truth. "You will not be able to become a dragon, and you definitely will not grow wings and fly in the sky." The male dragon saw that the boy was disappointed upon hearing his statement; PateraThrakon was pleased with that. "You are still a human, and humans do not have wings, so you will not be able to grow them. In time, you will be able to alter your body so that you will have increased strength, since dragons are stronger than humans. As well as the scales that will appear on your body will protect you. There are very few weapons in existence that are capable of even scratching the scales of a dragon, and you will have the same trait.

Kord, disappointed that he would not be able to fly, was still happy with the thought of having his body covered with scales that could stand up against weapons. He looked at his finger, then a concerned look appeared on his face, which he relayed to the male dragon, "Um, can my finger go back to being human, if I want it to, or am I going to be stuck like this forever?" He may not have realized it, but in a way, he had just insulted the King of Dragons.

PateraThrakon lowered his head so that he was once again a handbreadth away from the boy's face. "And what is wrong with looking like a dragon all the time?"

Kord realized what he had just said, "Um, nothing, it's just that I was wondering if I could change my finger back to looking human." Kord was ready to let his finger look the way it was for the rest of his life, just as long as the dragon did not eat him because he was offended.

"Think of how your finger looked when it was in human form," MiteraThrakena said, to stop the two males from bickering again. They had spent enough time with the boy's blessing, and she wanted to show Keia the gift she had bestowed upon her, but as usual, the two males were always holding things up.

Kord looked at his finger, which still resembled that of a dragon. To help him focus, he closed his eyes and thought about how his finger looked when it was in human form. "Open your eyes," he heard Keia say, and when he did, he saw that his human finger was once again on his hand. Which he was glad for. It was fun to be able to change it to that of a dragon, but he had been human his whole life, and he thought that was what he wanted to be.

"If we are through with Kord's blessing, may we now focus on Keia?" MiteraThrakena asked, and with her tone, both Kord and PateraThrakon knew it was time for them to remain silent and let the females speak.

Keia did not hesitate. "I am ready, My Lady," she said to let the female dragon know that she wanted to see what blessing she had received.

"Extend your arm out with your palm facing upward." Keia did as she was instructed, her excitement showing in the shaking of her hand. "Now think of a flame of fire in your palm."

Keia, having seen what Kord did to help him focus, closed her eyes. She then thought of a flame of fire resting in her palm. She did not need anyone to tell her to open her eyes; somehow, she knew that what she had pictured in her thoughts was there waiting for her to see. She opened her eyes, and sitting in the middle of her palm was a small flame of fire. It was only about a handbreadth in height, but it was big enough to bring an even bigger smile to the little girl.

"You will be able to call upon the forces of nature. You will be able to control them and use them," MiteraThrakena said.

Keia was confused. "What are the forces of nature?" she asked.

MiteraThrakena lowered her head so that she was directly in front of Keia's outstretched hand. "Fire is only one force of nature. The others are Water, Wind, Ice, and Lightning." MiteraThrakena saw the girl shudder at the mention of the last word. The dragon then raised her head, looking at the child watching the flame. The female dragon had no trouble sensing that the child would have a problem with the one.

"It doesn't burn," Keia said when she finally realized that the flame was not causing her any pain at all. In fact, the flame felt comfortable.

"The blessing would not do you much good if it harmed you, my child," MiteraThrakena said to let Keia know that she was safe with the blessing granted to her. "However, you must be cautious," the female dragon continued, and the girl took her focus off the flame and placed it on the dragon, whose tone had changed to match the importance of what she was about to relay. "The forces of nature are powerful. They can be controlled, but at any moment, that control can be lost. If you lose control, others will suffer from the devastating results."

With what the female dragon said, Keia began to think that maybe what she was holding in the palm of her hand was too much for her. Then she told herself that she would not lose control of the blessing given to her. She would not disappoint MiteraThrakena. "How do I use the other forces of nature?" she asked, wanting to see what the other gifts were like, all of them except for maybe one.

"It will take time for you to master all five forces. Fire will be the least difficult for you to learn because it is part of the everyday life of a human. You cook with fire, you use it to stay warm, and you use it to light your way. Fire is a tool mastered by humans, yet the others: Water, Wind, Ice, and Lightning, are forces which humans have less or no use for," MiteraThrakena explained to Keia, and did not miss the child's reaction to the word Lightning. Yes, that would be the most difficult for the child. "Close your palm, and the flame will go out."

Keia followed the dragon's instructions, and when she opened her fingers, the flame was no longer present, but Keia thought that all she had to do was think about the flame again and it would appear. "Thank you, Your Majesty," Keia said and bowed to the Queen of Dragons.

MiteraThrakena nodded to show the girl her approval, then spoke to the children, "You have both received our blessings, and in time you will come to master them. We hope that you will use what we have entrusted you with to bring blessings to others."

As if on cue, both children spoke together, "Yes, My Lady," they said, and bowed to her; then they both bowed to the male dragon. "My Lord," they said to show their gratefulness to him as well. Even Kord responded with honor to the two dragons, and PateraThrakon thought that maybe there was hope for him yet.

"There is one last part of the blessing that we have," MiteraThrakena paused to wait until she had the children's full attention. "When you both have completed your training, you will each be given a title. One which is in accordance with the gift you have received." The Dragon Queen placed her attention on Keia, "You will be called the Dragon Kastera. The word *Kastera* is used in reference to a female caster, who can control the forces of nature and what you will be able to cast."

"Thank you, My Lady," Keia said and bowed to the female dragon.

"And you will be called..." PateraThrakon began but was interrupted by Kord, who thought he had the perfect title for himself.

"Dragon-man!" Kord thought that it was a very good name, and to show it, he had taken up the pose with his arms brought up in front of him, bent at his elbows with both hands clenched into fists.

PateraThrakon thought that maybe the hope he had for the boy just a few moments ago was already gone in the wind. "You will not be called Dragon-man." When Kord realized that the male dragon was serious, he went back to his original stance before the dragon, and PateraThrakon continued with what he was going to say, "You will be called the Dragon Klau. The word *Klau* represents that which you will use. It is the claws of a dragon that defend the ones they protect."

Kord thought about it and did agree that maybe Dragon Klau did sound better, but he would decide later what he really wanted to call himself. Dragon-man still at the top of the list, but for now, "Thank you, My Lord," is what he said to the King of Dragons, and even gave him a bow.

Now that he had informed the boy of the true title, PateraThrakon could continue. "Do not take these blessings lightly. They are to be used for good, never for evil."

With the tone he had used, even Kord did not think it was wise to respond in his usual humorous way. "We will, My Lord," Kord and Keia said to him, then bowed to him, then to MiteraThrakena.

The two children looked at each other with smiles on their faces. Happy with what they had just gone through and ready to begin their training.

The two dragons looked at each other, trusting that they had made the right decision. Their hopes rested on the two children standing before them.

ELEVEN

It did not take long for Kord and Keia to fall asleep when they finally returned to their hut once the King and Queen of Dragons had given their blessings to them. From the long trek to the dragons' den, along with the rite they partook in, and the long trek back to their hut, as soon as they had settled in for the night, they were fast asleep, worn out from everything they had been through.

Unlike other mornings, MiteraThrakena allowed them to sleep well past their normal rising time. Usually, she would wake the children up to begin their daily routine, but since she knew that the blessings given to them was a lot for the children, she did not wake them, giving them time to recover.

Kord was the first to wake. He sat up and looked down to his left to see Keia still sleeping. She had her head resting on her arms and looked as if she was still going to be a while before she woke. Kord could not wait; he wanted to know if what he thought happened last night really did take place or was it all a dream.

He brought his right hand up so that he could

look directly at it. He thought he remembered what occurred, but a part of him also believed that it was all a dream. He had to find out.

What he saw were his normal human fingers, but he was sure that last night he was able to turn one into that of a dragon. He remembered how it looked. It had scales like a dragon. It was a copper color. It had grown longer than his own finger, and it had a claw at the end of it. He could visualize it perfectly in his mind. That memory was fixed in his thoughts so realistically that he knew that it could not have been a dream. There was only one way for him to find out.

Kord closed his eyes. He remembered that is what he did last night when he stood before the dragons. He concentrated on the image in his mind, and when he saw it clearly with his eyes closed, he opened them, and the vision he had in his mind was now directly in front of him. It was not a dream. He was able to turn his finger into that of a dragon's.

"Keia," he said to wake her, but he did not take his eyes off his finger, afraid that if he did, it would turn back to its human form. "Keia," he said again, but all he got as a reply was a groan from her, to let him know that she was not ready to wake up yet. "Keia," he said once more, but this time he reached over with his left hand and shook her, yet he continued to keep his eyes on his dragon finger. "Keia, you have to see this," he said as he shook her more to get her to wake up.

Not really knowing what he was talking about, since she was still groggy from sleeping, she sat up so that she was sitting next to him. She saw what he was looking at, and to make sure that she was seeing what she thought she was seeing, she rubbed her eyes with her hands to clear them so that she could get a better view of what she was looking at as well.

"Do you see it?" Kord asked her without taking his eyes off his finger.

"Can you move it?" Keia asked.

Kord had not even thought about trying to move it, and when Keia mentioned it, he was hesitant to do so, afraid that the dragon finger would revert to his own human finger.

"Try to bend it," she said to get him to do something more than just stare at it.

For the first time since his finger had changed form, Kord looked to his left to see Keia. He wanted to get her final opinion on the situation, and she nodded her head to let him know that he should do as she suggested. Kord nodded back to her then put his focus back on his finger. He took a deep breath, held it, and then he slowly bent his finger.

It moved just like it did when it was in its human form. When he had curled it up as much as it could, he extended it back out, then repeated the process two more times. By then, Kord was almost sure that the dragon finger was real, and more importantly, it was his. "It wasn't a dream," he said, then turned to look at Keia. "It wasn't a dream." He did not repeat himself because he thought that she had not heard what he had said. He did so because he wanted to make sure that what he was seeing was real, and now he believed it.

He continued to bend and unbend his dragon finger, and as he did so, he turned his hand so that he could see it from different angles and get a better look at it. While he continued to look at his finger, he remembered that he was not the only one who had received a blessing from the dragons, and since his was real, then Keia's must be as well. He stopped looking at his finger and looked at Keia. He saw that she was just as fascinated with his blessing as he was, but he wanted her to think about what she should be able to do. "It's your turn now." She stopped looking at his finger and looked at him directly. "They gave you a blessing also. Remember?"

She raised her right hand and looked at it, remembering what had happened last night. Even though she had just witnessed what Kord was able to do, Keia wondered if she would be able to repeat the act that she had done when she was with the dragons. Would she be able to make a flame of fire appear in her hand?

"You can do it," Kord said to take away any doubts she was having. When she looked at his face, he smiled and nodded at her to let her know that it was her turn.

She nodded to Kord to let him know that she was ready. At least most of her was. Like Kord, there was still a part of her that felt as if everything she went through last night was nothing more than a dream, but she had to try. She had to see if she would be able to make a flame appear in her hand, just as she did before.

She first brought her hand close to her face so that she could look at her palm. She saw that there was no mark left from the flame that she had brought forth last night, and part of her began to doubt if she could do it again. She looked at Kord, who was smiling with excitement, waiting for her to repeat the act of making a flame. With his smile, her confidence grew, and she was ready to try.

She extended her arm out in front of her with her palm facing up, just as she had done in the dragons' den. She then closed her eyes and pictured in her mind a flame in the middle of her palm. It took no more than a thought, and immediately the flame appeared. She could sense it there; however, it took Kord to make her trust herself. "Open your eyes."

She slowly opened her left eye, but when she saw what she was holding in her right hand, she opened her other eye as well. There, sitting in the middle of her palm, was a flame of fire. It flickered just like any other flame, glowing in the colors of red and orange, and even though she could sense the heat coming from it, it did not burn her.

Kord, being curious like any boy, reached up with his left hand and moved it closer to the flame. He stopped before his fingers came in contact with it.

"It's hot, I can feel it." He moved his hand back, then looked closer at the flame. "Doesn't it burn you?" he asked.

"No, I can feel it, but it isn't burning me. It feels warm and..." She paused for a moment to think of the best word to describe what she was feeling. When she was sure she had it, she continued, "... comfortable." Kord looked at her directly to try to get a better understanding of what she was saying. "That is the only way I can tell you what it feels like." She brought her hand up closer to her face so that she could look at the flame. "It's like when you are cold, and you sit next to a fire. The heat from it just makes you feel better." She did not know how to explain it any other way.

"Let me try something," Kord said, and Keia looked at him with a puzzling look on her face. "Stretch out your arm." She did and held her arm out just as she had when she first conjured the flame.

Now that she was ready, Kord proceeded to the next test he wanted to try. He lifted his right arm and reached out with his hand. He had already curled up his fingers that were in human form, leaving only the one that resembled that of a dragon's extended. When his hand was about two handbreadths away from Keia's, he stopped, hesitating on whether what he was about to do was a good idea or not. Curiosity got the better of him, and he once again started moving his hand closer to the flame.

"Wait!" Keia said, and Kord instantly stopped

moving his hand forward. "What if it burns you?" she asked.

Kord looked at her, then back to his finger and the flame in Keia's palm. "I don't feel any heat from the flame. As soon as I do, I'll stop."

Keia was not sure if she was comfortable with what he was about to do. The flame did not hurt her at all, but she was uncertain if it would harm Kord or not, and that was something she did not want to happen.

Kord saw the worried look on her face, and even though he understood her concern, he had to see what was going to happen. He nodded to her, then continued to move his finger closer to the flame.

When it was just a handbreadth away, he still could not feel any heat coming from the flame, then he realized that was not completely true. He did not feel any heat on his finger that was covered with scales, but for the ones that he had curled into his palm, he felt the heat from the flame on them. Even though he had them as tight as possible, he put more pressure on the three fingers and his thumb to see if he could get them even tighter; it did not happen, so he decided that he would just have to keep them away from the flame as much as possible.

He once again moved his finger closer to the flame, when he was just two finger lengths from it, Keia started to slowly pull her hand away. "Don't move," Kord said, and she froze where she was. She did not want Kord to get hurt because she reacted carelessly.

Kord suddenly stopped moving his hand forward. It was not because he was too scared to continue, but because now, where he had his hand positioned, his finger, the one in dragon form, was directly in the middle of the flame. He left it there, and even though he could feel the heat from it on his human fingers, since they were not in the flame itself, he was able to withstand the flame.

"Does it hurt?" Keia asked.

"No, I don't feel a thing." Now more comfortable with what he was doing, he moved the dragon finger across the flame. "I think the dragon scales protect my finger." He ran his finger a couple more times through the flame, then removed it. It was now time for another test.

He remembered what he did last night, so he tried it again. He moved his finger closer to him so he could get a better look at it. Without even closing his eyes, he thought about his finger and the way it looked when it was in human form. It immediately turned back to its original form, but Kord was not done yet. Still with his eyes open, he thought about the finger in its dragon form and the scales and claw reappeared. He then altered it back to its human form.

"See if you can make the flame go out," Kord said to Keia.

She looked at her hand and thought about the

flame. To help her, she curled her fingers into a fist, sealing up her palm. It was as if she smothered the flame in her hand, and when she opened her fingers, the flame was gone.

"Try to bring it back," Kord said.

Keia looked over at him, then focused on her palm extended out in front of her. She did not close her eyes like before, wanting to see the flame appear in her hand.

She took a deep breath and thought about the flame, which seemed to her as if it had appeared just as soon as she thought about it. As if every time she tried to bring forth the flame, it occurred faster and easier than the previous time. Then, with a thought, she extinguished the flame in her hand, and with her next thought she made it reappear.

"Come on, let's go outside," Kord said, wanting to perform his next test. Keia did not know what he was planning, but was just as eager to continue with what they were doing. Before she stood up, she extinguished the flame once again.

They walked out of the hut and Kord began to look for what he needed. It did not take him long to find what he was looking for. It was nothing but a small stick, no longer than the length of his arm. He took one last look at it, then turned to face Keia. "Ok, make the flame," he said.

Keia extended her palm out, and without hesitation or difficulty, the flame appeared in her hand.

"Go ahead," she said to Kord, knowing what he wanted to do.

Kord walked over to Keia but stopped when he thought he was far enough away that he would be able to stretch his hand out and allow the stick to come in contact with the flame sitting in Keia's palm. "Ready?" he asked. When she nodded, he continued.

He did not move as slowly as he did when he tested whether or not the flame would burn his finger, but he did not rush either. Maybe because part of the excitement was in performing the act, and he wanted to make it last, but eventually the stick touched the flame, and it immediately caught fire.

As soon as he saw the embers come from the end of the stick, he removed it and brought it up closer to his face to look at it. Keia extinguished the flame in her palm and moved closer to where Kord was standing, both of them looking at the burning stick.

Kord switched the stick to his left hand and brought up his right. Before he had even started moving his arm, he thought about his finger, and it immediately took on its dragon form. He then moved his finger and touched the end of it to the still burning stick, but it did not burn him at all, the dragon scales protecting him. He then had another idea about what his next test would be.

With his finger still in dragon form, he positioned the claw against the stick near the middle, and with a little amount of pressure and no resistance from the stick, the claw sliced the stick in two. The top half, the part with the burning end, fell to the ground. Even though Kord was impressed with how easily he cut the stick in two, he kept his wits about him, and as soon as the stick hit the ground, he stomped on the burning end with his foot to make sure the embers were completely out.

He looked at the burnt stick lying on the ground for a moment then looked up at Keia. They waited a moment, then neither of them could stop themselves from laughing. Even though they could have caused a fire that could have gotten out of control, they both thought that what they were able to do was exciting, and that brought joy to them. They were happy with what they were able to do.

Kord tossed the other end of the stick on the ground, then lifted his right hand toward the sky, and yelled, "I am the Dragon Klau!"

Keia then raised her right hand over her head and brought forth a flame in her palm. "I am the Dragon Kastera!" she yelled toward the sky.

They both brought their arms down, then Kord started running around with his arm halfway raised and his finger in its dragon form. To join in the fun, Keia began to run around as well, all the while having her palm raised, facing upward with the flame sitting in the middle of it.

They continued with what they were doing and only stopped when they felt a heavy wind blow down upon them. Then they heard something land a few paces away from where they were, and whatever it was, it landed with a loud pounding noise, causing the ground to shake.

They did not have time to even think about what it was, because the next thing they heard was the overbearing roar of a dragon. It was PateraThrakon who had landed enough distance away from the two children so that he would not crush them, but he was close enough to let them know that he had arrived with power, anger, and urgency. When he finally ceased his roar, the two children removed their arms from in front of their eyes, which they had positioned to guard them against the wind and the roar. It was obvious that the King of Dragons was not pleased with them.

TWELVE

In the legends of Eirene, it is said that dragons could cast a spell over the species of the world that would make anyone who heard the roar of a dragon become immobilized with fear. It was only a legend. Dragons did not need to cast any such spell. It was the roar of the dragon alone that placed the individual in such a state.

His anger was so great that he roared a second time. The two children could only stand motionless as the deafening blast from PateraThrakon engulfed them and traveled throughout the entire land of KhoraThraks. They could not move due to the sheer strength and power in the roar and the awe that they felt from such a tremendous force. If they had not been so frozen in fear, they would have fallen to the ground and waited for their lives to come to an end.

The King of Dragons finally ceased his roar, but the words that boomed out of his maw did not ease the children's dread that came upon them. "Foolish and impudent humans. You dare treat what we have given you as if it is but a plaything for your enjoyment." To express his disappointment in the two children, he lifted his head toward the sky and blasted out another roar. If he had focused it in the direction of the children, the force would have knocked them back into the hut behind them.

When he was done, he lowered his head to look at the two children who had not moved from where they had been standing since the arrival of the dragons. MiteraThrakena had come along with her mate, but on this matter, she would not interfere with the King of Dragons. Her concern about what the children had been partaking in was just as great as his, as well as the disappointment with the humans.

PateraThrakon began his chastising of the children once more. "We grant you the blessing of the dragons, and this is how you repay our trust in you. You think that what we have done is for your amusement, so that you can use it as if they are simple parlor tricks meant to entertain foolish humans." To show his displeasure again, he lifted his head toward the sky and let out another tremendous roar.

When he ended, Kord thought that he would give his explanation, "We only..."

"SILENCE!" PateraThrakon roared once he had lowered his head to look directly at the children, the moment Kord began to speak. The sheer force of the word caused Kord to close his mouth and hope that he was not about to be eaten, and this time, he thought that the King of Dragons would do just that. "We saved your life; we brought you to our land. We provided you with food; we made sure you were safe, and when we thought that you would be worthy of accepting our blessings, you revealed to us what all humans are. Nothing more than self-centered, arrogant, foolish beings, who know nothing of what it means to be a dragon. You have no honor, you have no respect, you have no reason for existence outside your own self-worth, and meaningless life."

PateraThrakon once again raised his head to the sky and released another roar to vent out his anger. This one was louder than the ones before since he had enraged himself while letting the two children know exactly what he thought about humans in general.

He lowered his head and looked directly at the two children. "I should have known that it would be a worthless effort to entrust you, *humans*, with the honor of being a part of something greater than yourselves." PateraThrakon had finished with what he wanted to say to the two children. He opened his wings, and with a twist of his body, he took to the sky to distance himself from once again another failure. Not one made by the children, but one of his own.

Kord and Keia stood where they were, not making a single move, so that they would not bring any attention to themselves, which might cause the gold dragon to return. It was only when they heard MiteraThrakena speak that they even realized that she was present during the entire incident. "You should both go inside the hut and wait there until I call for you." The Queen of Dragons made no mistake in what she said. She knew that her mate would have nothing to do with the children, and she would be the one who would have to deal with them and the outcome that they had set in motion. "Go, now," she said when Kord and Keia did not make a move. "I will speak with you when I am ready." She then turned away from the children, opened her wings, and sprang into the sky, following her mate, with as much regret as he had, or maybe even more. She had hoped with all her heart that she and her mate had made the correct decision, yet the two children had shown that humans treat power as if it were nothing but a toy.

As she flew away, she could not help but hear the sound coming from the hut where the children had retreated to. It broke her heart that the children had to be reprimanded, but it was necessary. It broke her heart even more as she heard Keia crying.

A dragon's hearing is far greater than any other creature in the world, and the crying of the young girl made MiteraThrakena's heart sink. Not only for the hurt that Keia must be feeling, but for the hurt the Queen of Dragons felt in her own heart. She had grown so fond of the children and especially of Keia. The kindness and gentleness the human girl had in her heart were something the female dragon cherished greatly, for so few humans possessed such a quality, and with most, if they did have those qualities, they lost them as they grew older, when the influences of the world changed their hearts forever.

MiteraThrakena was disappointed in the children, but she was also disappointed in herself for letting the hope she had in her heart grow greater than what the expectations of a human could be. As her mate had felt when he flew away, she felt the same. Once again, another failure. Not one made by the children, but one of her own.

By the time she arrived back at their den, PateraThrakon was already curled up on his dais. MiteraThrakena was not fooled by the way he was presenting himself, as if he were sleeping. She knew that he was thinking about all that had taken place. Not just with Kord and Keia, but since their troubles started many seasons ago.

MiteraThrakena stepped up onto her own dais and curled up as if she were positioning herself to sleep as well. Once she was settled in, with her tail, neck, and head all wrapped around her body, she spoke to her mate. "The ringing does not cease."

PateraThrakon knew what she was referring to. He, along with his queen, had continually heard the ringing since the moment it began. They could not even escape its sound when they slept. It was constant, and it bothered them more than anyone could ever imagine.

"What shall we do with the children?" she asked her mate. Not only did she want to discuss the matter, but she wanted his involvement as well. She knew that he preferred to lie there and sulk instead of dealing with the issue they were facing, but that did not resolve it. "You could eat the boy," she said as a small attempt at humor.

"Do not tempt me," the gold dragon replied. This time more serious of the notion than ever.

It was not much, but at least she was able to get a response from him, and that would allow her to continue with the conversation. "We thought they were the ones. We erred in our decision."

"It will be our lack of judgment that will cause many to suffer the cost of our mistake."

She had to agree with his reply. As the only two dragons, they were responsible for the outcome of what they had set in motion. "We cannot take back the blessings."

PateraThrakon let out a long sigh before he spoke, "If we could and we did, we would be no better than the humans. We are dragons. Once a blessing is given, it would be dishonorable for us to take it back."

Once again, she agreed with her mate. A dragon would never go back on a promise or their word. "What shall we do with the children?" That was the question she wanted an answer to. As the Queen of Dragons, she had a say about what happened to the children, but she would discuss it with her king and together they would decide what the best solution was to a bad situation.

PateraThrakon was silent for a moment. When he had thought about the problem and finally came up with an answer, he informed his queen. "They must never leave KhoraThraks. We cannot take back what was bestowed upon them, but we can ensure they do not use it against the other races of the world. We will not train them, and in time the gifts they have been given may leave them permanently; even so, they will remain here where we will guard them from causing harm to themselves or others."

"Like prisoners," MiteraThrakena said to let her mate know what exactly he was deciding.

He lifted his head and turned to look at his queen, "Prisoners they may be, but at least they will be allowed to live." He then lowered his head back down to continue with the conversation. "They will have food; they will have shelter. That is more than what some humans can claim."

"They will not have a life," MiteraThrakena said.

"Nor will they take one without cause."

Once again, she had to agree with her mate. It was better for the two children to live in isolation than to allow them into the world where they could possibly do harm with the blessings they had been given. Even if the children are not trained by the dragons to use what was bestowed upon them, it was possible that they could learn to develop them on their own, and that could be even more disastrous.

The queen thought that the discussion was over, so she settled in for a nap. There was not much else she could do or would do when it came to the children. They would stay in KhoraThraks, but as for what they had planned for them, it had come to a complete and utter halt.

"Inform them tomorrow of what we have decided," PateraThrakon said without moving from his resting position. "I do not wish to see them for as long as they remain. Let them know that they are to stay away from our den and are to keep to themselves. They may roam freely in the land as long as they distance themselves from me. Let them know that they should be grateful for what we have decided." He then closed his eyes, ready to sleep for a very long time. He had no reason to remain awake. Now that the children were no longer a concern of his, he would sleep, maybe for a few hundred seasons or so. At least he would try, because the ringing he constantly heard always disrupted his sleep.

MiteraThrakena also decided to take a nap. She would meet with the children tomorrow and inform them of what their lives would be from now on. They may not enjoy staying in the land of the dragons, but at least they would be able to live their natural human lives. She closed her eyes to drift off to sleep; only the ringing in her ears caused her to have trouble doing so.

The sun had left the sky when she caught the scent of someone approaching the den where she and her king dwelt. She knew what it was, and she also knew that her mate would not be happy.

"Why do they approach?" PateraThrakon asked, not even moving from the position he was in. Yes, he had caught their scent as well.

"I do not know. I instructed them to remain in the hut."

"Just like humans to do as they please. Their minds tell them they are right, but their minds are so small they cannot even follow simple instructions from their betters." She did not reply to his comment. She knew that he was still brooding over the fiasco that took place earlier in the morning. "Send them away. Their smell disturbs my sleep."

As much as she loves her mate, even she had her limits as to how much she could take his almost childish human behavior. She was about to let him know just what she was thinking when she realized that the children were not moving any closer to the den. From what she could tell, by their scent in the breeze that entered the den, they were standing at the entrance. This intrigued her, so she decided to ignore her mate and handle the situation in her own manner. "I did not call for you, so why have you come?" With her voice, it might have seemed as if she was speaking in a normal tone, at least for a dragon, but her words echoed through the long chamber leading to the entrance and made it sound as if she was in a fouler mood than she was.

"May we speak with you?" Kord asked to reply to her question.

"Send them away, I am trying to sleep," PateraThrakon said, not wanting to be disturbed, especially by the humans.

"Silence," MiteraThrakena said to him, and she made sure that he understood that at the moment she was in charge of the gathering, and he was not to interfere. Which was okay with him; he just hoped that their visit would be brief so that he could go back to sleep. "You may enter," she spoke, and her voice carried down the chamber to the entrance of the cave.

A few moments later, Kord and Keia came into her sight. She had lit the torches in the chamber as well as in the cavern so the two children would be able to see. They reached the area of the two daises but stayed a distance away from them, not knowing the mood of the two dragons.

Kord stood there holding Keia's right hand in his left. MiteraThrakena did not know if he was doing so to guide her along as they walked through the cavern or for support, or maybe both. The female dragon saw that Keia had her left hand behind her back. When the two children had reached their position, they stood there waiting for one of the dragons to acknowledge them, and of course, it was MiteraThrakena.

"What is it you wish to say?" She had permitted them to explain why they had come to the dragons' den, yet neither of them did so. "Speak what you have to say or return to your hut." MiteraThrakena saw Keia slightly squeeze Kord's hand, giving him the courage he needed.

"We come here and ask that you hear us out," Kord said, his voice cracking because he was nervous.

"Go on," MiteraThrakena said, giving him permission to continue.

"We know that we were wrong in what we did, and we are sorry," Kord said to begin with what he and Keia had come to say to the dragons.

"And you believe that will fix everything?" MiteraThrakena asked.

Kord looked down for a moment, then put his eyes back on the female dragon. "No, it will not. Only that we know that we were wrong and we ask..."

PateraThrakon lifted his head and voiced his opinion on what the children had to say. "What right do you have to ask of anything? We gave you all that you have, and you dare come to our den and ask to speak with us, and now you dare to ask for something else."

Kord looked down at his feet, but when he looked back up, he was determined that he was going to say what the two children had decided on. "We ask that you take back your blessings."

The two dragons were not prepared for what they heard. They looked at each other, then at the two children. It was PateraThrakon who spoke next, intrigued by what the boy had said. "You want us to take back the blessings we gave to you. Is that what you want?"

"Yes," Kord said without hesitating. "You gave it to us, so you can take it back. We do not need it."

"You do not want what we have given you?" PateraThrakon asked.

"I said we do not need it. That is not the same as not wanting it," Kord said with honesty and humbleness.

There was silence in the chamber, so MiteraThrakena decided to see just where the boy was going with his comment. "Explain yourself, child."

In that moment, Kord, whether he knew it or not, stood just a little bit straighter, a little bit taller, as if he were addressing a true king and queen, and he began his explanation. "When I was five seasons old, I asked my father for a knife. He said that I was too young, and I had to wait until I was older. I asked him why. He said that a knife, if not used properly, can hurt not only the one who wields it, but also, if that person does not know what they are doing, they can hurt someone else. He said that when he thought I was ready, he would buy me one and show me how to wield it the correct way." Kord stopped for a moment, took a breath, then continued. "If we are not old enough to use the blessings you gave us, then we ask that you take them from us. We do not need it, because we were happy without them. So please take back your blessings, but we ask that you allow us to stay here with you and that we go back to the way it was, before the other night. We'll do the chores, and I'll even take a bath every day, just please do not make us leave, we have nowhere else to go."

Kord looked to his left and nodded to Keia, who was looking at him. She let go of his hand and walked up to the dais where the female dragon was. When she reached it, she pulled her left hand from behind her back and brought out the bouquet of flowers she had picked on her way to the den. She then divided the bouquet into two parts, placing one half at the base of the dais MiteraThrakena was lying on, then walked over to stand in front of the dais of PateraThrakon. She laid the remaining flowers in front of it, then returned to stand in the middle of the two. She then said the only thing she could think of, which was the most important thing in her heart, "Please do not make us leave, we love being with you." She gave them a curtsy, then returned to stand next to Kord, taking his hand in hers.

Once again, silence filled the chamber. "Return to your hut," MiteraThrakena said.

Both Kord and Keia bowed to the two dragons, then turned and left the cavern. MiteraThrakena waited until she was sure they were away from the den before she spoke so that the two children would not hear what she had to say.

"They would rather give up their blessings and remain here than keep what we have given them," MiteraThrakena said to her mate, who had already returned to the position he was in before he was interrupted by the visit of the two humans. "They said they do not need the blessings we gave them. That they would be happy to go back to the way they were." She still did not get a response from her mate, so she curled her neck and head up against her body to go back to sleep, but not before she said one last comment. "That does not sound like two humans desiring power for their own gain." With that, she closed her eyes, and she was not sure, but she thought she heard her mate whisper a comment of his own. Something that sounded like, *Stubborn humans.*

Kord and Keia both rose early the next morning. Kord told her that if they must leave, they need to get an early start so they will be able to find a place to rest before nightfall. Keia did not want to leave, and neither did Kord, but he decided that no matter what happened, wherever they went, he would make sure that Keia would be taken care of; he would always be there to protect her.

As they were packing, they heard the sound of something landing outside of their hut, and a moment later, they heard the booming voice of PateraThrakon, "Come out here, boy."

Kord looked at Keia and nodded to her. They took each other's hands and went outside to face the male dragon.

He saw the two humans and, for a moment, wondered if he was making the correct decision, but since he had made it, he would follow through with it. “Boy, you will follow me,” PateraThrakon said, looking directly at Kord.

“I am not going to leave Keia behind,” Kord said and made sure that the male dragon knew he meant what he said.

PateraThrakon was almost ready to change his mind right there and then, but he knew that the human was only trying to protect the girl, something the dragon could admire about the boy; however, he was still in charge. “Keia will stay here,” he paused for a moment, then continued, “You will come with me. I will take you to where you will begin your training to become the Dragon Klau.”

The two children looked at each other and smiled, then looked at the male dragon. It might have been hard to tell, but for a very brief moment, PateraThrakon smiled as well. It did not last long; he still had to present himself as the mean and nasty dragon.

MiteraThrakena flew down and landed next to the gold dragon. Keia did not hesitate to ask her question, “You are going to let us stay?”

MiteraThrakena, not worried about putting on a gruff attitude, smiled and answered, “Yes, you both can stay, and I will train you to be the Dragon Kastera.”

Keia, happy that she was going to be able to stay, ran over to PateraThrakon and did the best she could to wrap her arms around his enormous leg and gave him a hug, "Thank you," she said, then ran over to MiteraThrakena and hugged her leg as well.

Kord stayed where he was. Yes, he was grateful that he and Keia would be allowed to stay and happy that they would be trained in becoming the Dragon Klau and Dragon Kastera. He did not hug either of the dragons, but he did nod to PateraThrakon to express his gratitude. Surprisingly, the male dragon gave him a nod to reply. Because of that, Kord decided to keep the comment to himself about how he thought Dragon-man still sounded better than Dragon Klau. He did not want to test his luck, nor PateraThrakon's patience.

THIRTEEN

Keia watched as Kord walked off with PateraThrakon. She was not sure why, but for some reason, she missed him, even though he had just left and would be back. As he was about to cross over the top of the hill and walk out of her sight, he turned around and waved to her. She waved back, and even though he was too far away to see it, she smiled.

"Do not worry," MiteraThrakena said, and Keia looked to her right and upward to face the female dragon. "He will be back before the night is here."

Keia smiled and nodded. She was sure that Kord would be back; he had just said that he would not leave her behind.

They had only been together for two moon-cycles, but Kord was the only one she had. The only one who had been with her since that frightening day. She had become used to him being around and making her laugh. Even though he could be a bit foolish at times, she felt an absence in her life as he wandered beyond the point she could see him.

"Come, it is time that we start your training."

MiteraThrakena could tell what the child was thinking, so she decided that it was best to take her mind off the male child and put it to better use. "Let us go for a walk," she said to Keia, then turned and began walking toward the forest.

They were walking on the path that went through the woods, one that both Keia and Kord had taken many times to collect firewood. It was wide enough for her to walk next to the dragon that stood higher than the little girl. MiteraThrakena did not move fast since Keia was just a small child and would not be able to keep up with the dragon if she had not slowed down her pace.

They walked in silence, Keia allowing the dragon to lead her. She decided not to speak until the female dragon spoke first. She thought it was best since the incident that enraged the two dragons had just been resolved, it was still fresh on their minds, and Keia did not want to bring the topic up again. Never in her short life had she ever felt as if she had disappointed someone in a way where she would not be able to live with the guilt if she was not forgiven. Yet, MiteraThrakena did not mention the incident. She knew that the young girl had learned from her mistake, and that is the most important lesson from the entire situation, so it was time to move on to the next one.

They had been walking for a while, and when MiteraThrakena noticed that Keia had begun to slow down, she decided that it was time to show the young girl another example of what she would be learning as the Dragon Kastera. "Are you growing tired, child?" MiteraThrakena asked but already knew the answer.

"No, I am fine," Keia replied, but even her words lacked the energy to be convincing.

MiteraThrakena stopped walking, and when she did, Keia stopped as well. The dragon looked down to her right and saw Keia looking up at her. Without warning, Keia was lifted off the ground. The surprise of what was happening caused her to make a high-pitched squeal because all of a sudden, she was flying in the air and was positioned over the dragon. She hovered there for a moment, and then she dropped down onto the back of the dragon just at the base of her neck. "Hold on to me so that you do not fall."

Keia did not hesitate to do as she was instructed. She had no desire to fall from the height of the dragon's back. To verify just how high she was, she leaned over to her right to see the view. As soon as she caught sight of the ground, she quickly leaned back to sitting in an upright position and tightened her grasp on MiteraThrakena's neck.

"You may want to keep your eyes forward until you get used to the height," MiteraThrakena said, knowing that the child was a little overwhelmed from what had just happened. "Do you know how you flew through the air?" she asked Keia.

Keia thought about it for a moment, then gave her answer, "No."

"I gathered up the wind and used it to lift you into the air. Wind is a part of nature, and as the Dragon Kastera, one day you will be able to use it as well."

"I remember when you gave me the blessing that you said that Wind was one of the forces of nature."

"Do you remember the other four?" MiteraThrakena asked.

Keia took a moment, then answered the dragon's question, "There is Fire."

MiteraThrakena decided to just briefly remind Keia of the wrong she had done, "Yes, child, we both know that you remember Fire." Keia grew silent, thinking that she was about to be scolded once again, but MiteraThrakena only wanted to make sure she did not forget what she had done. "Wind and Fire, what are the other three?" the dragon asked to let the child know to continue.

"There is Water, and..." Keia had to stop for a moment to think of the next one, which she did, "... oh, there is Ice."

"Correct," MiteraThrakena said to encourage the young girl. "And what is the last one?" She had a feeling that Keia did remember the final force of nature, but she just did not want to mention it. The dragon remembered how the girl reacted during the blessing. The child would have trouble with it, so to help the child, she spoke the word herself. "Lightning is the last force."

"Yes," Keia said in a whisper, and MiteraThrakena

could feel the girl grab tighter around the dragon's neck. It was obvious to her that Keia had a fear of the one force, and that would be a problem when it was time for her to learn it. Fear can cause anyone to fail.

"Do you know why they are the forces of nature?" MiteraThrakena asked.

"No, My Lady," Keia replied in her respective voice, and the dragon could not help but smile.

It was time for her first lesson. "The forces have a life of their own. They themselves have movement. Do you understand?"

Keia did not hesitate to answer, "No, My Lady."

MiteraThrakena was pleased to hear the child admit that she did not know. Most humans, especially males, would rather put on an act instead of admitting that they did not know something. It will be easier to teach the child since she was aware that she did not know, so the dragon continued. "You can see Fire move. The flames dance around, and I am sure there were times when you would stare into the flames of a fire as the wood crackled."

"Yes, My Lady."

"You have seen Water move. It flows in the rivers. Ripples on the ponds and lakes, and of course, when you and Kord are bathing, it seems to splash everywhere." When she made the last statement, MiteraThrakena turned her head and neck so that she could see Keia behind her, who was smiling at the dragon's comment. She then turned her head forward and continued with the lesson.

"Wind moves, and even though you do not see it, you can feel and see the effects it has on other objects. Wind blows your hair into your eyes. It blows on the ground, causing leaves to move. It blows in the sky, causing the tallest trees to bend."

Keia looked around and saw exactly what MiteraThrakena was speaking of. Keia had never seen the wind, but she saw now how the trees were moving, not on their own but because the wind was blowing against them. At that moment, Keia began to feel as if a new world was being opened to her. "But how does Ice move?" she asked.

MiteraThrakena was pleased that the young girl came up with a question. It showed that she would seek knowledge, and for the Dragon Kastera, that was the most important learning tool. "Ice forms when it grows cold. Have you ever seen a lake freeze over during the cold seasons?"

Keia thought back. She had a vague memory of something from her past. "I remember seeing a bucket of frozen water."

"There are parts of the world where Ice covers the entire land. In a single night, a lake can become completely covered with Ice, and you would be able to walk across." It was time to see just how Keia would react to the last force of nature. "What do you know about Lightning?"

She did give her answer, even though the dragon could barely hear it. "It scares me."

"Why?"

"I don't know, it just does."

MiteraThrakena would not press the issue of her fear; there would be time for that later, but she would give Keia something to think about. "Without Lightning, we would not survive. There are things called nutrients; Lightning breaks these nutrients up, and they mix with other nutrients and enter the soil, which in turn helps the plants to grow. Which, in turn, allows food to be made for you to eat. Do you understand?"

"No," Keia answered, and it was the truth. She had no idea what nutrients were and still did not know why Lightning was needed for them. All she knew was that it scared her.

MiteraThrakena understood that her answer was probably too much for the human child. As a dragon, her knowledge of how everything worked in nature was only surpassed by Creator himself. If Keia lived to be one hundred seasons old, she still would not have had the time to take in all the knowledge the dragon had. "It is okay that you do not. Just remember that Lightning, like all the forces of nature, Fire, Wind, Water, and Ice, is needed. They can be useful, but they can also be dangerous, and that is what you need to remember most of all."

"Yes, My Lady," Keia replied.

They continued to walk in silence. Well, MiteraThrakena walked, and Keia rode on her back. It took some time, but they finally reached the destination they were making their way toward. When they came to a stop, MiteraThrakena spoke again, "Look, my child."

Keia, while still holding onto the dragon's neck, leaned to her right to see what the dragon wanted her to observe. They stood at the top of a hill overlooking a valley. The floor of the valley was covered with flowers of every color imaginable. Keia could also see deer wandering around, eating the vegetation. She saw birds flying through the sky. Off in the distance, she saw a mountain whose peak was covered with snow. She saw the river running through the center of the valley, providing the water needed to allow the flowers to bloom and the animals to drink.

"This is the epitome of nature," MiteraThrakena said.

Keia did not know the meaning of the word *epitome*; however, she described it in her own way. "It is beautiful." She then began to rise off the dragon's back; MiteraThrakena used Wind to place her gently on the ground. When she landed, Keia walked a little further to be able to see into the valley below. The dragon moved to stand next to her.

"Nature is everything that lives and thrives in the world of Eirene. What you see here is because we dragons protect this part of the world. In the outside world, the other races have changed nature to suit their needs. In many ways, those needs have corrupted nature and cannot be mended." MiteraThrakena turned and looked down at Keia, who looked up at the dragon. "You must remember that nature depends on us, and all living things depend on it. There must be a balance, and even though some things in nature may frighten you, they are necessary for all to survive."

Keia was not sure if she understood what the dragon was saying. A part of her did not. The part she was trying to figure out in her mind was what nature was exactly. She put her focus back on the valley below, and when she saw the beauty of nature, it was her heart that understood what her mind did not. The sight below placed a feeling in her that made her want to be a part of what she was seeing; it did not matter if she did not understand everything about it.

"Are you ready to begin your training as the Dragon Kastera?" MiteraThrakena asked.

Keia took one last look at the valley, then turned and faced the silver dragon. "Yes, My Lady. What is the first thing you wish to teach me?" Keia asked, eager to begin her training.

"The first thing is the most important, and that is to learn how to read."

Keia was confused. She thought that she would learn about nature. Fire, Wind, Water, Ice, and yes, even Lightning. Once she thought about it, she realized that reading was something that she really wanted to learn. So, she smiled and said, "I am ready."

FOURTEEN

To Kord, it seemed as if he had been walking forever. He was sure that since they had traveled for so long, it had to be at least time for his midday meal. To verify what he had determined, he looked up into the sky, and to his surprise and disappointment, the sun had not even reached its midway point, which let Kord know that he had not been walking as long as he thought, but also that it was not time to eat yet.

"How much farther do we have to go?" Kord asked again, having lost count of how many times he had questioned PateraThrakon regarding the distance they had journeyed.

"Seven," the male dragon said.

Kord did not understand the dragon's reply to his question. "What does seven have to do with how much farther I have to walk?"

"It is the number of times you have asked me how much farther. We will get there when we get there," PateraThrakon said.

To display his dislike for the dragon's response, Kord silently mocked him by whispering, "We will get there when we get there," in his best impersonation of the dragon's deep voice. Unknown to Kord, the dragon's hearing was better than he could have imagined.

"I suggest if you wish to speak as I do, you should wait until you are much older; perhaps then you may at least sound like a man and not a troublesome child."

Kord decided that would be the last time he tried to imitate the dragon, at least while he was within earshot of him.

They continued to walk, and eventually they reached the place where PateraThrakon was leading them. "We have arrived."

Kord looked around and was not impressed with what he was seeing. The first thing he saw was that they had come to a part of KhoraThraks where he had never been. He saw a river, and even if it was part of the river he used near the pond where he bathed, he knew that he had travelled much farther than where it was. There were a few fallen trees in the area, and none of them were sprouting leaves, which led him to believe that the trees had been there for some time. Other than that, all he saw was the landscape behind him, which PateraThrakon had led him along.

"What now?" Kord asked because he had no idea why the dragon would lead him to the area where he was.

"This is where you will begin your training in

becoming the Dragon Klau. With the rising of the sun, you will make your way to this place and train. When you see the sun reach the treetops, you may make your way back to your hut. I will accompany you for the next three sun-cycles to ensure that you do not get lost."

"I won't get lost," Kord said, even though he was not exactly sure of the correct path they took to arrive at their destination, since he was so focused on how long they had been walking. "What about food? If I am here until the sun is almost out of the sky, where can I get my midday meal from?"

PateraThrakon could not help but sigh. Here he was, trying to teach the boy how to be the Dragon Klau, which is a great honor, and the only thing the child can think about is food. "There are plenty of berries and fruits in the forest for you to eat. If you feel you cannot go a single moment without filling your belly, then feel free to forage for your meal."

Kord looked around, then walked further into the area where he would be training. When he made his way to the center, he turned around in a circle, trying to take in what he was seeing, which in his opinion, was not much. "What do you want me to do?" Kord asked, wanting to get on with his training since he was becoming bored.

PateraThrakon stared at the boy, and for a moment, Kord thought that he was about ready to become the dragon's meal, but he soon felt the ground beneath his feet begin to shake. He looked down and saw the dirt and rocks move on the ground as if something was coming up from beneath him, and in a moment, there was.

A mound of dirt began to rise in front of Kord, and it only stopped when it was the same height as him. When he thought that the mound could not do anything else, it began to change its shape, and after a few twists and turns of the dirt, Kord was staring at a replica of himself. Every detail matched him perfectly. The nose, the lips, the eyes, everything, even the hair, except that the duplicate was completely formed out of dirt. He took one last look then asked, "What is it?"

"This is a golem. It will be the one that trains you."

"It's made of dirt," Kord said to make sure that the dragon was aware of the fact.

"Yes, it is, and since you are covered in dirt most of the time, you and it have something in common."

Kord was not happy with the dragon's comment. He was sure there was no way that he ever had the amount of dirt on him that made up the golem. "How is this thing going to train me?" Kord did not see how a mound of dirt could do anything except be a mound of dirt. The golem began to move by taking a step backward. When he saw the golem move, Kord jumped back as well from the shock of seeing a mound of dirt move all on its own. "It's alive!" Kord said to state what he was seeing as well as to get clarification as to what he was witnessing.

"It is a mound of dirt," PateraThrakon said to remind Kord just what was in front of him. "A mound of dirt cannot be alive. I have created it to train you. You will do as it instructs you." The dragon added one final statement. "You will obey it without failure."

Kord looked at the golem but was not impressed with what he saw. Yes, it looked exactly like him, but other than that, he did not see how it was going to be able to train him. "What does it want me to do?" Kord asked, and for a reply, the golem turned and began walking away from him, heading off in the direction that would lead him into the forest. Kord was still not sure of what to do, so he remained where he was.

"What are you waiting for?" PateraThrakon asked.

Kord turned to look at the dragon. "He didn't say anything, so how am I supposed to know what to do?"

The dragon once again let out a sigh, having to deal with the limited intelligence of the human boy. PateraThrakon had made the golem with some of his own essence and will. It would train the boy the way the dragon wanted it to. When he created it, he did not realize that the boy did not have the intelligence to follow a mound of dirt. "The golem is made from dirt. It does not have the capability to speak. It can move around, and it will be able to train you; all you must do is perform as it does."

Kord saw that the golem had stopped at the edge

of the woods, so he figured that the golem wanted him to follow. He watched as the golem stood there waiting for him, then looked at the dragon. "Why don't you train me?"

"I have better things to do than to train you." To make his point, PateraThrakon made his way closer to the river, where he found the perfect spot to curl up and take a nap in the morning sun.

Kord watched as the dragon made himself comfortable, and since the dragon had closed his eyes, Kord knew that the discussion was over. He looked at the dragon, then at the golem, and decided that following the golem would be more fun than staying there and watching a dragon sleep all day. At least if he went with the golem, he could go exploring a part of the land he had not been to before, and exploring was something Kord enjoyed.

He started making his way over to the golem, but before he reached it, it turned and began making its way into the woods. Kord did not hesitate to follow it.

PateraThrakon was happy that he would have some time away from the annoying child, even if it would not be long.

By the time the golem returned, the sun was already below the tops of the trees. Since PateraThrakon created it, he could always sense where it was, so it was no surprise to him when it came back to where he had been napping. He was also not surprised when he saw Kord stumbling into the area sometime after the golem. When he exited the woods and made his way to the nearest clearing, with no items to lie on, he fell first to his knees, then fell forward onto his chest, lying on the ground, exhausted from his trek with the golem.

The dragon lifted his head and looked at the boy lying on the ground. If he did not sense the child's breathing, he would have thought he was dead, but since he was still alive, he would still be able to move.

PateraThrakon uncurled his body and stood up. "Come along, boy. Your training is over for today, and we need to get you back before it gets dark."

Kord heard the dragon, and even though he did not want to move, he lifted his head and looked at PateraThrakon as he passed him. "You never said there was a big hill that I had to climb."

To the dragon, the boy spoke the truth, so he would as well, "I never said there was not one either." Maybe it was because he was exhausted, but for some reason, the dragon's statement made sense to him. "Come along now, we still have one more stop to make before you head back to your hut for the night."

Kord found the energy to lift himself off the ground and stand when he heard the word hut. Once inside, he would be able to sleep, but he realized that it had taken them a while to reach the location where they were, and it would take just as long, if not longer, to make their way back, and PateraThrakon had said they had one more stop to make as well. He knew that if he did not start now, he never would, so he forced himself to take the first step and followed it with another. He was not sure how many he would have to take before he could finally rest.

Just before he walked out of the area, he turned back to look at the golem. Just as he did, he saw it shrink back into the ground where it had come from. Kord was jealous because the golem did not have to move from the area, but he did.

Somehow, Kord was able to continue walking even though he kept his eyes closed for most of the time. He even had them closed when he heard PateraThrakon speak, “We are here.”

Kord opened his eyes and saw where the dragon had led him. It was the small pond where he and Keia took their baths. A part of him was upset because, after all he had gone through, the mean dragon expected him to bathe. Yet a part of him thought that maybe a nice warm bath was exactly what he needed to feel alive again.

He made his way over to the pond, stripped down to his undergarments, and waited. When what he expected to happen did not, he spoke up. “Aren’t you going to warm the water like MiteraThrakena does when she brings us to bathe?”

“I have no concern whatsoever if you bathe in warm water or not,” the dragon said to make sure that Kord knew that he was not there for the boy's comfort.

Kord thought that he would be smarter than the dragon. "Oh, I didn't know you couldn't breathe fire."

PateraThrakon knew exactly what the boy was trying to do, but would not take the bait. To show Kord that yes, he could breathe fire, the dragon lifted his head toward the sky and released a wide stream of fire into the air that made it look as if the entire sky had been set ablaze. He then lowered his head and looked down at Kord. "As you can see, I can breathe fire."

Kord did not say it, but with the display of raw power the dragon just presented, the young boy was impressed. He still wanted to take a warm bath, so he stuck his toe in the pond and pulled it out immediately. "It's too cold, I can't take a bath in it."

"Well then, let me help you," PateraThrakon said and moved closer to the pond and Kord as well. He took a deep breath, and just as it appeared he was about to release a fiery display, he used his tail to nudge Kord on his back, causing him to fall into the cold water.

From the shock of the sudden dip in the water and the surprise as to what the dragon had done, Kord quickly regained his balance and stood up in the middle of the pond, where he landed after being pushed in. "That wasn't funny," Kord said, not amused, as he wiped his face to remove some of the water.

"From where I am standing, it was," PateraThrakon said. "Now hurry up and take your bath, it is getting late."

Kord, having been shocked awake by the cold water, decided that since he was already in the pond, he might as well take a bath. "We could have just gone back to the hut. I didn't need to take a bath."

"You may be comfortable with your own stench, but I am not, and if I brought you back smelling like a boar who has been wallowing in the mud, MiteraThrakena would insist that you take a bath before you enter the hut. Then you would have to travel back out. Since it was on the way, it is simpler to take care of it now."

Kord had to agree. Not with the *smelling like a boar* portion, but the part where he would not have to come back out once he reached the hut.

By the time he had finished with his bath and put his clothes back on, he saw MiteraThrakena making her way to where he and PateraThrakon were. When she had finally reached them, he heard someone speak, "Hello, Kord." It was obvious that it was Keia's voice, but he did not see her. He looked around but could not find her anywhere. "Up here!" Keia yelled to him.

At first, he was not sure what she meant by *up here*, but he soon realized that there could only be one place, so he lifted his eyes to look at the silver dragon, and there on her back, Keia was sitting, waving to him. The thought of riding on the back of a dragon was very exciting to Kord.

"I saw the fire display in the sky, so I thought that I should come and check on the two of you," MiteraThrakena said to give her explanation on why the two females had arrived.

"Were you afraid that I had decided to roast the boy in flames?" PateraThrakon asked. "Believe me, I thought about it."

The two dragons smiled at each other, knowing that neither one would ever hurt a human, even if PateraThrakon had thought about it, especially since he had met Kord.

"Come along, we need to get the children home. It is getting late, and they still need to have their evening meal." Having given everyone their instructions, MiteraThrakena turned around and started making her way back to the children's hut. All the while, Keia looked as if she was having the time of her life riding on the back of a dragon.

Kord could not resist; he had to ask. "Can you give me a ride?"

"I will not give you a ride," PateraThrakon answered.

"But I'm tired."

"Then perhaps you need to wake up."

Kord was not sure what the dragon meant until he was nudged in his chest by the dragon's tail, knocking him back into the pond, dry clothes and all. Kord quickly stood up, and by the time he got his balance and wiped the water from his eyes, the male dragon was already walking away. It would not have done any good to say anything, so Kord just climbed out of the pond and started following the others back to the hut. At least he would be able to get something to eat and get some sleep, that is, after he dried himself off again.

The next morning, Kord woke up when he heard PateraThrakon calling for him from outside the hut. "Come along, boy. It is time for your training."

Kord stood up from the straw mat he was lying on, and since Keia was getting up as well, he walked outside the hut and saw the dragon waiting for him. He then lifted his arms and looked at them, then looked over his body.

"What is wrong with you, boy?" PateraThrakon asked.

Kord took a moment, then gave his explanation, "I thought that I would still be tired from yesterday, but I feel good. Like I had the best sleep ever."

"That is because you are training to be the Dragon Klau," PateraThrakon said, and Kord looked up at him. "You will face a lot of challenges, and there will be times that it will take all of your strength just to make it through one sun-cycle, but after a night's sleep, your strength will replenish itself, and you will feel better than you did before." The dragon gave Kord a moment to take in what he said, then continued, "What do you think about becoming the Dragon Klau now?"

Kord looked at himself, then back at the dragon, "I think I'm ready to train some more," Kord said, smiling. More eager than ever to find out just what it meant to be the Dragon Klau.

FIFTEEN

Kord stumbled out of the forest and was able to take five more steps before his exhaustion took over, and he fell to the ground. At least this time, he made sure that he ended up lying on his back instead of face-first like the last time. Now he was able to look up at the sky even though he did not see anything because he had his eyes closed and was not even sure if he had the strength to open them.

"You took longer this time," Kord heard PateraThrakon say, from the same position he was in when Kord had started his morning training. "I would think that since it was your second attempt at having traversed the forest and the hill, you would have been faster, although I suppose I should not have such high hopes for a boy the likes of you."

Kord stayed where he was on the ground, not caring what the dragon said to him. He was just thankful that he was still able to breathe. His training consisted of following the golem PateraThrakon created. It would lead him through the forest and up the hill, but the landscape was covered with trees, some of which had fallen, so Kord had to climb over some, and others he had to go under them. Their girth was at least twice the size of Kord's height, which made maneuvering around them more difficult.

Something else that was abundant were rocks and boulders. One area in particular was covered with them, and with the incline of the hill, Kord was forced to make his way upward using his hands as well as his feet.

Once they had reached the top of the hill, the golem allowed Kord a moment to eat some fruit from the trees that grew in the area, then he had to make his way back down the hill. Kord thought that it would be easier going downward, but he had to be even more careful because he could easily stumble and lose his balance, causing him to fall down the hill in a manner that would not be good for his health.

Kord had finally rested enough to where he had the strength to stand. He looked over his shoulder and saw the golem standing a few paces away. When they had returned to the training area that morning, PateraThrakon once again called forth the golem to lead Kord in his training. It ran through the forest and up the hill with no problems at all, never tiring and always making sure that Kord did not stop to rest. Every time he tried to take a break, the golem would pick up stones and throw them at him, most of them hitting him on the side of his head. Kord soon realized that if he did not want to be pummeled with stones, he had to keep moving.

He looked from the golem over to the dragon, who had stood up from the position he had been resting in. Kord could not help feeling some hostility toward the dragon. He had to run all through the forest over trees and boulders, and all the dragon did was take a nap.

"It is time we return to the hut," PateraThrakon said as he started walking in the direction that would take them home. "But first..."

"Yes, I know," Kord said to cut the dragon off from what he was going to say, then continued. "But first I will need to bathe," Kord said in the voice he used to try to sound like the dragon and what the dragon was going to say.

PateraThrakon turned his head and looked at Kord. "At least you can be taught something, and I do not sound like that." The dragon then began walking again.

He knew that his impersonation of PateraThrakon was not accurate, but it was his small way to annoy the dragon. Kord took one step, then stopped. He lifted his right arm and took a whiff. The pungent smell that came from himself made him realize that maybe this time the dragon had a point. Even Kord thought that his own smell was a bit offensive.

After the much-needed bath, PateraThrakon told Kord that he could make his way back to the hut on his own and did not hesitate to fly away, more than likely back to his den for another nap. Kord knew the way; he had gone from the hut to the pond where he bathed and back to the hut ever since he and Keia arrived in KhoraThraks.

As he was approaching the hut, he saw Keia out in front with a bucket of water. That was when he realized that in the two sun-cycles that he had begun his training, he had not had time to perform his chore of fetching water and filling up the water jar. His first thought was that Keia was the one who was taking care of it, and that made him feel guilty.

He ran past the front of the hut, not even greeting Keia, and ran to the back of the hut. When he reached the water jar and looked inside, he was surprised to see that it was almost full. From the looks of it, it was only missing about a bucket full of water, and that was what he saw Keia with. Without performing his chore for the past two sun-cycles, the jar should have been only filled about halfway. He thought that Keia had to take over his chore.

"What are you doing?"

He turned his head and saw Keia standing at the corner of the hut, staring at him. He then turned around and looked for the buckets he used to fetch the water. When he located them, he grabbed them up. "I'm sorry, I forgot to fill the water jar. I will get some now and make sure I fill it up before I leave for training in the morning."

He was about ready to do as he had told her when she stopped him, "You don't have to do that anymore."

Now he really felt bad about her having to haul

the water from the stream to the water jar. "It's too far away for you to carry the buckets. I will do it." He started walking toward her, and when he reached where she was standing, she grabbed his arm. "I'll go and fill it up now."

"MiteraThrakena filled the water jar. She said that you would be busy training."

Kord looked at Keia, then at the buckets. He was trying to figure out how the female dragon carried the buckets. "Did she carry them in her mouth?" Kord asked, holding up the two buckets to let her know what he was thinking.

Keia smiled, took the buckets out of his hands, and placed them on the ground next to where they were standing. She then took hold of his hand and walked him over to the water jar. She looked inside it, then looked at Kord. "She used the force of Water to make it rain over the water jar. That is how she filled it."

Kord looked at the water jar and was glad that Keia did not have to make the trip to fetch the water. It was his chore to do, but what he would have felt bad about was that even though he was able to do the chore with no problem, he did not want Keia to have to lift the heavy buckets. Now that he knew that she did not, his guilt was gone.

Keia turned and started walking away, but stopped and turned to face Kord when he realized something and began to voice his enlightenment. "If she could fill it up, then why did I have to fetch the water with the buckets?"

It was an interesting question, and to answer it, Keia shrugged her shoulders, turned around, and headed back to what she was doing before Kord arrived and interrupted her. He took one more look at the object of his animosity, then followed Keia, not wanting to think about all the trips he had to make to fill the water jar for two moon-cycles.

When he was back around at the front of the hut, he saw Keia leaning over a black cooking pot, stirring the contents within. He walked over to where she was and looked inside for himself. “What is that?” he asked.

Keia continued to stir the pot while she answered his question. “It’s soup.”

Kord was surprised by what she said. They had eaten nothing but berries and fruit from the bushes and trees since they had arrived, and now, they were going to have soup. “What’s in it?” Kord asked.

She stopped stirring, stood, and looked at Kord. “Potatoes and carrots.”

Kord could not help but feel disappointed with her list of ingredients. When she had told him that it was soup, he immediately thought back to the soup his mother would fix, and even though it had potatoes and carrots as well, it also had chicken and sometimes pieces of beef. Two things that Kord would love to taste again.

“There is one more thing,” Keia said, and Kord could not wait to hear the words he was hoping she was going to say. “There is also wild rice.” Those were not the words he wanted to hear.

Having had his dream of meat taken away from him, the thought of having any type of soup was new to him. "Where did you find all of those things?" he asked.

Keia went back to stirring the soup but answered his question. "MiteraThrakena showed me where they were and had me gather them." She continued to stir the contents of the pot while talking to Kord. "She also showed me where to pick some wild herbs that would give it more flavor." She then dipped some of the broth out with the spoon and sipped it. Smiling, she placed the spoon back in the pot and continued to stir.

The list of ingredients was not some of Kord's favorites, but he did decide that at least the soup was something different, instead of the same fruits they had been eating. He also saw how happy Keia was at making the soup, and with the way she was smiling, with what she had accomplished, he did not want to hurt her feelings.

Keia stopped stirring and took another sip of the broth. "I think it is ready. Grab the bowls and spoons from inside."

Kord went into the hut and looked around, but did not see the items Keia had mentioned. He went back to the door and yelled to Keia, "I don't see them."

Keia stopped what she was doing, walked into the hut, and over to the left wall, where she retrieved the two bowls and two spoons that were on the shelf. She then walked over to Kord and handed him the items. "They were right there," she said in a manner to let him know that if they were a snake, it would have bitten him.

Kord followed her out of the hut and back over to the pot with the soup simmering over the fire. With her hands wrapped tightly in a cloth, she lifted the pot and placed it down on a flat stone next to the fire so that it would stay warm but would not burn the soup.

"Where did you get the cooking pot from?" Kord asked, since he just realized that he had never seen it before.

"MiteraThrakena showed me where there were some things that we can use." She looked over her shoulder at Kord, "That is where I got the bowls and spoons you have." Kord looked at what he was holding and was about ready to ask where the place was, but the next words he heard forced that thought out of his mind. "Time to eat."

He walked over to Keia and handed her one of the bowls. She took it from him and filled it with the soup, handed the bowl back to Kord, who then handed her the empty one. She filled it as well, then they both took a seat on the ground, ready to begin their evening meal.

Kord stirred the soup with his spoon and saw the contents move within the broth. Yes, he was glad that the meal consisted of something other than the normal fruits they had been living off of, but to him, potatoes, carrots, and rice were not much of an improvement. "Taste it," he heard Keia say, and he looked over to her. She was watching him and had not tasted her soup either. Kord was certain that she wanted him to be the first to try what she had cooked. That thought alone encouraged him to stir the contents one last time, fill his spoon with the soup, and sample it. To his surprise and delight, he enjoyed it. To make sure that his mouth was not playing a trick on him, he took a second taste of the soup, and then a third. "Do you like it?" Keia asked.

Kord stopped eating for a moment and gave his answer, "It's great." The smile he saw on her face was almost as pleasing as the soup, almost.

Keia then tasted the soup from her own bowl. The smile she had when she saw that Kord liked it was nothing compared to the one she had from feeling proud of what she had accomplished.

She took another taste of the soup, and before she could taste it a third time, Kord asked, "Can I have some more?" She looked over and saw that he was holding his bowl out to her, and she saw that even before she had a chance to empty a small portion of her bowl, Kord had emptied his.

She placed her bowl down next to her, took his, and went over to the pot with the soup. She filled his bowl for a second time, then returned to where they were sitting, handing the bowl back to him. Kord immediately began to eat. Keia picked up her bowl and went back to eating her meal, only with more self-restraint than the boy sitting across from her.

"Did MiteraThrakena teach you to make this?" Kord asked, now that he had slowed down to eat his meal with more human-like speed and not like some wild animal gorging on its most recent kill.

"Yes. She told me to boil the water, and when to add the wild rice and vegetables."

Kord was happy that she had done so. The soup was a pleasing meal, especially after he had trained all day, which brought up another question he had for Keia. "Is that what she is teaching you, how to cook?"

Keia finished swallowing the food she had in her mouth, then answered him. "No, she is teaching me about the different plants. She said that it is easier to start with the ones that I can use to cook with, then she will teach me about the ones that can be used for medicines."

"Medicines for what?" Kord asked.

"To help people," Keia said, then swallowed another spoonful of her soup.

Kord took another taste of his, then asked another question, "Is that what the Dragon..." He stopped to think of what the title was that MiteraThrakena had given her. When he remembered it, he continued, "Is that what the Dragon Kastera does? They make medicines. I thought you were going to learn how to use fire and wind and things like that."

Keia set her bowl down next to her, having

finished her meal after just one bowl. "She said that I cannot learn how to be the Dragon Kastera until I am older."

"Why?" Kord asked.

"She said that when I become a woman, then I will be able to learn what I need to."

Kord thought about what she said, then gave his opinion on the subject. "It will be many seasons before you are a woman."

For her reply, she simply stuck her tongue out at him, which caused him to laugh, which in turn she did as well.

He finished the contents of his bowl, and to make sure that he ate every last drop, he skipped using the spoon and brought the bowl up to his mouth, slurping the remaining broth. To his credit, he did not allow any of the broth to run down his chin. Once he was done, he set the bowl down at his side. "What else are you learning?"

Keia looked around but did not see what she needed. She stood up, took a few steps, and when she found the item, she returned and took her place across from Kord. She then used the stick she brought with her to write something in the dirt in front of her. When she was done, she looked over to Kord and said, "I learned how to write my name. I still have to learn the rest of the letters, but MiteraThrakena said once I do, she will teach me to read."

Kord looked at the ground and could read what she had written, but it took him a moment to work the letters out. Not because of the way Keia had written them, but because he had to concentrate and sound out each of them.

He was seven seasons old, and his mother had started teaching him to read and write, but it was something that did not come easily for him. Now that his mother was gone, he was not sure if he would ever get any better than the level of learning from where he was.

He stopped thinking about reading and writing because he had another question for Keia. He picked up the bowl sitting next to him and extended it out to her, and asked, "Can I have some more?"

Keia nodded and was happy to get him another bowl of the soup she had made, happy that Kord enjoyed it.

It was the third sun-cycle of Kord's training, and like the two before, it was no easy task. By the time he had come down the hill and landed in his normal spot, tired and worn out, he did not feel any different since his training began.

"Why am I doing this every day?" he asked, and since the golem could not answer him, PateraThrakon did.

"You need to strengthen your body. The only way to do so is to put you through the rigorous training." He was doubtful that the boy would understand and decided it was time to leave. "Come, you will take your bath, then return to the hut."

It was not the bath part that excited Kord, but the mention of going back to the hut. Just the thought gave him the energy to pick himself off the ground and begin heading back. Even if he had to stop to take a bath first, he would eventually get to the hut, and hopefully, Keia would have made more of the soup she had fixed before. Something that Kord enjoyed very much after training so hard.

Before he even reached the hut, he saw Keia standing over the small fire she used to cook the soup, and to his delight, she was also stirring something in the pot. He had trained all day, and even though he was worn out, he found enough energy to pick up his pace to reach Keia and whatever it was she was cooking.

To his delight, it was the same meal as before. "I'll get the bowls," he said without being instructed to, and went inside the hut. When he returned, she took the bowls from him, which was a good sign to let him know that the soup was ready.

They sat down and ate their meal, and when Kord had finished his second helping, while Keia was still on her first, he set the bowl down next to him and asked her the question he had been thinking about since their last meal, "After we eat, do you think..." He paused for a moment to get the courage to continue, "...do you think you can teach me to read and write?" While she still had her last spoonful of soup in her mouth, she smiled at him and nodded. More than happy to help him. Kord, also happy that he would be able to learn to read and write, decided that he had one more question for her. He picked up his empty bowl and extended it to her. “Can I have some more?” Once again, Keia smiled at him.

SIXTEEN

A moon-mark had passed since Kord began his training. PateraThrakon had no longer gone with him to the training area, and in a way, Kord was thankful for it. The only thing the male dragon did when he was around was make comments on how useless Kord was and nap while he trained.

When Kord arrived at the training area, the golem would rise out of the ground and lead him into the woods, where he would once again navigate the rough terrain of trees and boulders. Kord was certain that this day would be no different, so when he saw the golem take form, Kord started making his way toward the forest, but stopped when he realized that the golem had not moved from where it had appeared.

Kord turned around and walked over to where it was standing. Since it was not moving, Kord decided to find out what was wrong with it. "Are we going to train today?" he asked, knowing that the golem could not reply but thought that the question alone would cause it to start to move, and move it did.

The golem lifted its right arm just enough to point toward the ground at Kord's feet. Kord looked down but did not understand what the golem was trying to relay, so he looked back at the golem. "What do you want me to do?" The golem continued to remain in the position it had taken up, pointing toward the ground at Kord's feet.

Still confused, Kord looked from the golem to the ground, then back to the golem. He did this a couple of times, but did not know what the golem was trying to relay to him. "I don't understand," Kord said, and to try to express what the golem wanted him to do, it raised its arm and then extended it again with more force and pointed toward the ground at Kord's feet. "Yeah, that helped," Kord said sarcastically, not coming any closer to understanding the golem.

He decided that there was no need to continue the one-sided conversation, so Kord turned and started walking toward the woods. When he reached the edge, he turned to look at the golem. "We need to get started." Kord had been training for a moon-mark, and it had become his daily routine. Now that the golem was interfering with that, Kord was beginning to lose patience, so he decided that he would enter the forest on his own, and the golem could remain where it was. He knew what he had to do. Run through the forest up the hill, then come back down. He did not need the golem for that.

Just as Kord was about to enter the forest, he felt something hit his back. He turned around and looked at the golem, thinking that it had thrown something at him. When he took in the sight, he saw that the golem was standing exactly where it had been, only there was something that caught Kord's attention, or better yet, the lack of something.

Kord looked down at the ground where he was standing, and sure enough, lying at his feet was the foot of the golem. When Kord looked at the golem, it was standing where it was, but it was standing only on one foot. Its right foot was missing, but that was not actually true since it was on the ground in front of Kord.

"Why did you do that?" Kord asked, not seeing the point in the actions of the golem. Kord looked at the foot at his feet, then back to the golem. Then it started to walk over to him, and since it was missing one of its feet, it walked with an uneven step every time its right stump touched the ground.

When it reached Kord, it pointed at the ground at its own foot. Kord looked at what it was pointing at, then informed the golem what he saw. "Your foot." The golem adjusted his arm to point at the next item. Kord looked down, and when he was sure he knew what the golem was pointing at, he looked back at the golem. "My foot," Kord said.

Kord looked at the separated foot of the golem, then at his own. Once he thought he had deciphered what the golem was trying to relay, he informed the golem. "You want me to take off my foot!" Kord shouted in a manner to let the golem know that what he thought the golem wanted him to do was out of the question.

The golem pointed back at its own foot on the ground, then at Kord's foot. Once again, Kord looked between the two items, and he soon figured out what the golem was trying to tell him. "You want me to take off my boots?"

The golem lowered his arm to confirm with Kord that he now understood what the golem wanted him to do, finally.

Kord, not knowing the reason why, but just glad that the conversation had come to an end, did as the golem instructed. He pulled off his boots and let them fall to the ground beside him. "There," Kord said, but the golem once again pointed at Kord's feet. He looked down again, and this time he believed he knew what the golem wanted. "You want me to take my socks off too?" The golem lowered his arm to let Kord know that he was correct.

Kord decided that he would do as the golem instructed and remove his socks as well. Now barefoot, Kord looked at the golem waiting for his next set of instructions. The golem, having prepared Kord for the next part of his training, walked around Kord and entered the forest, the same as it had since it started Kord's training.

"I can't go in there with no boots, I will cut my feet," Kord yelled to the golem. It stopped, turned slightly to face Kord, then waved him in to let him know that he was to follow. Kord looked down at his bare feet and thought that it was a bad idea, but he went ahead and took the first step into the forest. By the fifth step, he had already felt the small twigs and pebbles press against his feet, and he was not happy with having to make the entire trek through the forest with no boots on. Nevertheless, he continued to follow the golem.

After the training, when Kord finally made his way back to the entrance of the forest and into the training area, he once again fell to the ground exhausted. Since PateraThrakon had not accompanied him, he had no one to talk to except the golem, and it could not talk back. Hesitant to do so, Kord sat up, thinking about the concern that he had.

When he had entered the forest earlier, it took only about twenty steps before Kord could no longer feel the sharp bite of the debris that covered the forest floor. He thought that it was because his feet had become so numb that he no longer felt the pain. Now that he was sitting down, he thought for sure that when he looked at the bottoms of his feet, they would be cut, scraped, and more than likely covered with blood.

He drew up his courage and pulled his right foot closer to him. When it was in range, he grabbed it with his hands and moved it even closer so that he could see how badly his foot was injured. To his surprise, there was not a single scratch on his foot. To verify what he was seeing, he took his left hand and wiped it across his foot. He then looked at his hand and saw that there was no blood on it. He then looked at his right foot again to make sure that it was okay. He then let go of it, pulled his left foot up to inspect it, and saw that, like his other foot, there was no sign of injury at all.

"Boy, what are you doing?" PateraThrakon asked as he landed in the clearing and saw Kord fiddling with his own feet.

Kord, while still holding his foot, turned his head to look at the dragon. He then looked at his foot, then back to the dragon, and realized that it may seem odd with the way he appeared to the dragon.

He quickly let go of his foot, stood, and faced the dragon, "I was just..." Kord stopped with his explanation because he really did not know how to continue. Only this time the dragon wanted him to.

"Tell me what you were doing." Kord truly did not know what to say, so he remained silent. However, PateraThrakon was running out of patience. Any other time, the boy would speak when he should have remained silent, and now that the dragon wanted him to speak, he kept his mouth shut. "Tell me," PateraThrakon said one last time, and the sound of his voice let Kord know that the dragon was out of patience.

Kord looked down at his feet, then back to the dragon. "The golem had me take off my boots and socks before I began my training today. I thought that with the rocks and branches on the ground, they would have been cut and bleeding."

He stopped talking, so the dragon spoke, "They were not." His statement was not a question; however, Kord nodded his head to agree. "It is progress, even if it is not much," PateraThrakon said to let Kord know what he thought of Kord's observation.

"What do you mean?" Kord asked.

The dragon let out one of his normal sighs as he did a lot when talking to the boy, then explained what he meant. "For the past moon-mark, you have been training. Going up and down the hill and over the rough terrain has strengthened your body. Most of all your legs. The golem had you remove your foot coverings so that you would have direct contact with the ground." The dragon stopped talking to give the boy a moment to take in what he had said so far, then continued. "There were no injuries to the soles of your feet because you were protected by the blessing of the Dragon Klau."

"I don't understand," Kord said.

Surprisingly, PateraThrakon was not upset with his answer. In fact, this was one of the few times when Kord admitted that he did not know something. To a dragon, that shows intelligence. "Sit back down on the ground," PateraThrakon said, and without hesitation, Kord did as instructed, and the dragon was once again surprised by the obedience of the human. "Now take one of the stones next to you and push it against the bottom of your foot." Kord did, and as he watched what he was doing, he was amazed at what he saw.

To see the results of his actions again, he pushed the stone into the bottom of his right foot once more, only this time, he not only put more pressure on it, but he also held it in place as well, so that he could use the thumb of his other hand to feel the texture of his sole. "It's like..." He knew what he wanted to say, but did not.

"It feels like dragon scales," PateraThrakon said, and Kord looked toward the dragon and nodded. "The reason you did not injure your feet when you were training is because the dragon scales protected them."

"How come it never happened before?" Kord asked.

"You had no need of them. You wore your boots, so your feet were protected. In the time you have been training, you have become stronger, especially your legs, since that is what the golem has been training you on."

Kord thought about the past moon-mark and what he had been through. Repeatedly, he had run up and down the hill and through the forest. Over and under trees, on top of rocks and boulders, all the time he was using his legs and all the time he was strengthening them, and now he had something to show for it. However, since Kord is the child he is, it was not enough.

"You mean that's it! I've been killing myself all this time, and all I can do is make the bottoms of my feet be covered with scales."

"That is an improvement," PateraThrakon said. "What, you thought that in just the short amount of time you have been training, you would be able to have your entire body covered with scales?"

Kord thought for a moment, then gave his answer, "Yes!"

Just as quickly as he had gained some respect for the child, PateraThrakon's thoughts went right back to thinking that Kord was nothing but a stubborn human. "It will be quite some time before you come into your full potential. Until then, continue with your training. The more you train, the stronger you will become, and the sooner the results you desire will present themselves."

Kord understood what the dragon said, but he was not happy with it. He wanted to be able to do everything the Dragon Klau could do now, but he knew that he would have to train more to make that happen.

"Remember," Kord heard PateraThrakon speak and looked back at the dragon. "As you grow stronger, your body will react to situations without you having to think about it."

"Like the way the bottoms of my feet changed without me even knowing it," Kord said.

"Yes. Your body will react by instinct. To protect you. It will take some time, but continue with your training, and it will happen."

Kord nodded and walked over to where he had left his boots and socks and proceeded to put them on. All the while, PateraThrakon watched him, surprised that the boy was already showing results from his training. It had only been a moon-mark, and Kord's instincts had already begun to interact with the blessing. The dragon was impressed, although he did not tell the boy what he was thinking.

"If you continue with the way you are training, you will gradually see more results. First, it was the soles of your feet, next it could be your feet completely. Then your legs. Keep doing what you are doing; it will come in time."

"Yes, My Lord," Kord responded, and the dragon was not sure if he even realized how he did so.

Kord, having finished placing his socks and boots on, began walking away from the area. "Are you heading back to your hut?" PateraThrakon asked.

Kord continued walking but answered the dragon's question, "First, I have to go take my bath."

The dragon did not stop him. If the boy was willing to take a bath on his own, then maybe there was hope for him yet. Of course, PateraThrakon was not going to get his hopes up. The boy still had a long way to go.

When he finally made it back to the hut, what he was most anxious to see was if Keia had fixed some more of her soup. He had eaten it twice in the last two sun-cycles, but if he had to eat it again, that would be fine with him. He enjoyed it that much.

He did not see the pot hanging over the fire, and his thoughts of the soup were crushed. His stomach must have agreed with him because it started growling.

Just before he reached the hut, he saw Keia exiting it. To his delight, he saw that she was holding two bowls in her hands. “Is the soup ready?” he asked before he walked to where she was standing.

“We are not having soup,” Keia said, and Kord’s stomach announced its own displeasure. “We are having seasoned fried potatoes in honey.” She held out the bowls to him so that he could see what they contained. There in the bowls were the fried potatoes with some type of green leaves, and they were sitting in honey.

“How did you fix that?” Kord asked.

“MiteraThrakena told me how.” She turned and walked over to the spot where they normally ate their evening meals.

Once they were done and Kord had his second helping, Keia showed him what MiteraThrakena had taught her with her daily lesson in writing her letters. She would draw one letter at a time, and then Kord would do the same. They practiced their writing until the sun was out of the sky, then went into the hut to rest for the night.

Kord exited the hut and looked up into the sky. Feeling refreshed from a good night’s sleep and having gone to bed with a full stomach, he was ready to begin his training.

He took a couple of steps to make his way to

the training area, but stopped suddenly. He remembered what PateraThrakon had said about if he continued his training, he would become stronger. He looked down at his feet, then bent over and took off his boots and socks. He figured that since he could walk in the forest without them, he could walk to the training area as well. Every bit of training would make him stronger.

He then started walking again, ready to continue with his training in becoming the Dragon Klau.

SEVENTEEN

It had been a little over a moon-cycle since Kord began his training. As soon as the sun rose, he would make his way to the training area and head straight into the forest. The golem would be in front of him, but Kord had maneuvered through the obstacles of trees and boulders so many times that he knew the fastest way around them. Now he could reach the top of the hill way before the sun was mid-way in the sky and be back at the entrance of the forest with plenty of time left before he needed to head back to the hut.

Once he was done with his physical training for the day, Kord would remain in the training area and practice what Keia had taught him the previous night. He now knew all of his letters and was able to write quite a few words. He would use a stick to write words in the dirt, erase them, and start again. After about a sun-mark, he would head back to the hut, but not before he stopped off at the pond for his daily bath.

Kord was on the last stretch of his run out of the forest, and when he saw the edge of the woods, he increased his speed. He gave every last bit of energy he had to finish his daily training to the best of his ability.

He had one more obstacle to clear, which was one of the fallen trees. It was leaning against another tree that was still standing, so the fallen one was not completely on the ground. Normally, Kord would go under the tree because there was plenty of room for him, but today, just before he reached the tree, he decided to try a different method.

When he was almost to the fallen tree, he slightly changed his direction to his right. Instead of heading straight for the tree, he positioned himself so that in front of him was a boulder that was just a little shorter than he was. As he reached the boulder, he jumped toward it and made sure that he allowed his right foot to make contact with it first. He then immediately used that same foot to push himself off the boulder a little to his left, where he cleared the top of the fallen tree with ease. He touched down on the ground with his left foot, and to make sure he did not lose his balance, he sprang forward and did a headfirst roll on the ground, ending in an upright position, then continued with his run.

When he made it out of the forest, he stopped and looked behind him, then looked up into the sky. From the position of the sun, he could tell that he still had five sun-marks left before he needed to be back at the hut for his evening meal. He was sure that his latest run was the fastest he had ever made since he started training.

Kord walked over to one of the logs he used to sit on and practice his letters. When he reached it, he sat down on it and stretched out his legs. He had previously torn off the bottom part of his trousers, so now his legs from his knees to his feet were bare, since he did not wear his shoes when he trained. He looked at his legs and saw that they were still covered with dragon scales from his calves to the end of his toes, with them extending out into little claws on each one.

He ran his hand over each of his legs and felt the scales. If he brushed downward, the scales felt smooth, but if he brushed upward, he could feel the edges of the scales that overlapped the ones below them.

He had come a long way since he had started his training. The first sign of his progress began with the scales appearing on the soles of his feet, and now they have reached the top of his calves. Kord was sure that within another moon-cycle, the scales would be up to his knees.

He was pleased with himself, but he knew that he had a long way to go, and he had other things to learn as well.

Kord picked up the stick that he used to practice his letters. He sat on the log and leaned over so that he could write in the dirt. The very first word that he always started with was the same. It was his name.

He would write *Kord,* and once he finished, he would use the stick to spread the dirt around to erase his name. He would then write the second word that he always wrote, and that was *Keia*. He did not wipe her name away as fast as he did his own.

When he was ready, he spread the dirt and started to practice the word Keia last taught him, which was PateraThrakon. After they had eaten their evening meal, she had shown him how to write it and was able to copy it easily from what she had written. Now he was trying to remember how it looked. He pictured the letters in his mind as he sounded out the word. That is how MiteraThrakena had instructed Keia, and that is how Keia taught him. Only he did not pick up on it as quickly as Keia did. She was able to recite all her letters and write quite a few words. She was even able to write complete sentences, something Kord was still having trouble with. He was able to recite his letters, but it was the writing part that he had trouble with.

He looked down at the ground and decided that maybe he would have to have Keia show him again how to write the male dragon's name, so he decided to work on an easier word. He just could not decide on what to write.

He lifted his head and saw the golem standing a few paces away from him. It would remain in the area while Kord was there, but as soon as he left, the golem would merge back into the ground and only return when Kord arrived at the training area.

Kord had an idea, and he thought that it would be interesting.

"Hey, golem," Kord yelled, and the golem lifted its head and looked at him. He was not sure if the golem could actually see with its eyes, since it was not able to talk either, but it gave the appearance that it did. "Come over here." The golem walked over to where Kord was sitting and stood in front of him.

"You understand what I am saying," Kord stated, not expecting the golem to reply. Kord knew that the golem understood because when he told it to come over to him, it followed his instructions. Kord decided he would start with the basics.

"When I ask you a question, you nod your head if the answer is yes." To let the golem know what he wanted him to do, Kord nodded his head. "If the answer is no, then shake your head like this." Kord shook his head from side to side to show the golem. He was now ready to see if the golem would do as he instructed, so he asked his first question. "Do you understand?" The golem did not move at first, but after a moment, it nodded its head to let Kord know that it understood.

Kord smiled and was happy with what he came up with. He was ready for his second question. "Do you have a name?" he asked, but the golem did not reply with a nod or a shake of its head. Kord knew that even if it did have a name, it would not be able to tell him since it could not speak, so he thought that he would be able to figure it out with a couple of questions. Only it was not going as easily as Kord thought it would.

He decided to try again. "Do you understand what I am saying?" To his delight, the golem nodded its head. Kord then realized that he was confusing himself. He had asked the last question in reference to the question he had asked the golem about a name, but Kord was not sure if the golem was answering the question about the question he just asked, or if the answer to the question was about whether the golem understood what he was saying about the question about the name.

Kord closed his eyes and shook his head. With what he had just thought, he was confusing himself. "Let's start again," he said to himself more than to the golem. Kord knew that the golem could only answer by moving its head up and down or from side to side, so the questions had to have an answer of yes or no. Kord thought of his next question. "Do you know what a name is?" Surprisingly, the golem was quick to respond by shaking its head from side to side, which pleased Kord greatly.

"Now we are getting somewhere," Kord said and rubbed his hands together to show his excitement, then proceeded to explain what a name is to the golem. "A name is what other people call you by. Like my name is Kord, and Keia's name is Keia." He thought about it, then realized that the golem probably did not even know who Keia was since it never left the training area. "Never mind that. When I called to you, 'golem', you looked at me, so is your name Golem?" It did not reply in any manner.

Kord thought that maybe it just did not understand enough to be able to answer the question. Then he thought that the golem just did not know, which brought another idea to Kord.

"If I ask you a question and you do not know the answer, I want you to do this." Kord tilted his head to his right, then straightened it. "Do you understand?" Kord asked, and the golem nodded its head. Now there were three replies the golem could respond with. Kord realized that, like him, there were questions he did not know the answer to, so he had to come up with a way for the golem to relay just that. He was ready to continue, "Do you understand what a name is?" The golem nodded its head to let Kord know that it did.

Kord, excited with the golem's response, leaped up from where he was sitting and went over to the golem. When he first asked the question, the golem did not know what a name was; then Kord explained it, and now it did. That let Kord know that the golem could learn.

Kord was ready for the next question. "Is Golem your name?" For a reply, the golem tilted its head to the right, then straightened it up again.

"You know what a name is, but you don't know if Golem is your name." He then decided to go back to one of the first questions he had asked before he explained to the golem what a name was. "Do you have a name?" The golem shook its head from side to side.

Kord now knew that the golem did not have a name, and the entire conversation, as much as it could be, was all about the golem and its name. Kord then asked his next question, "Do you want a name?" At first, the golem did not respond, then just when Kord thought that it had confused it, the golem nodded its head to relay its answer to him.

Kord smiled, happy with what he and the golem had accomplished. It had been with him for over a moon-cycle, and apart from pointing at the ground to relay the instructions about removing his boots, they had not communicated in any other manner. Now they were having a conversation.

Kord looked at the golem and realized that they had just arrived at what was going to be the most difficult task. Trying to decide what name he could give the golem. Then he thought that maybe the golem could decide on its own. "Do you have a name you want to be called?" Kord asked, and to his disappointment, the golem shook its head to let him know that it did not. It was going to be up to Kord to come up with one.

At first, he thought he would just call him Dirt, since that was what it basically was, but then he thought that would not be a good name. Dirt is what the golem was created from. It was like when PateraThrakon referred to Kord as *boy*. It was what he was, not who he was, and it sounded more like an insult than a name.

Kord realized just how hard it was to come up with a name. He looked directly at the golem to see if its appearance would help him, but it did not because PateraThrakon had made the golem to look exactly like Kord, and calling the golem Kord would be confusing. More for Kord than the golem.

He tried to think of names that he had heard, then he remembered that there was a boy he used to be friends with when he was growing up. When Kord and his family left the city where they were living to make a new life for themselves, he had to leave his friend behind, probably never to see him again. Then Kord thought that even though the golem did not look like his friend, at least he could give him his name. "How about if we call you, Vrom?"

The golem did not respond at first, but after it appeared that it had thought it over, the golem nodded its head to let Kord know that Vrom would be its name.

"Ok, Vrom it is," Kord said, happy that the task of giving the golem a name ended with success. It was now time for the next part.

Kord went back over and sat down on the log. He picked up the stick he had used to write his and Keia's names, then looked at the golem. "Come over here and sit next to me." The golem did as Kord had instructed. "This is how we write your name." Kord thought about how the name Vrom sounded and was glad that he had not come up with a more difficult name to spell, something like PateraThrakon. He then drew the characters in the dirt to spell out the name Vrom.

"You see, that is how you write your name," Kord said and looked at Vrom, who was looking at the letters on the ground, which brought another idea to Kord. "You try," he said and handed the stick to Vrom.

Vrom looked at the stick, and at first, Kord thought that writing would be too much for the golem, but after a moment, Vrom took the stick and began to scribble its own name on the ground at their feet. When it finished, it looked over to Kord and handed him back the stick. He was ready to teach Vrom the next word. "This is my name," Kord said, then used the stick to once again write his name on the ground. When he finished, Kord looked at Vrom, and the golem nodded to let Kord know that he understood the word.

Kord was amazed at what he had accomplished, but there was more to it. When he had first started training, PateraThrakon had come along with him, and even though the dragon slept while Kord and Vrom went into the forest to train, at least when he arrived back at the clearing, he had someone to talk to. On the fourth sun-cycle, PateraThrakon stopped accompanying him, and Kord had no one to talk with. Keia always stayed at the hut, and it seemed as if she was having fun learning from MiteraThrakena how to read and write, about plants, and about how to cook, which Kord was really thankful for.

Over the past moon-cycle, Kord had no one to talk to, and even if Vrom could not speak, Kord had come up with a way to converse with the golem, and maybe in time, they would be able to communicate even more.

Kord realized that he had better start heading back to the hut. He still had to stop and take his bath, but he wanted to head back to let Keia know what he had done and how he had given Vrom his name. He had told Keia about the golem before, but what he accomplished with the golem was something new. He was sure that she would be impressed that he was able to teach the golem how to write its name.

Kord stood up and started heading to where he would take his bath. Before he left the clearing, he turned back to look at Vrom. "Why don't you come along with me?" Kord did not see any reason why Vrom had to stay in the training area by himself.

Vrom walked over to where Kord was standing just on the outside edge of the clearing but did not go any further. When he stopped, he pointed at the ground, and both he and Kord looked down. Kord then looked up and saw that Vrom was looking at him.

He realized what Vrom was trying to convey, and to let him know that he understood, Kord said what he thought he was telling him, "You can't leave this area, can you?" Unfortunately, Kord understood correctly. Vrom was made to assist in Kord's training, and that took place in the training area PateraThrakon had brought him to. "Ok, I'll be back tomorrow," he said, then turned and started making his way to the pond to take his bath.

Usually, once Kord left the training area, the golem, now called Vrom, would disappear back into the ground. This time, he did not. He walked back over to the log, sat down, picked up the stick, and wrote his name in the dirt. Then next to it, he wrote the name *Kord*. He did not know why, but for some reason, Vrom felt different.

Kord arrived at the hut but did not see Keia. He looked around and even went inside the hut, but she was not there either. He went back outside and called out her name, "Keia!"

"I'm back here," Kord heard her reply, her voice coming from behind the hut.

Kord went around to the back and saw that she was working in a large area where the ground had been plowed up. "What are you doing?" Kord asked when he reached where she was working.

Keia was bending over, but to answer Kord, she stood up. "I'm planting vegetables."

Kord looked around and now realized that what he was seeing and what Keia was standing in the middle of looked like a garden. It was as long as the hut and was twice as wide as its length. It had not been there when he had left in the morning, but now there was the beginning of a garden. “How did you do all this?” Kord asked. Since Keia was only six seasons old, he was not sure how she could have completed such a massive task.

“I didn’t, MiteraThrakena created the garden. She used magic to dig up the soil, but she told me that I was to plant the vegetables. If I take some of the seeds of the vegetables that we eat and plant them in the soil, they will grow more vegetables,” Keia said, smiling at what she was doing and what she had accomplished.

Kord started to feel bad about leaving her alone all the time. “I can help if you want.”

Keia went back to what she had been doing before Kord arrived, but continued to talk to him. “No, I can do it by myself.”

Kord felt a bit hurt at what she said, as if she did not need him. He looked at the size of the garden and wondered about it. “Why is it so big? We don’t eat that many vegetables.”

Keia continued with her work. “Half of it is for vegetables, and half of it will be used for other plants.”

“What types of plants?” Kord asked.

“Ones that I can make medicines with.”

Kord watched as Keia continued to work in the garden. Then he realized that he was missing something. “What did you fix for our meal?” Every time he came back from training, she had their evening meal ready for him, which was one of the highlights of the day.

Keia stood up and looked around her. When she saw what she wanted, she went over, picked up the items, and took them to Kord. “Here. I was too busy today to fix a meal, so you can eat these.” She handed him the items, then went back to working in the garden.

Kord looked down at what he was holding in his hands. Two raw potatoes and two raw carrots. It definitely was not the meal he was hoping for.

EIGHTEEN

Kord ran toward the training area. He had started doing so after the second moon-cycle since he began. The dragon scales now would appear up to his waist whenever he would train, and with them, his legs became stronger. Whenever he made his way in the morning to train, he would take off his boots and run. When he was finished for the day, he would run from the training area to the pond, where he would take his bath. After his bath, he would walk the rest of the way back to the hut, not wanting to sweat again, then have to take another bath. One bath a day was enough for him.

As soon as the training area was in sight, Kord was surprised at what he saw. There in the middle of the area stood PateraThrakon. He had not seen the male dragon since he had begun his training over two moon-cycles ago. Now there he was waiting for Kord to arrive.

PateraThrakon watched as Kord ran toward him. He did not tell him, but the dragon was impressed, not only with how rapidly he was developing his skills but also with how Kord was devoted to his training.

The gold dragon was starting to believe that there was still hope for the boy, but he would not make a final judgment yet; Kord still had a long way to go.

Kord stopped running when he reached the location with PateraThrakon. The dragon noticed that even though the trek from the hut to the training area was some distance away, the boy was not even breathing hard. "Could you not arrive any faster?" PateraThrakon asked, even though he saw improvement in Kord, he was not going to go easier on him. "I have been waiting for you since the sun was in the sky. I have more important things to do."

Kord had not seen the dragon in a while, and with the comment the dragon made, Kord was ready to reply with his own sarcastic response, but he did not want to waste his time. He came to train, and that was what he was going to do. "Sorry, My Lord," was all he said, then turned to enter the forest to begin his daily training.

As soon as he turned around, PateraThrakon spoke, "You will no longer be training in the forest." Kord turned and faced the dragon, not knowing what he meant. "It is time for you to move on to the next stage."

Kord was surprised at what the dragon said. The forest training was the only thing he had done, and he thought that was all he was going to do. He knew that he had made progress since he began because the dragon scales appeared all the way up to his midsection. He thought that if he continued to train, then one day he would be able to have his entire body covered with them.

Kord was pleased with what he was able to do, even though he knew he still had more to learn. He especially liked the way that when the dragon scales appeared, his legs, all the way to the bottom of his feet, could not be cut by anything that he had tried. A sharp stick, a rock, not even the dagger that he had back at the hut. Nothing could scratch the scales. Along with the protection they gave, they allowed him to have more strength in his legs. He was able to run faster, leap higher, and his kicks were more powerful. He found this out while he was running through the forest, and he used his right leg and foot to kick off a tree, and it fell over. Kord was now wondering if he was not going to train in the forest, then what was he going to do?

As if he knew what the boy was thinking, PateraThrakon spoke, "Come and stand over next to the golem."

Kord looked at where Vrom was standing, and he thought that he would show him what he was supposed to do. Vrom was the one who trained with him anyway, so he figured he would continue to do so.

Kord moved to stand next to Vrom, but when he was in position, the golem moved away from him. Kord started to follow, but was stopped by PateraThrakon. "Stay where you are." Kord looked at the dragon but did not understand what he was supposed to do. “Prepare yourself,” PateraThrakon said.

“Prepare myself for what?”

Kord did not have time to hear an answer because the next thing he knew, he went flying backward some distance from where he was standing. He was lying on his back, and the way he felt, he was more than happy to remain there.

“Stand up,” PateraThrakon said, but Kord did not move. “Do not tell me that you are broken just from one swipe of my tail.”

Kord now knew what had hit him, and he was surprised that he was still breathing, even though that act alone came with trouble since part of the dragon’s tail struck him in the chest.

“Golem, help the boy up.” Kord heard the dragon give the command to Vrom, and the golem went over to Kord and helped him to move into a sitting position so that he was looking at the dragon and not the sky. “I told you to prepare yourself,” PateraThrakon stated to remind Kord that he had given him some kind of warning.

“You could have told me that you were going to hit me with your tail. You could have killed me.”

“Yes, I could have, but I used as little of my strength as I could, and as you can see, since you are speaking, you are still alive.” Kord thought that he would have hated to have seen what would have happened to him if the dragon had used all of his strength. “Now, stand up, so we may continue.”

Kord did not want to stand up, and he did not want to continue. He wanted to lie there until his body stopped tingling from his head to his toes, but he did not have a choice. Vrom lifted the dazed boy off the ground to a standing position but held onto him until Kord stopped wobbling. He then let go of him but remained next to the shaken boy.

"You did not prepare yourself," PateraThrakon said.

"What does that mean?" Kord asked angrily. "If I knew what you were going to do, I would have run behind a tree or a boulder so you wouldn't hit me with your tail."

PateraThrakon hoped that Kord would have figured it out on his own, but at the same time, he decided that the boy would not have known what to do; he wanted to test him anyway. Now that he saw him in action, the dragon would proceed. "What have you been doing for the past two moon-cycles?"

Kord thought about it, and the answer was simple. "I was training in the forest. I was running up the hill, over boulders and trees." That was essentially all he had done.

"Because of that, what has come about?" PateraThrakon asked.

Kord thought, and even though it took a moment for the answer to come to him, it did. "My legs grew stronger, and they can now take on the likeness of a dragon."

PateraThrakon was impressed that Kord's

answers were accurate, and it was time to educate the child on more than what he knew. "The legs of a dragon are solid. It would take a great deal of force to knock one off its feet. Unlike what just happened to you." The dragon waited a moment to let Kord take in his last remark. "Now that your legs are stronger, you need to train your body so that you are unyielding in your stance."

Kord did not understand. "What do you mean?" he asked.

"The success of any fighter begins in their stance. The way they place their feet and position their body will help not only in their defense but in their attack as well." After he was done explaining, PateraThrakon could tell that Kord did not grasp the concept of what he had relayed to him. "Stand there with your legs and feet together."

Kord looked down at his feet, then at the dragon, "You're not going to hit me again, are you?" he asked, not wanting to feel the power behind the dragon's tail for a second time.

"I might if you do not do as I say," was all PateraThrakon had to say to him, and Kord hurried to stand as the dragon had instructed. "Golem, you may proceed."

Not sure what was going to happen, Kord tried to stand as stiff as possible. Vrom took a position in front of him, facing the boy, and then the golem used his hands and pushed Kord backward. Since he was sure that he was going to be struck in some manner, Kord was able to take a step back with his right foot, but he did not fall over.

"Now stand with your legs and feet apart, at the same distance between your shoulders," PateraThrakon instructed. Now that Kord knew that he was not going to be hit by the tail of the dragon, he quickly took up his new stance. "Golem, you may proceed," PateraThrakon said.

Vrom moved closer to where Kord was standing, then reached out and pushed Kord backward. With his legs apart, he did not have the same balance as he had when his legs and feet were together, even though he stumbled back more than the last time, he did not fall.

PateraThrakon relayed his next set of instructions. "Now stand with your right leg extended from your body, and your left leg slightly behind you."

Kord was not exactly sure what the dragon wanted him to do, so by the time he positioned himself to what he thought was correct, he looked as if he was trying to step over a wide stream without falling in. "Golem, show the boy the stance he should be in."

Vrom positioned himself beside Kord and assumed the stance the dragon wanted from Kord. His right leg and foot were a step in front of him, with his left leg and left foot a step behind his body. Once he saw the way the golem was standing, he adjusted his legs to match Vrom.

"Golem, you may proceed," PateraThrakon said, and Vrom moved to stand in front of Kord and pushed on his chest. Even though Kord's body moved from the force against him, he did not take a step back. "Do you see the difference?"

Kord did. With the way his feet and legs were positioned in the last stance, he was able to maintain his balance better and held the position as well. He looked down at his feet and legs to see just how he was standing, and just barely had time to hear the dragon's next statement. "Prepare yourself."

He did have enough time to look up at the dragon just before he went flying backward, landing on his back, once again.

Right there and then, if he had a sword, Kord thought that he would have attacked the dragon and fought him until one of them was dead. The two things that stopped him were that Kord did not have a sword, and he was in too much pain to stand up on his own, let alone attack the dragon. Once again, Vrom helped Kord to a sitting position, even though Kord thought that he was more comfortable lying down.

"I told you to prepare yourself," PateraThrakon said as if that relieved him of all responsibility for placing Kord in the agony that he was in. "This is your next level of training." Kord, trying to get air into his lungs, looked up at the dragon. "Your legs are strong, now you need to learn to use them so that your stance is strong as well. Remember, the stance of any fighter is the first step for them in winning the fight." Kord was not sure if the dragon was telling the truth or not. All he knew was that being hit by the tail of a dragon was not something he wanted to feel again. "Golem, assist the boy," PateraThrakon said to let them both know Kord had rested long enough.

Vrom helped Kord to stand, and when he did, Kord decided to let PateraThrakon know something had changed. "His...name...is...Vrom," Kord said with a short breath between each word, since he was still having trouble breathing.

"What?" PateraThrakon asked, referring to the comment Kord had made.

Kord stood up straighter and on his own. It was not much, but he tried to regain some of the dignity he had lost from being knocked down by the dragon twice. "You keep calling him golem, but that is not his name. It is Vrom," Kord said, and would have seemed a bit more valiant if he did not have to place his hand on his chest to help him breathe. He also felt a sharp pain in his side. What he did not know was that from the second blow of the dragon's tail, a couple of his ribs had been broken.

"Did you give him that name?" PateraThrakon asked. Kord gave a nod for his answer since he was having trouble breathing. "Why?"

"Why what?" Kord asked, being able to force those two words out.

"Why did you give him a name?"

Kord did not reply immediately, but it was not because he could not breathe. He thought about the question, then answered it. "Because everyone needs to have a name. Even if he is a golem, he is someone."

Surprisingly, PateraThrakon was impressed with Kord's answer. It meant nothing to the dragon if the golem had a name or not, but the way Kord stood up for him was honorable, and honor was important to a dragon. PateraThrakon also knew that giving someone, or even something, a name can change the person or object. The name alone can give life.

"Very well. Vrom will show you what you will need to do for the next stage of your training." The dragon tilted its head and looked at Kord. Once he was sure he had a clear assessment of the boy's condition, he decided to postpone the boy's training for a sun-cycle. "You may stay here until you are feeling better, then I suggest you head back to your hut and rest. When you wake, your wounds will be healed, and you will be able to continue with your training."

"I'm fine," Kord said, not wanting to show any weakness to the dragon even though he felt as if he was about to fall over.

"If that is your decision, so be it," PateraThrakon said, then spread his wings and took to the sky. Having given the boy his next instructions for his training.

As soon as the dragon was out of his sight, Kord fell to the ground, lying on his left side with his knees curled up to his chest. The pain he was feeling went from the top of his head to his feet. He felt Vrom come over to him and place his hands on his arm as if to say he would help Kord to stand, who was not ready for that yet. “Just let me rest here on the ground for a moment. I’ll be fine.” Kord was not sure if he would be or not; he could only hope.

He closed his eyes, thinking that it might ease the pain, which it did not, but he felt Vrom pat him on his arm as if to say he would be alright. To Kord, at least Vrom showed him some pity. Not like the mean dragon.

Kord finally had the strength to walk back to the hut. He did as PateraThrakon had suggested and did not partake in any training. Keia was in front of the hut and saw that Kord had returned earlier than he usually did. “You’re back early. It will be a while before I have our meal ready,” she said to let him know that he would have to wait.

“That’s ok, I’m not hungry. I’m going to go lie down and rest,” Kord said as he walked past her.

“Do you want me to wake you when it’s time to eat?”

“No,” was all Kord could say, and headed into the hut to rest and pray that what PateraThrakon had said about him healing after he rested was true. If not, Kord hoped that he would just die in his sleep.

When he woke, he was surprised at how well he felt. He could breathe normally, and his side did not hurt. He could not wait to begin his training. When he stepped out of the hut, he saw MiteraThrakena standing outside. "Keia will be out in a moment," Kord said to the female dragon.

"I am here to see you as well," MiteraThrakena said and waited for Keia to exit the house.

"Good morning, My Lady," Keia said to greet the dragon.

"Good morning, my child," MiteraThrakena replied, always happy to speak with Keia.

"What did you want to see us for?" Kord asked, ready to hurry up and leave so that he could begin his daily training.

"You will both come with me today," MiteraThrakena said and looked directly at Kord to let him know that yes, she was speaking to him as well.

"Where are we going?" Keia asked, excited about whatever it was the dragon had planned.

"We are going on an outing. Kord, there will be no training for you today, and Keia, you can let your chores go for today as well."

"An outing, that sounds like fun," Keia said.

The dragon had decided that the two children had had enough time with what they were doing. Kord had been training for over two moon-cycles straight, and Keia, even though she was not performing her actual training in becoming the Dragon Kastera, she was performing tasks that would help her when the time came for her to do so.

Today, especially since she found out what

happened to Kord with his training, MiteraThrakena decided that the children needed a day to just be children. She would take them where they could have a nice midday meal and play in the pond, where they took their baths just as they had done before they took on the blessings of the dragons.

"Come, I want to show you both a place where there are a lot of deer and rabbits," MiteraThrakena said, and Keia was quick to step alongside the female dragon.

Kord decided that it might be fun, so he walked over to Keia, and when he was next to her, he said, "I'll race you," then took off running.

"That's not fair!" Keia yelled and took off after him, wanting to join in the fun.

MiteraThrakena had informed PateraThrakon what she had planned to do, and when he told her that the children needed to continue with their training, she simply told him that the children needed to remember that they are still children, which ended the conversation between the king and queen.

MiteraThrakena watched the two children running. Kord slowed his pace to allow Keia to catch up to him. The female dragon knew that one day, without training or chores, would not interfere with them becoming the Dragon Kastera and Dragon Klau. It was just for one day, where they did not have to think about anything except being children.

NINETEEN

Kord's training took on a variety of methods. From allowing Vrom to attack his upper body with large thick sticks, to him swimming from one side of the river to the other and back. With all of his training, in the seven seasons since he began, he had increased in strength, and now, when his body reacted to an outside force, the scales covered him from his neck all the way to the bottom of his feet.

During his training, most of the time, Kord would strip down to his undergarments. When he was not training, he wore a long, loose-fitting tunic that reached past his waist, with a rope tied around it, along with loose-fitting trousers and a pair of boots. The clothing allowed him to move more freely when he trained and kept his outer clothes on, because they did not hinder his movements.

Keia took him to a cave where she showed him a hoard of items that they could use. There were clothes for both of them, along with boots; however, Kord seldom wore anything to cover his feet, because by reflex, whenever he walked without boots, the scales would react to protect him. Keia herself found a few dresses that fit her quite well, and some boots also.

He asked Keia where all the items came from, and she told him that MiteraThrakena said that many, many seasons ago, humans would come to KhoraThraks, and some even lived there for a while to receive training. Nothing compared to what he was partaking in to be the Dragon Klau, but the dragons would pass their knowledge on to some of the humans whom they felt were deemed worthy of it. Unfortunately, a human's heart can change, and sometimes that knowledge was used for the wrong reasons and in the wrong way.

Kord came up out of his roll, landing on his feet. He quickly turned around to face his wrestling opponent, who looked exactly like him. As Kord grew and his appearance changed, Vrom's did as well. In height and build, they were mirror images of each other. Only that Vrom was the color of dirt.

Kord looked at Vrom, who was standing in the same position as he was, with his fists and arms out in front of him and slightly bent upward at his elbows. His left foot was slightly extended out behind him, with his right placed in front of him. Kord knew that this was the best position to stand, no matter if he decided to run toward Vrom or if Vrom came at him. If he chose to run toward Vrom, he would push off with his left foot. If he decided to stay and wait for Vrom to advance, his stance would allow him to brace for the impact.

What they were currently partaking in was one of Kord's favorite training methods. They would take turns running toward one another, and when they made contact, they would slam their bodies against their opponent. Even before the first time they collided at the start of the training, Kord's reflexes reacted, and the dragon scales formed on his body. They helped to reduce the impact and gave him strength as well. Scales did not appear on Vrom, yet whenever Kord's strength increased, whether it was because his body naturally grew or because of the abilities of the Dragon Klau, Vrom's strength increased to match Kord so that his opponent would be a suitable training partner.

Vrom made the first move and took off running toward Kord. He prepared himself for the golem's attack and decided that this time, Vrom would go high, attacking his upper body. He had misjudged the golem. Instead, just before he reached Kord, Vrom bent low and bowled into Kord's waist, wrapping his arms around his midsection. Kord, having seen the attack numerous times, was not surprised. To begin his counterattack, he extended his arms and wrapped them around Vrom's back and chest. It was now time for both of them to try to knock their opponent off their feet.

Kord tried to lift Vrom off the ground and toss the golem over his head and behind him. Vrom was ready for the move, and just as Kord was about to lift him off the ground, Vrom put all his force in his arms and lifted Kord, and with a twist of his body, tossed Kord slightly to his left and to the ground, with Vrom on top of him, pinning him under the golem.

Kord landed on his back, and even though the scales covered his body, the force of the impact from hitting the ground caused him to lose his breath. When they trained, Vrom did not go easy on him, but Kord had no problem with the intensity of the training. In fact, Kord was the one who came up with their current training method after he watched two mountain rams butting heads together. He did not want to try to butt the golem's head; he was sure that after a few hits, he would be the one with a pain in his head and not Vrom.

Kord tapped Vrom on the shoulder while they were lying on the ground to let his opponent know that he surrendered, and the golem won their last round. With Kord submitting, Vrom stood and extended his hand down to Kord to help him up. His pride was not hurt in the least, and he accepted the help and rose to stand facing the golem. "How many was that?" Kord asked.

Vrom lifted his right arm with his hand in a fist. He opened and closed it three times, then, with his left arm and fist raised, he did the same, but on the third time opening his hand, he only held up two fingers.

"Are you sure?" Kord asked, wanting to make sure Vrom had kept an accurate count of the wins and losses between them. To answer the question,

Vrom nodded his head. Kord decided to see if maybe the golem had miscounted. "I think I won more than twelve rounds." Vrom, sure that the boy was incorrect, shook his head. "Ok, I believe you." Kord was sure that Vrom had kept an accurate count, but he wanted to have fun with the golem, and to show that he had no hard feelings about losing the most rounds, he smiled at his opponent, who returned his own smile.

Kord had never stopped teaching Vrom words and letters, and even though the golem still could not speak, the more Kord taught him, the easier it was for them to communicate. Kord had come up with different ways for Vrom to reply, like when he opened and closed his hands to let him know how many matches he had lost, and the golem had won.

Kord looked up into the sky and saw that it was time for him to head back to the hut. He looked back at Vrom and saw that he had already taken up his stance to begin the next round of their wrestling match. "No, you've won today. I have to be going." He was not surprised when Vrom extended his arms up into the air to announce that he was the victor for the day. Kord could not help but laugh because the golem was only imitating him, since he was the one who first expressed his victory in the same manner the first time he had won the most rounds against Vrom. Now the golem celebrated his victories the same way.

Kord walked over to where he had laid down his

clothes when he began the day's training. He did not put them on; he would do that after he took his daily bath. He did not need the garments for protection because the dragon scales would cover his body, and with them, he had not suffered a single scratch. On the days he swam, he would remove all his clothing to allow him to move through the water at a quicker pace, but even he felt uncomfortable wrestling and rolling on the ground completely naked.

Kord looked over to the golem who was now watching him. Vrom looked exactly like him, and he could see the way his body had changed over the seasons since he arrived in KhoraThraks and began his training. He was now twice the height he was when he was seven, and even though he had trained almost every day and had increased his strength, his body was not muscular, yet he was fit and lean. His hair had grown and reached down past his shoulders since he never cut it. So that it would not get in the way of his training, Keia had plaited it into a tail. The very first time she fixed his hair the way he wore it, she told him that it was his dragon tail. They both laughed, and that was what they called it from that day on. With that thought, he was ready to go back to the hut. Always eager to see Keia, even though he could not express why he did so.

"It's time for me to head back," he said to Vrom to let him know he was leaving. As he always did, before he was completely out of the golem's sight, he turned around and waved to him. Something he did to let the golem know he always enjoyed their time together.

Vrom, as usual, went over to the log and sat down, picked up a stick, and began to write on the ground. He was now able to write complete sentences.

Kord, having taken his bath, was now approaching the hut. What was odd was that outside the hut, he saw MiteraThrakena lying on the ground, and it appeared as if she was waiting for him. "Hello, My Lady," he said to greet the female dragon. It had been a while since he had seen her, even longer since he had seen her mate, who was supposed to be the one training him, but left it up to Vrom. He looked around but did not see who he was looking for. "Where's Keia?" he asked.

"She is inside resting," MiteraThrakena said to answer his question.

Kord thought that the statement was strange. Every time he came back from his training, Keia would always be either working in the garden, cooking dinner, or doing something else around the hut. "Is she tired from working today?" Kord asked, thinking that maybe she had just decided to go to bed early, but even that was not like her, so he decided to go in and talk to her, but before he could reach the door, MiteraThrakena placed her tail out to block his way. He turned to face her, and the look he gave her let the dragon know that he wanted an explanation.

MiteraThrakena knew the time would come, and she was not surprised when it had. She had long ago explained to Keia what being a woman was about, and for Keia, it was even more important. Now it was time for her to explain to Kord. "Keia is going through changes."

"What do you mean, changes? Is she alright?" Kord asked, and the concern he had for Keia was obvious to the dragon.

"Yes, she is fine. Her body is adjusting to becoming a woman, and with that, there will be times she does not feel well." Kord turned his head and looked toward the hut, then looked back at MiteraThrakena. He did not understand exactly what she had told him, so she continued to explain. "It has been seven seasons since the two of you arrived; in that time, you have grown into young adults. With that, your bodies have changed as well."

Kord understood some of what she was saying. He had grown taller and stronger; however, he was still ignorant of some of the aspects of being a man and a woman. The two children had spent more time with the dragons than they had with humans, and in that respect, with their parents. It was common for the parents to teach their children about the differences between boys and girls and about what it means to be a man and a woman, and for Keia, that meant even more changes to her body.

Kord was not concerned at the moment about what the dragon said about their bodies changing;

all he wanted was to make sure Keia was okay. He turned and tried to head into the hut, but MiteraThrakena continued to block his way with her tail. “I want to see Keia,” he said when he turned back to face the dragon, and his voice had more force in it than a moment ago.

MiteraThrakena was not upset with him; in fact, she thought that the way he was acting was commendable. She could tell that he was worried, and that was only because he cared about her. How much he cared, the dragon was uncertain of, but she decided to leave that topic for later and began teaching Kord about the birds and the bees. As the children’s guardian, it was her responsibility. “I will allow you to speak with her, but only after I explain to you what is happening with her and some things that you might be experiencing as well.”

When their talk was over, Kord entered the hut as quietly as he could. It took MiteraThrakena some time to explain what she wanted to, but he now understood what was happening to Keia, at least he thought he did. The dragon told him that no matter how many times she explained it to him, he would never know what it was like when a woman went through her cycle. He was a male, and that was that.

He saw Keia lying down on the mat with her legs slightly curled up to her chest. He walked as quietly as he could and sat down next to her. He thought that she was asleep, but she opened her eyes and looked at him. “I didn’t mean to wake you,” he said, feeling guilty about disturbing her rest.

“I wasn’t sleeping. I just had my eyes closed.” With the sound of her words, Kord could tell that she was not her usual self. Keia was always full of energy and always performing some type of task. Now she looked as if she did not have the energy to move. “I will not be able to fix your evening meal. I’m sorry.”

Now Kord felt even more guilty. Here she was lying down and sounding as if she had no strength, and she was worried about him eating. Something she always did. “That’s ok,” Kord said, “I was getting tired of potatoes and carrots anyway.” To his delight, she laughed at what he said, but also to his disappointment, when she laughed, Kord could see that it caused her discomfort. “Do you need anything?” he asked to see if there was something he could do for her.

“No, MiteraThrakena gave me some medicine to help with the pain, but she said that I should rest until I feel better.”

Kord thought that maybe what Keia and MiteraThrakena said was for the best, so he decided that he would leave and let her get some rest. Before he stood, he gently placed his hand on her shoulder and said, “I hope you feel better soon.” He felt bad that she was not well, but the smile she gave him made him feel a little better. He then stood and walked over to the door, looking back at Keia just before he left the hut.

Once outside, he saw MiteraThrakena still there, and she was looking at him. He remembered what the dragon had told him, that Keia would be this way for seven sun-cycles. To him, that was a long time. He also remembered that she told him Keia would feel the way she did once every moon-cycle. He did not like that at all, but MiteraThrakena said that in time she would be able to deal with what she is going through better and that it was just part of being a woman. Something Kord would never understand.

To his greater disappointment, MiteraThrakena told him that he would not be allowed to lie next to her while she was experiencing her cycle. Kord was not happy with that at all. Ever since the two had met, whenever they went to bed, they would end up lying with their backs touching one another. MiteraThrakena said that Keia needed to get her rest and that his presence would cause her to be uncomfortable, so he would have to sleep outside. He did not like that idea. Sleeping outside was no problem for him; he and Keia had done so many times, but still, he was able to lie next to her. Kord did not have a say in the matter, since MiteraThrakena used her tail to block the entrance of the hut so that he could not enter. There was nothing he could do.

On the second sun-cycle since Keia had stayed inside the hut, Kord did not go to train. He remained at the hut but was only allowed to enter when MiteraThrakena gave him permission. Since she was too big to enter, she allowed Kord to take Keia medicine to help with the pain and to take her water and food to eat. She took the medicine and drank the water, but ate very little.

On the third sun-cycle, Keia exited the hut before Kord had even woken. As soon as he heard her, he jumped up and rushed over to greet her. He thought that since she was walking about, she had recovered. "Are you feeling better?" he asked, smiling because he was happy to see her.

"I'm fine," she said, but did not look at Kord, and to him it sounded as if there was still something wrong.

"Do you need anything?" he asked. More than happy to get her some food or water.

"No," she said and looked around, then asked, "Shouldn't you be off training?"

Kord thought it was a bit strange with the way she sounded. "I decided to stay here and help you." He thought that would be the right thing to do.

"I don't need your help," Keia said and turned to walk away from him.

"Yeah, but I can help you with whatever you need. I can..."

Keia quickly turned to face him and made it clear what she wanted, "I don't need your help. What I need is for you to leave me be. Go off and do whatever training it is you do." Without any more words, she turned and stomped off out of his sight.

Kord did not know what he had done wrong. Keia had never yelled at him in that manner, and he thought that she was angry with him, but all he wanted to do was make sure she was alright.

"Come along," MiteraThrakena said, and Kord looked at her. "I will walk part of the way with you to your training area, and I will explain to you what you should not do when Keia is having her cycle."

Kord did not understand. He just wanted to help, and he hoped that MiteraThrakena would be able to tell him what was happening. For he had no idea how to deal with what Keia was going through.

By the time he arrived at the training area, Kord decided that the best thing to do when Keia was not feeling well was to keep his mouth shut. He wanted to help her, but MiteraThrakena told him there was nothing he could do, so it was best for him to allow her the time she needed.

Kord went through his training, and every night he went back to the hut. He only spoke to Keia to ask her if she was feeling any better or if she needed anything. For the most part, she replied in a kind and thoughtful manner; however, there were a couple of times when he felt as if he had done something wrong and did not know what it was. Her words came out fast and furious, and it was at those times that he decided to leave her be.

It had been eight sun-cycles since Keia had begun her cycle, and Kord was making his way back to the hut. When he saw that Keia was outside leaning over the pot she used to cook with, he ran up to her. "Are you feeling better?" he asked, hoping she would say yes and not tell him to go jump in the river as she had a couple of times before.

"Yes, I am feeling much better now." She looked down at the pot, then back at Kord. "I made potato and carrot soup for us. I know you like it."

Kord smiled at her. Not just because he was happy that she was feeling better, but also because she had made his favorite meal. MiteraThrakena had told him that Keia would be better within a moonmark, and she had been right. It looked as if Keia was back to her old self again, and things would return to normal. "I'll get the spoons and bowls," Kord said, eager to taste the soup.

"Wait," Keia called to him before he entered the hut. He turned around and looked at her. "There is something I need to tell you." Kord did not like the way her voice sounded, and he was afraid it had something to do with what she had been through, and in a way, it did. "MiteraThrakena said that I cannot stay in the hut with you any longer. Now that I am a woman, it would not be appropriate."

Kord did not understand what she was saying, "But you're better now, so everything is alright." She did not answer, so he asked, "Isn't it?"

She walked over to where he was standing. "I am a woman, and you are becoming a man. We cannot live as our parents lived together. That is the way it must be."

Kord thought about what she said, but was still confused. He looked at her and asked his next question, "Where are you going to stay?"

For her answer, she walked around him and stood in front of the door to the hut, turned and faced Kord, who had turned to face her, "I am going to stay in the hut. You will have to find another place to live."

Once again, Kord was not sure what was happening. He looked at her with an expression of confusion on his face. First, he did not understand why they could not stay in the hut together, and second, he did not know why he had to leave. The hut was both of theirs, and he was not the one who decided they could not stay there together, so why was he being forced out?

Keia walked over to him and placed her hand on his chest, then tried to explain what was happening. "This is the way it must be from now on. I will miss lying next to you, and I am grateful that you have been with me all these seasons to give me peace when I sleep." Kord knew that she was referring to when she had trouble sleeping because she would dream about what had happened to her parents, but she had not had a frightful night in over a season. "I have changed, and I need to live by myself now. That is the way it must be." Keia finished speaking, but she gave him one last expression of her appreciation to comfort him. She leaned upward and kissed him on his cheek. She then turned around and walked inside the hut, leaving Kord alone.

He did not know what was happening. He was not allowed to sleep in the hut, so where was he going to sleep? Keia was acting differently, and the word he thought best to describe her was *strange*, especially the part where she placed her hand on his chest. It made him feel uncomfortable and comfortable at the same time. He then remembered what else she did, and that was the kiss on his cheek. Only his mother had ever done that, and Keia was not his mother. Too much had happened since he had just arrived at the hut, and he was more confused than he had ever been.

Kord turned around and started walking. He had to find MiteraThrakena and talk to her. Maybe she could explain to him about everything that was going on. Someone had to.

Keia closed the door behind her, knowing that Kord had walked away once she was inside. She also knew that he was more than likely confused. In a way, she was as well. She wanted to continue to lie next to Kord when they slept and let things be the way they were before, but MiteraThrakena told her that change is a natural part of life, and it cannot be stopped, or there will be no growth. Now that she was the one who had grown, her way of life, along with Kord's, would have to change as well.

She had waited seven seasons, and now that she was a woman, MiteraThrakena told her what she had been waiting so many seasons for. It was time for her to become the Dragon Kastera.

TWENTY

They had been walking ever since the first rays of the sun had entered the sky. When she was a child, MiteraThrakena would allow Keia to ride on her back, but once she got older, the female dragon told her that she needed to walk so that each step she took came in contact with the ground, and therefore with nature.

Keia did not mind walking. They slowed their traveling down to a pace where the dragon had to match Keia's because a human's steps are far less than those of a dragon, but MiteraThrakena was very patient. She has lived for many seasons, and time meant very little to a dragon, so there was no rush to get to where they were heading.

The sun was not quite at its midday point by the time they reached their destination. When they did, Keia was quick to notice that it was another entrance to a cave. It seemed that there were quite a few caves in KhoraThraks. Keia remembered entering the cave all those seasons ago when she and Kord first found their way to the land where the dragons live. There was a cave that Keia and Kord would go to if they were looking for something they needed. That cave was where all the possessions of the people who used to be able to visit KhoraThraks were now kept. Then there was the cave where both the King and Queen of Dragons lived. In all the time Keia and Kord have been with the dragons, they have only entered that cave twice.

Now Keia was standing at the entrance of another cave, and like all the ones that she came upon before, there was only one thing to do, and that was to enter.

The ceiling of the cave was high enough and wide enough to allow the dragon to walk inside. It was not wide enough to let the two traveling through to walk next to one another, so Keia walked in front of the dragon. As they walked through the cave, MiteraThrakena lit the torches that were hanging on the walls. She did not need the light, but Keia would not be able to see without it.

They finally came to an opening, and when Keia took her first step through, fire came forth from the torches located on the walls of the semi-circular chamber. Keia watched as each torch awakened with light starting from her left and moving around to end at her right. Once the light was as bright as it could be, Keia put her focus on what was in the center of the chamber.

Five stone pillars stood five paces away from Keia. They rose from the floor of the chamber and came to the height of Keia's chest. When she first noticed them, she did not pay much attention to the pillars themselves, because her focus was on what was located at the top of each of the pillars.

"Enter," MiteraThrakena said to let Keia know that the entrance of the inner chamber was not their final destination.

Keia did not turn around to look at the dragon; she simply took her next step on her journey to becoming the Dragon Kastera.

She made her way to stand two paces from the pillars, positioning herself so that she was in front of the one in the center. She turned her head to her left so that she could inspect what was on each of the pillars. She continued to put her focus on the next pillar in line, and when she came to the one farthest to her right, a feeling inside her made her take her eyes off the item just as soon as she realized what it was.

The female dragon had entered the chamber behind the young woman. It was now time for MiteraThrakena to begin Keia's training. "These are the forces of nature. These are what you will learn to control and use them as the Dragon Kastera." The dragon watched as Keia continued to study each of the objects before her, and it did not go unnoticed by the Queen of Dragons that after Keia's initial sight of the furthest pillar to the child's right, she did not put her focus on it at all. The dragon knew that the final item would be the child's most difficult test. That is why the dragon would save it for last.

"Stand before the first pillar," MiteraThrakena said, and Keia did not hesitate to step forward and to her left, placing her at the farthest distance away from the fifth pillar as possible. "What do you see?" MiteraThrakena asked.

Keia did not hesitate to reply, "Fire."

"And what do you see of it?"

Keia took a moment to gather her thoughts. She knew what MiteraThrakena was asking; she wanted more of an explanation as to what she was seeing. The flame floated over the top of the pillar. It was not coming out of it, because Keia could see the space between the flame and the top of the pillar. The flame was about two handbreadths high and about one handbreadth wide. Keia knew that the dragon wanted a description of the flame, but also what Keia noticed about it, which made it one of the forces of nature. When she was ready, she gave her answer.

"It is hot because I feel the heat coming from it. It is bright because, like the torches on the walls, it gives off light." She took a moment, then added to her answer. "It moves, but not like we do."

The dragon understood Keia's comment, but she wanted her to elaborate, "How does it move?"

Keia took a moment and thought about the question, then replied. "It moves on its own, as if it is alive." Keia thought about fire in general, then added to her answer. "Fire is not human, but it can grow. It does not have legs or feet, but it can move fast and spread over a distance. It can burn someone, and even kill them, yet we use fire to cook our food, to light our way, and even to make things. So even though it can harm us, it can help us."

MiteraThrakena was impressed with Keia's answer. Humans have been using fire for a very long time, so it is the force of nature that is most familiar to them. It was now time to move on. "What about the next one?" the dragon asked, and Keia took a step to her right to stand before the second pillar.

"Water," Keia said without hesitation once she was standing in front of the second pillar. A ball of water was floating over the top of it. As soon as Keia had her eyes focused on it, the ball of water began to move. It altered its shape so that it was now stretched out vertically, but before Keia could say anything, the water altered its shape again and was now stretched out horizontally over the top of the pillar. Just as quick as it took on the third form, it returned to its original shape of a sphere.

"What do you see?" MiteraThrakena asked.

Keia looked at the floating ball of water, and as she did, it continued to change its form. It stretched itself so that it was in a circle with the center hollow. Keia could see the water moving in a circular pattern, then it altered its form again. It was now moving in a way that Keia thought it looked like a river flowing. Keia took a moment and thought about the question, "It moves on its own, as if it is alive."

"What else?" MiteraThrakena asked.

Keia continued to observe the flow of the water. "It flows, but it only flows in the shape that it is in. Like a river or stream." As soon as she finished speaking, the water over the top of the pillar started moving erratically. Keia did not understand what it was doing.

"You have never seen the ocean before, have you?" MiteraThrakena asked.

Keia turned her head to look behind her, "No, My Lady." She then put her focus back on the water over the pillar.

MiteraThrakena continued with Keia's training. "You are correct. Water flows according to its surroundings, like a river or stream, but the ocean is vast. The water of the ocean can be wild and dangerous. Waves can rise to heights that can overturn a ship that can hold hundreds of humans. Waves can crash onto land that can not only engulf a single person but also an entire city." It was now time to lead Keia to what water can really do. "What happens if a person remains underwater for too long?"

Keia continued to look at the water over the pillar, which was still moving erratically, but answered, "They drown." She then turned around to look at the dragon behind her. "Water can kill us, and yet we need it to live. If we do not drink enough water, then we will also die." She turned back to look at the pillar with the water, which was now back in its spherical form. "Like fire, water can kill us, but we need it as well."

"Yes, my child," MiteraThrakena said. "And what of the next?"

Keia took another step to her right, and as she watched the item over the third pillar, she realized that she did not truly understand what she was looking at.

"What do you see?" MiteraThrakena asked.

Keia did not hesitate to answer, "A leaf."

MiteraThrakena asked her next question, "What do you not see?"

Keia watched the leaf move over the top of the pillar. MiteraThrakena had told her what the forces of nature were, and the leaf was not one of them. Keia knew what it was that she did not see. "Wind is moving the leaf around. It is because the leaf is moving that I know that there is wind."

"Correct," MiteraThrakena said. "What do you know of Wind?"

Keia continued to look at the leaf, because that was the only thing she was able to see that let her know that the wind was present, and she relayed that to MiteraThrakena. "Since I cannot see the wind itself, the only way I know it is there is because I see the leaf move." She stopped talking, and an idea came to her. She did not know if what she wanted to do would be acceptable to MiteraThrakena, but she wanted to test her theory.

She moved forward, and when she was less than a step away from the pillar, she turned her head and looked over her right shoulder at the dragon behind her. MiteraThrakena nodded to her to let her know that she could continue with what she had planned. With MiteraThrakena's approval, she turned her head and put her focus back on the leaf. She then stretched out her arm and grabbed hold of it. Once she had it in her hand, she did not pull back her arm. She kept it there, holding the leaf, but it was not the item of her focus. She felt the wind on her hand. She held it over the top of the pillar and could feel the wind brushing against her closed fist. She moved her fist around, and no matter how she held it, she could feel the wind against it. When she felt she had studied the wind enough, she opened her fist and let go of the leaf. It went back to floating over the top of the pillar, then Keia pulled her hand back and turned around to look at the dragon.

"Even though I cannot see the wind itself, I can feel it." Keia took a moment and thought about what she wanted to say. When she was ready, she spoke to the dragon about wind in general. "It blows things around, and that is how I can tell it is there. I can feel it on me, but without those two things, I would not know it existed."

MiteraThrakena did not disagree with Keia's remarks. Even so, Keia's thoughts on the aspects of Wind were not complete. "Then what is the wind?" MiteraThrakena asked.

Keia thought for a moment but could not come up with anything to add to her previous statements about Wind.

MiteraThrakena knew that she would now have to teach Keia the rest of what Wind is. "Take a deep breath." Keia did then let it out. "What did you breathe in?"

"Air," Keia said with certainty.

"Did you not breathe in wind?"

Keia thought for a moment, then gave her answer, "No, humans breathe in air. That is what we need to live."

MiteraThrakena did not disagree with Keia because the child was correct. "Then what is air?"

Keia took a second to think about the question, then gave her answer, or at least the best she could, "Air is air."

MiteraThrakena held back her laugh after hearing Keia's answer. The child's answer was not wrong, just not complete. "Air is part of nature, and yes, all living things need it to live. So even though air is a part of nature, what is wind?"

Keia thought for a moment and did not have an answer, but she had a question. "Are air and wind the same?"

MiteraThrakena could hear the confusion and doubt in her words and knew it was time to explain what Wind was. "Air exists because Creator created it so that living beings can breathe. Wind is a force of nature. It is the movement of air. That is how you can feel the breeze on your skin. How the tops of the tallest trees move. It is how ships can sail across the great oceans, by catching the wind in their sails."

Keia had never seen ships before or even the ocean, but she knew what they were. It was now time for MiteraThrakena to tell her the rest of what Wind can do.

"The same wind that moves those ships across the ocean is the same wind that can capsize those ships. The same wind that blows the tops of the trees is the same wind that can uproot those trees from the ground. The same wind that you feel on your skin is the same wind that can lift you off the ground and send you flying to your death."

Keia now understood more about Wind. She had not known about the harshness of it. She had never seen any of the circumstances that MiteraThrakena had just told her about, but she knew what would happen if she did. "Wind can kill me. Just like Fire and Water," Keia said to let the dragon know that she understood.

"Yes, it can," MiteraThrakena said to let Keia know that she was correct. She could now continue with Keia's lesson on the third force of nature. "Wind, when it comes in contact with Fire, will allow the fire to move faster. This can cause great damage to even a forest that has been in existence since the beginning of creation. Wind, when it comes in contact with Water, can cause the water to become so fierce that it can rise so high that the waves can cover the tallest of ships and send them to the bottom of the ocean, never to rise again. Windstorms, cyclones, tornadoes, and hurricanes are all destructive forces of wind. That is why it is a force of nature. One that can give the slightest of breezes, or one that can bring complete and total destruction."

Keia turned around and looked at the pillar with the leaf floating over the top of it. With everything that MiteraThrakena had just explained to her, she now understood more about Wind. Although she did not fear it, she did have a greater respect for it.

TWENTY-ONE

There were still two more pillars for Keia to examine. "Move on to the next one," MiteraThrakena said to let Keia know that it was time to continue. As Keia turned to her right and walked over to the next pillar in line, it did not go unnoticed by MiteraThrakena that Keia forced herself not to look at the last pillar to her right, even though she knew that she would eventually have to deal with it.

Keia faced the fourth pillar, and she saw what looked like some type of crystal. Since MiteraThrakena had told her about the forces of nature, she knew that it was not a crystal, but Ice. "I have never seen ice like this before," Keia said to let the dragon behind her know what she thought of the item before her.

"Where have you seen ice?" MiteraThrakena asked.

Keia continued to look at the shard of ice but answered the dragon. "During the cold season, my father..." Keia stopped for a moment as she spoke the word. It had been many seasons since the death of her parents, but that did not mean that Keia did not still miss them. When she composed herself, she continued. "My father would have to break up the ice every morning in the water bucket from the well during the cold season. He would also have to break up the ice in our well just so he could fill the bucket." Keia stopped looking at the ice and turned around to face the dragon. "Ice is water that is frozen," Keia said to state what she knew of Ice.

"You are correct," MiteraThrakena said, but there was more to Ice than just being frozen water as the dragon was about to explain. "You have never seen a river or stream frozen, have you?"

"No," Keia replied.

MiteraThrakena was not surprised by her answer. Keia had come to her when she was very young and had not had the time to see many of nature's behaviors. As for the dragon, MiteraThrakena has had plenty of time to see them all. "Ice is water that is frozen. There are places on Eirene where there is ice constantly because it is so cold. In most areas where humans live, ice only forms during the cold seasons. It can become so cold that an entire river can become ice in a matter of sun-cycles."

"But how is Ice a force of nature?" Keia asked, not knowing much about Ice. "Fire can heat our food and give us light when it is dark. We need water to drink, and you said wind allows ships to move. So, fire, water, and wind help us, but does ice?"

MiteraThrakena thought that Keia's question

was a very clever one. It showed that she had seen the uses of the first three forces of nature, but Ice was different. "Ice does not benefit humans. There are some places far away where the entire land is covered in ice, and there are some creatures that use that area as their home. Other than that, ice does not serve much use to humans."

"Then why is it a force of nature?" Keia asked.

"Ice is a force of nature because it can grow, it can move, it can consume." It was obvious by the look on her face that Keia did not understand and that MiteraThrakena would have to explain it further. "Ice can form on a single spot of a river. As it becomes colder, the ice can spread. It can continue to spread until the entire river is covered. Do you know what an icicle is?" MiteraThrakena asked.

"Yes, they would form on our home during the cold season." Once again, Keia thought about how her mother would break off the icicles on their house and give them to Keia so she could play with them.

MiteraThrakena gave her a moment, seeing that Keia's thoughts were focused on her past. When she thought Keia was ready, she continued with the lesson. "An icicle starts with a single drop of water. That drop of water freezes and becomes solid. Then another drop of water freezes onto the first drop. This continues until an icicle is formed. Ice can spread and grow."

Keia then realized something about Ice. "Ice is

a form of water, but it can only take form when it is cold. For ice to even exist, there must be the presence of water, and it must be cold enough for the water to turn to ice." Keia understood more about ice, but she did not fully understand. "I still do not see how Ice is a force of nature."

It was now time for MiteraThrakena to explain just how devastating Ice can be. "You are young, my child, and I am very old. I have seen many events in this world come to pass. I have watched rivers of water turn completely to ice. I have seen lands that were once brimming with life, and in time, they have become entirely covered in ice. Any living being can freeze to death if they are left to the effects of the cold, and even their blood can freeze. Ice can kill. As you can die by Fire, you can also die by Ice." MiteraThrakena was not finished with Keia's lesson on Ice. "Wind cannot be seen, but you see the effects of it by the movement of a leaf, or you feel it against your body. Ice can be seen, but it is announced by the coldness of the world. Make no mistake in underestimating Ice, child. Ice is a force of nature that cannot be overlooked."

Keia believed that MiteraThrakena was telling her the truth. As the dragon said, she has seen much more than Keia or any other human has. Keia understood more about Ice than she had before she entered the cave, and that was what learning was about. To know more than what you did before you started.

"Move on to the last pillar," MiteraThrakena said to let Keia know that it was time to learn about the last and final force of nature. One that she knew Keia would have a problem with.

Keia looked over her left shoulder at the dragon behind her. When she did not move as instructed to do so, MiteraThrakena moved her head in the direction of the last pillar to let Keia know that it was time to face what she did not want to.

Keia knew that she had to move to stand before the last pillar, but as she stood there in front of the fourth one, she could not bring herself to do so.

"The pillar is not going to come to you, and we will not leave this place until you stand before it and know about the last force of nature," MiteraThrakena said to Keia since she had not moved from where she was.

Keia closed her eyes. Maybe it was because she did not want to see the dragon staring at her, or maybe it was because she did not want to see what was waiting for her, or maybe it was both of those reasons. It did not matter because she knew that she had no choice. With her eyes closed, she turned to her right and took the step to place her in front of the fifth pillar. She did not open her eyes, even when she turned her body so that she was facing the pillar.

"Open your eyes," MiteraThrakena said to have Keia look at the pillar before her. When she did not open them, MiteraThrakena spoke again, and this time it was not the gentle, soft-spoken dragon that

Keia had come to know. It was the voice of a teacher telling their pupil what they needed to do and to do it immediately. “Open your eyes, now.”

Keia heard the command. She had never heard MiteraThrakena speak to her with the tone she used. She knew she had to obey the dragon, and there was a part of her that felt she could not resist the command even though she wanted to.

Keia took a deep breath and then opened her eyes. She had her head tilted downward so that she was looking at the base of the pillar.

“Raise your head,” MiteraThrakena commanded.

Keia could not resist the voice of the dragon. She was now sure that MiteraThrakena was doing something to force her to do as the dragon instructed. Keia lifted her head and kept her eyes open, even though she wanted to close them. When the item over the top of the pillar came into her sight, all she could do was stare at it.

“What do you see?” MiteraThrakena asked, and once again she put power into her words to insist that Keia do as she commanded.

Keia looked at the pillar in front of her. She felt the power in the words the dragon had spoken, and even though she was trying to speak, what she saw in front of her was causing her to overcome the command.

“What do you see?” MiteraThrakena asked again and put even more power into her words.

Keia continued to look at the pillar in front of

her, but not even the strength in the dragon's words could overcome the fear Keia was feeling within herself.

"What do you see?" MiteraThrakena asked again, with even more authority in the words and louder than she had before.

Keia did not speak. Keia did not move. Keia was trapped in her own fear, and nothing could break her away from it. "Keia!" MiteraThrakena called out to her, but she did not respond. "Keia!" the dragon called out again, but Keia did not move. "Keia!" MiteraThrakena yelled a third time, and whether it was from the dragon trying to force Keia to face her fear, or the fear itself, Keia could not handle the strain on her body, mind, and spirit. It was her body, mind, and spirit that decided that the young woman could not take the torment any longer, and Keia fell to the ground unconscious.

"Keia!" MiteraThrakena shouted and extended her head and neck over Keia, who was lying on the floor of the cave. She could sense the young woman's life force, so she knew that she was not dead and was very thankful for that. Keia had fallen unconscious from looking at what was over the top of the fifth pillar. There, small bolts of lightning continually struck the top of the pillar. They were so fast that a single bolt of lightning came and went in the blink of an eye. Lightning was the fifth force of nature, and Keia was terrified of it.

TWENTY-TWO

Keia had woken up a while ago but remained silent and kept her eyes closed. With every step MiteraThrakena took, she could feel her own body rise and fall as she rode on the back of the dragon. She kept her thoughts to herself, thinking about how she had failed in the cave. How she froze when she had to face her fear.

"You do not have to pretend you are asleep," MiteraThrakena said, thinking that the young girl had gone on long enough with pitying herself.

"I'm not pretending," Keia said.

"Then are you sleeping?" MiteraThrakena asked to let Keia know that if she was not pretending to be asleep and she was not actually asleep, then what was she doing?

Keia decided that she could not fool the dragon, so she sat up but kept her head bent down. She may not have been sleeping, but she was disappointed in herself.

"There is no shame in being afraid of something," MiteraThrakena said.

"Are you afraid of something?" Keia asked.

MiteraThrakena did not answer the question. The female dragon was afraid of one thing, and if she told Keia what it was, it would not help the child. "Being afraid of anything does not make someone weak. It allows that individual to overcome their fear, and when they do, they are stronger for doing so."

"Will I have to overcome my fear of Lightning?" Keia asked.

"Yes."

"Can't I become the Dragon Kastera without learning how to control it?"

"The Dragon Kastera must learn to control all five forces of nature. If they do not, they cannot be the Dragon Kastera. If you were to learn only four of the five forces, then you would not be complete; and anything that is not complete is futile."

"What does futile mean?" Keia asked.

"It means, ineffective, useless, unsuccessful," MiteraThrakena said to answer her question. She did not want Keia to think that she was being hard on her, but she had to know the truth. "There must always be balance in nature, and between the five forces, there is balance. If you were to only learn four, then there would be no balance within yourself, and that is very dangerous."

"How is it dangerous?"

MiteraThrakena was always pleased with the way Keia would ask questions, but her questions now were taking her to a dangerous area. The female dragon would answer the question and hope that Keia understood, or better yet, her heart did.

"Do you know the difference between good and evil?" MiteraThrakena asked.

Keia did not hesitate to answer. "Yes, I think I do."

"Then what is the difference?" MiteraThrakena asked.

Keia did not answer as quickly as she had the previous question. It was easy to say that she knew the difference, but explaining it was a little more complicated. "Good is when you do good things, and evil is when you do bad things." Her statement was the best answer she could think of.

MiteraThrakena did not laugh at the simple answer, because even though it was simple, it was also the truth. Keia was still young, and even though she might have seen bad things in her life, what the dragon had seen since the beginning of her existence was substantially greater than what the girl of a few seasons had ever set her eyes upon. MiteraThrakena thought that the next lesson Keia needed to learn should be the difference between good and evil. "Good and evil come from the hearts of those who choose to do them. If an individual has a heart of good, then they will do good; if they have evil in their heart, then they will do evil things."

"So, it depends on someone's heart if they are good or evil?" Keia asked.

"Yes," MiteraThrakena said, and she had a

deeper question to ask. "Answer me this. If someone has good in their heart, but they think evil thoughts, does that make them good or evil?"

Keia thought for a moment, then answered the dragon's question. "If they have evil thoughts but do not act on them, then I do not think that they would be evil. If they acted on them, if they thought about hurting someone, and they did, then they might be evil."

MiteraThrakena was not surprised by Keia's answer. It was the typical way most humans view the difference between good and evil. Even her parents might have taught her about good and evil before they were taken away from her. "Someone might do something that is evil, but we are all capable of making mistakes." The act of her greatest mistake that the dragon had ever made passed through her thoughts, and she had to close her eyes for a moment until it went away. When she was ready, she began the lesson again. "If someone commits an act of evil, that does not necessarily mean that they are evil. After they have performed the deed, if they feel remorse or regret in their heart, then they may not be evil. If, from that remorse or regret, they seek to right the wrong or swear they will not do the evil again, then they can move on with their life and still be good. If they do not feel remorse or regret, or if they do not seek to redeem themselves, then they may become evil. Do you understand?"

Keia thought for a moment, "I think so. It's like

the Mountain Raiders that killed Kord's parents and mine. They continue to do what they do, so they are evil."

MiteraThrakena was not impressed with the answer that Keia gave, but she was impressed with the way she gave it. It had been many seasons since the incident with the Mountain Raiders and Keia's and Kord's parents, but when Keia just spoke about what had happened, MiteraThrakena did not sense any fear, hatred, or animosity toward the Mountain Raiders. "Yes, because of what they do, the Mountain Raiders can be considered evil. It is in their nature to hurt others, and that is evil."

"But what does this have to do with me becoming the Dragon Kastera and me having to learn to control Lightning?" Keia asked.

"Do you remember what we were discussing concerning the reason you have to learn to control Lightning?"

Keia thought for a moment about the entire conversation that they were having since the moment she sat up on the dragon's back. When she remembered what they had been discussing, she gave her answer, "Balance."

"Yes, balance. As I said, everything is about balance when it comes to nature. When it comes to being the Dragon Kastera, balance is also everything. If you were to only learn four of the five forces, you would be unbalanced, and if that were to happen, your heart would also be unbalanced, and if that should happen, then you could fall to either side."

"Either side of what?" Keia asked.

"Of good or evil. Even if you were to fall to the side of good, you would be unbalanced and incomplete, and it would not be long before you fall to your death because you would be weak." MiteraThrakena did not hold back on what she had to tell Keia. The young woman had to understand every aspect of being the Dragon Kastera.

"So, if I fall to evil, would I fall to my death as well?"

MiteraThrakena still did not hold back on what she had to teach Keia. "Falling to the side of evil is worse than falling to your death. Yes, you would be incomplete, but evil does not need to be complete to do evil. All evil needs is the desire to do evil, and it will." MiteraThrakena remained silent so that Keia could ponder over what she had been told.

After a few moments of silence between the two, it was Keia who spoke. "I don't want to be evil, so I will learn to control Lightning. I'm still afraid of it, but I will do my best to become the Dragon Kastera."

"That is all I ask," MiteraThrakena said, happy with what Keia had told her. "We will arrive at the hut soon. Tomorrow we will continue with your training; you may rest for the night."

Keia looked up and saw that there was still plenty of time left before the sun was out of the sky. "I should have time to cook the evening meal for Kord."

"I believe he can go one night without you cooking his meal," MiteraThrakena said, all the while smiling at the fact of how Keia always thought of Kord and how to help him.

"While I'm training, there may be times that I won't be able to cook for him, so if I can, I want to. He likes it when I cook for him."

MiteraThrakena turned her head and neck around so that she could face Keia before she asked her next question. "Or is it that you like to cook for him?" Keia did not answer the question, at least not out loud. MiteraThrakena finally turned around to look in the direction she was walking when she saw Keia's face turn red from the question she had asked.

As they walked, MiteraThrakena thought about what she had to do. She knew that there was the possibility that Keia would not overcome her fear of Lightning, and if that were to happen, then she would not become the Dragon Kastera. Even that is not the worst outcome that could come to pass. Keia had asked her if she feared anything, but the dragon did not give her an answer. Yes, MiteraThrakena was afraid of one thing, and that was failing again. The ringing in her ears was a constant reminder of that failure.

TWENTY-THREE

Keia waited outside her hut for MiteraThrakena to arrive and retrieve her for her lesson. It would be the first day that she would actually train in learning to control the forces of nature. She had mixed feelings about the whole ordeal. She was happy that she would be able to start training, while at the same time, she was afraid. Not only afraid of having to learn about Lightning, but also afraid of failing at becoming the Dragon Kastera.

As soon as she saw MiteraThrakena flying through the sky, she was able to gain courage at the sight of the dragon. Keia knew that MiteraThrakena would not let her fail. She trusted the dragon to teach her everything she needed to know, including how to face her fears.

MiteraThrakena landed gently in front of Keia. "Good morning, My Lady," Keia said to greet the dragon.

"Good morning, my child. Are you ready to begin your training?" MiteraThrakena asked.

"Yes," Keia replied with a smile.

"Very well. Follow me." MiteraThrakena turned

around to face away from Keia. She then raised her right front paw, and with one of her claws stretched out, she sliced open the space in front of her. A line appeared from the height of the dragon's head all the way down to the ground. It then opened wider as it stretched to the left and the right. When it stopped, an image was in front of the dragon. MiteraThrakena then stepped through the portal she had created.

Keia could see MiteraThrakena on the other side of the opened space. When the dragon was completely through, she turned her head to look at Keia, still standing on the opposite side of the image in front of the hut. To let Keia know that she was to follow her, she just smiled, turned her head, and started walking away. MiteraThrakena knew that the thought of walking through the portal would be too much for Keia to resist, and she was correct.

Keia, having seen everything that the dragon had done since she landed in front of her, was not shocked at what she witnessed; she was amazed at what she saw. Now, after the initial excitement was over, Keia did not hesitate to run up to the portal and straight through it to catch up to MiteraThrakena.

When she was on the other side, Keia stopped for a second and turned around to look at the portal, which she had just walked through. She wanted to make sure that what she thought she had just accomplished actually happened, and since she could see the portal, and on the opposite side of it, she saw the small hut where she lived, she was sure of what she had partaken in. Before she took her eyes off the image in front of her, the sides of the portal closed, and once it had, there was nothing left. Not even the line that MiteraThrakena had made, it also disappeared.

Keia turned to look at MiteraThrakena, and the dragon was looking at her, knowing that the young girl would want an answer. "Do not worry, when we are ready to return, I will open the portal again for us. Now, come along," MiteraThrakena said, then turned and started walking away.

Keia took one more look at where the portal used to be, then turned around and started running to catch up with MiteraThrakena. She took a quick moment to look at her surroundings and realized that she did not know where she was and did not want to be left behind.

As they walked, Keia continued to look at the area they were in. "Where are we?" she asked because she had never been to the location where they were.

"We are far from where we began; although we are still in KhoraThraks."

Keia looked around and noticed that there was not much to see. All she saw were rocks and boulders, and the walls of the canyon that they were walking through. "Why did we come to this place?" Keia asked.

MiteraThrakena decided that they had traveled

far enough for what she had planned for Keia's training. "Here is where we will begin your training. Since Fire is the most common of the forces of nature which humans are aware of, then that is the one we will begin with."

Keia still did not understand. She looked around some more and still only saw rocks, boulders, and the walls of the canyon. Which were so high that they were at least three times the height of MiteraThrakena. "Why did we have to come here for me to learn about Fire?" Keia looked around again, not understanding the reason the dragon had brought her to where they were. "Couldn't I have learned it back where we started from?"

"What do you see?" MiteraThrakena asked.

Keia did not even have to take another look at her surroundings. A couple of times was enough to know that no matter what direction she faced, the scenery was the same, so she gave her answer, "I see rocks and boulders and the walls of the canyon we are in."

Keia had answered correctly, so MiteraThrakena presented her next question, "Now, what do you not see?"

Keia did take another look around her, hoping to see what she did not see to answer the question. When she thought she had looked long enough, she gave her answer, "I don't see anything."

"Exactly," MiteraThrakena said and saw the look of confusion Keia had. "In this area, as you said, there is nothing but rocks and boulders. There is nothing that will catch fire if something should go wrong with your training."

Keia understood what MiteraThrakena had said, but she had a question for the dragon. "What could go wrong?"

MiteraThrakena knew that it was time to begin her training. "The forces of nature are wild, and as I have explained before, they can be dangerous. If something were to happen while I was training you in how to control Fire, and you were to lose control, the results could be very bad. If we had remained near your hut, and you were to accidentally set fire to it, then you would have no place to sleep. That is, unless you wish to sleep where Kord now inhabits." MiteraThrakena was serious, but at the same time, she was having a little fun with Keia, and she knew that her comment stirred something in the young girl because her face turned red.

After teasing Keia, MiteraThrakena continued. "These surroundings are more suitable for learning to control Fire."

Keia saw the reasoning behind MiteraThrakena bringing her to their location. She would hate to accidentally set something on fire, and she quickly took her mind off the hut where she slept because it brought back the comment about Kord. "What do I do?" Keia asked to put her thoughts back on her training.

"First, let me explain to you about the abilities of

the Dragon Kastera." MiteraThrakena decided that since she was going to be talking more than performing actual physical training, she might as well make herself comfortable, so she lowered herself down on the floor of the canyon with her legs under her and her tail wrapped around her body. She kept her neck and head raised so that she could continue to talk to Keia.

"As the Dragon Kastera, you will be able to use the forces of nature in different ways. First is to conjure up the force, which is simply bringing it into existence. With that, you will be able to cast it in a variety of ways."

"That is why I will be the Dragon Kastera," Keia said, remembering back to the night MiteraThrakena had told her about the title she would receive upon completion of her training.

"Correct. For example, with Fire, once you conjure the force with your will, you will be able to cast it. The most common would be as a ball of fire. With more training, you will be able to cast it as a stream of fire. Once you become more efficient, you will be able to cast it in more intricate ways. Although it will take time."

Keia knew that she would have to go through a lot of training to learn to be the Dragon Kastera, but she was ready for it. "Can we begin now?" Keia asked excitedly, wanting to start learning how to control Fire.

"In a moment, there is something else you need

to know. When casting, you must only use your right hand to control the force."

"Why?" Keia asked. Since she was right-handed, she thought that would be the one she would use anyway, but since MiteraThrakena spoke of it specifically, she wanted to know the reason behind the rule.

"There is another way for the Dragon Kastera to cast a force of nature, and that is with their left hand."

Keia did not understand, and she lifted both of her hands so that she could look at them. "What is the difference?"

It was now time for MiteraThrakena to tell Keia the biggest secret of being the Dragon Kastera. "A human's heart is positioned closer to the left side of their body." Keia did not know exactly where her heart was actually located, but she did look down at her chest as if to confirm what the dragon had said. Since she could not see inside her body, she put her focus back on MiteraThrakena. "The Dragon Kastera, once they have mastered all five forces of nature, they will be able to cast a stronger force from their left hand. They draw on what is called the Dragon's Heart Force to do so. However, there are consequences to performing such an act."

"What do you mean by consequences?" Keia asked, wanting to know exactly what would happen.

"Once you cast the Dragon's Heart Force, whatever force of nature you choose to use, you will not be able to cast that force for a full sun-cycle. Not even the less powerful spells from your right hand."

Keia took a moment and thought about what MiteraThrakena had said. "If I use the Dragon's Heart Force, I would be powerless," Keia said to see if she understood the dragon correctly.

"Yes, but you will still be able to use the other forces. That is, unless you use the Dragon's Heart Force with those forces as well."

Keia understood what MiteraThrakena had explained; however, she did have one question that she really wanted an answer to. "What is the difference in power between using a force of nature with my right hand and using one with my left?"

MiteraThrakena smiled before she gave Keia her next instruction. "Come stand next to me." Keia moved to stand to the left, close to the side of MiteraThrakena. "Do you see that boulder over there?" the dragon asked while at the same time lifting her left front paw and using one of her claws to point to a boulder that was three times the size of Keia.

"You mean that one?" Keia asked and pointed to make sure she was looking at the same boulder.

"Yes, that one," MiteraThrakena said, and then she inhaled, and when she was ready, she released a stream of fire from her maw, which struck the boulder that was twenty paces away. When she finally cut off the flame, the boulder was red from the heat of the fire, and the edges of it were breaking off and falling to the ground. "That is about as strong a flame of fire that you will be able to create using your right hand.

Keia looked at the boulder and was surprised at what she saw. She did not think that she would ever be able to create a flame that was hot enough to burn a boulder, but she was going to do her best to succeed.

The dragon waited a moment to allow Keia to witness the force of Fire the dragon had unleashed, then continued with her demonstration. "This is what the flame created by the Dragon's Heart Force can do." MiteraThrakena inhaled again and then released another stream of fire. One that was even more intense than the one before. It was so hot that Keia had to raise her arm in front of her face because even though the dragon's flame was traveling away from her, she could still feel the heat from the fire coming from the dragon's maw.

When MiteraThrakena finally stopped releasing the stream of fire, Keia cautiously lowered her arm. She wanted to see how much damage was done to the boulder, because she knew that with the increased intensity of the flame, compared to the first one, the boulder was probably as red as the sun.

When she looked toward the boulder, Keia was amazed at what she did not see. She did not see the boulder at all. It had been completely destroyed by MiteraThrakena, but that was not all. The boulder had been twenty paces from where she was standing. There were still another twenty paces to the wall of the canyon. Further from the location where the boulder used to be, there was a hole in the canyon wall that was about five paces deep.

“That is the difference between the two,” MiteraThrakena said and looked down at Keia standing next to her.

Keia could not help but stand in awe at what she had just witnessed. After seeing the first of the dragon’s flame, she thought she would not be able to learn to control the force of Fire to heat a boulder. Now, with the hole in the canyon wall before her, she did not think she would ever be able to become so powerful. Although she thought to herself, it will be fun trying.

TWENTY-FOUR

Keia spent the majority of the day learning how to control the force of Fire. When she first began in the morning, she had no problem with creating a flame in the palm of her hand. She had been able to perform that task since the moment she was given the blessing of the dragon.

The next step in the process was to be able to toss that flame toward a target. Since there were plenty of boulders in the area, she was not short on finding one. The task of throwing the flame came very easily to Keia as well. To her, it was just as simple as throwing a small rock. Something which she and Kord would do when they were younger. While concentrating on holding the flame in her hand, she simply pulled back her arm, then quickly brought it forward and tossed the flame outward. She was able to do this with no problems. She did not even have a problem with hitting whatever boulder she chose as her target.

Both Keia and MiteraThrakena were pleased with how well she was able to perform the first steps in controlling Fire. Although MiteraThrakena knew that Keia would have fewer problems with casting Fire since it was common to humans, and Keia had spent her entire life in the presence of it.

By the time the sun was past its midpoint, Keia was able to cast four fireballs, one right after the other. She was able to summon a flame in her hand, release it, and before it was halfway to its target, Keia already called up the second and third fireballs. By the time the first one hit the target she had aimed for, Keia had already released the fourth fireball, which was just behind the third. All four struck her target, one right after the other.

MiteraThrakena had instructed her on her next step in controlling Fire, and it was the one that was causing Keia problems. She was now trying to create a continuous stream of Fire. One that would stretch from her right hand all the way to a target without stopping. It had been a few sun-marks since she began, and the sun would be out of the sky soon, for over three sun-marks, Keia had been attempting to create the stream of Fire with no success.

MiteraThrakena had been watching Keia and decided that it was time for them to head back to the hut. Keia had been practicing all day, and even though she had not accomplished her current task, she had taken a good step forward in becoming the Dragon Kastera. "That is enough for today, Keia. It is time we made our way home." Keia heard MiteraThrakena, but she was not ready to give up. She continued to cast fireballs, but even with her last attempt, she was only able to release six of them, which was far from being a stream of fire. "You can try again tomorrow."

Keia lowered her arm and looked at the boulder twenty paces away. She saw the number of scorch marks that she had made from throwing fireballs at it for the majority of the day. Even with so many, which was still an accomplishment, Keia felt that she had not succeeded since she was not able to cast a stream of Fire.

Not ready to admit defeat, Keia lifted her right hand once again, palm toward the boulder she had been using for a target. She concentrated on creating a stream of Fire. She conjured up a flame in the center of her right palm, and with a thought, she forced the flame to leave her hand. As before, she did not create a stream of Fire. All that she was able to release were six fireballs, and even though each of them struck her target, it was not what she was trying to accomplish, and once again, she knew that she had failed.

MiteraThrakena watched Keia, and even though the young woman was disappointed in herself, MiteraThrakena was not. Fire is the force that she knew Keia would be able to learn the easiest and fastest. She also knew that controlling the forces of nature takes time. How much time would depend on the individual, but MiteraThrakena did not expect Keia to learn everything in one sun-cycle. "Come now, you have practiced enough for today." To let

Keia know that it was time to go, the dragon stood up from where she had been sitting for the majority of the day watching Keia. She then started walking away.

Keia heard MiteraThrakena departing, and since she did not want to get left behind, she turned around to follow the dragon back home. Before she took her first step, she once again thought about how she was not able to make a stream of Fire. She knew it was only her first sun-cycle of actually training in becoming the Dragon Kastera, but she wanted to be able to accomplish more than she had. Creating a flame in the palm of her hand was nothing to her. After a few attempts at trying to throw a fireball, she was able to do so. Even casting six of them in a row. The problem she could not overcome was that when she tried to create a steady stream of Fire, she failed.

She looked back at the rock that she had been using as her target, then looked toward MiteraThrakena, who was still walking away. She took a moment, looked at the ground, and exhaled a long, deep breath to cope with her failure. Once she was through, a thought came to her. She was not quite sure what had started her to think along the path in her thoughts, but there was a small concept in the back of her mind. To bring it forward, while still looking at the ground, she took another deep breath and exhaled. The concept was there, in her thoughts, but it just was not clear enough for her to focus on it.

"Come, child. I will open a portal to take us back to your hut," MiteraThrakena said when she turned her head and saw that Keia was still standing where she had been.

Keia heard MiteraThrakena call to her, while at the same time, she did not. She was too focused on what she was trying to put together; however, with MiteraThrakena's voice in her ears, Keia looked up at the dragon standing a few paces away from her. When she saw the dragon, the thought that was in her mind became a little clearer. Keia took another deep breath and then exhaled. What she had been trying to contemplate was closer to the edge of her thoughts.

She then remembered back to earlier in the day when MiteraThrakena showed her the difference between casting a normal stream of Fire and the Dragon's Heart Force. She pictured the scene in her mind. She could see MiteraThrakena breathe fire and strike the boulder she had been aiming for. She saw the dragon breathe a steady stream without ever stopping. Without ever taking another breath after she inhaled just before releasing the fire. With that, Keia had her answer.

She put her focus back on MiteraThrakena, who was still standing off in the distance. Only she did not move to go to the dragon. Instead, she turned around and looked at the boulder that she had been using as a target. The same one she would use to test her theory.

She looked at the boulder, and when she was sure she had the image of it in her mind, she closed her eyes so that she would not be focusing on her target; no, she would put her complete focus on what she wanted to do.

With her eyes closed, she raised her right hand with her palm facing away from her. She then took a deep breath and released it. This was not the breath she needed to proceed with what she was attempting to do. The breath was to remove all her doubts and thoughts of failure. To put her mind at ease.

Once she felt the calmness wash over her, she took another deep breath and held it. When she was ready, she released it. Not just through her mouth, she released it through her mind, body, and soul, and with it, she released it through the palm of her right hand.

She had kept her eyes closed, but when she opened them, she still had her right hand up, palm toward the boulder. When she looked forward, she saw that the boulder had turned completely black. She knew that she had succeeded in what she wanted to do. Even though she did not see it herself. However, seeing the darkened boulder gave her more confidence in what she had done.

It was in her breathing. When MiteraThrakena had breathed the stream of Fire, she had released it with the exhaling of her breath, and that was exactly what Keia had just done. Now that she knew what to do and that she could do it, she once again took a deep breath, and when she was ready, she released it. Along with a steady stream of Fire from her right palm.

It lasted just as long as she was exhaling. Keia knew that she had performed the act twice, and she was confident that she could do so again. She took a deeper breath, and when she was ready, she exhaled while summoning the flame in the palm of her hand. Once again, a steady stream of Fire extended from the palm of her right hand to the boulder. This time, the stream lasted even longer than before.

With what she had accomplished, Keia did not even get excited. She just turned around and looked at MiteraThrakena, who had moved to stand closer to her. The dragon was smiling.

Keia looked back at the boulder that she had used as her target, then back toward the dragon. It was at that moment that Keia realized something. "You knew?" Keia asked MiteraThrakena, turned to look at the boulder again, then turned to face the dragon. "You knew what I had to do to create a stream of Fire, but you didn't tell me."

MiteraThrakena did not deny the accusation because she could not. She did have her own question for Keia. "Yes, that is true. The question you should ask yourself is, 'Why did I not tell you?'"

Keia took a moment, and when she had her answer, she relayed it to MiteraThrakena. "You wanted me to figure it out on my own."

MiteraThrakena once again smiled because Keia was correct, but the dragon had more to explain to her. "As the Dragon Kastera, you will have access to power, great power. It is with power that some humans will force their will on others because they believe that power gives them the right to do so. It is when humans disrespect power that they lose control of it and themselves. By learning to access that power on your own, I hope that you will realize that power is not something that is given freely. It needs to be earned by accepting that it is great and is something that should not be thoughtlessly misused. I will teach you the beginning of your training for each of the forces of nature, but as you learn, as you travel down the path and grow and control that power, I hope that you will also learn to respect it."

Keia understood what MiteraThrakena had told her. She understood it with her mind, but more importantly, she understood it with her heart. When she began to work through the process of casting a stream of Fire, she felt as if the force of Fire was guiding her. As if the force itself would lead her to the answer, but only if she was willing to accept it and the responsibility for it. She would be the one held accountable, and she would be the one to answer for her actions.

She looked back at the boulder and saw that it had blackened from the streams of Fire that she had cast upon it. She decided that the boulder would be a reminder of what her heart should not succumb to. She would respect the power that was given to her, and she would always remember that it was a blessing, one that came with accountability.

TWENTY-FIVE

The next morning, MiteraThrakena arrived at Keia's hut just as the sun was rising in the sky. Keia was already awake and had already eaten her morning meal. With eager anticipation, she waited for the next step in her training.

They walked until the sun was almost at its midpoint in the sky. When they finally stopped, they had come to a part of the river that MiteraThrakena had brought Keia many times when she was younger. Those were the days when the dragon would only explain certain things to Keia, but today, she had brought her to the location to train her on the next force of nature, Water.

Keia looked at the river, knowing why she was there. She also knew that somewhere upstream, Kord was training as well. He had not come back to the hut. Since the two of them no longer cohabited together, she figured that he had decided that it was easier for him to sleep wherever he chose to. Keia started wondering if he had eaten his evening meal, and if so, did he have enough?

MiteraThrakena had spoken Keia's name twice

before she turned and looked at the dragon. "I asked if you were ready to begin," MiteraThrakena said when she had the young woman's attention.

"Yes, My Lady," Keia replied to apologize for not paying attention to the dragon, who was there to teach her.

MiteraThrakena did not only see the absent-mindedness in the look on her face, but she heard it in her words as well. "What were you thinking about?" MiteraThrakena asked.

"Nothing, my mind was just wandering, that's all."

MiteraThrakena was more astute than Keia could ever imagine, so it did not take any great thinking by the dragon to know that Keia was thinking about Kord. "Pay attention to what I want you to do."

"Yes, My Lady," Keia replied and made sure she kept her eyes, ears, and thoughts on the dragon in front of her.

"Today I will teach you about the force of Water. I believe that you should not have a problem with learning it. Even though Water is the opposing force of Fire, as a human, you have been with it since even before you were born."

"Before?" Keia asked, not knowing what the dragon meant.

"Yes. I have explained to you how human women conceive a child, but I have not gone into the specific aspects of human birth."

"What do you mean, *specific aspects*?" Keia

asked, confused about what the dragon had said. MiteraThrakena told her about when a woman becomes with child by lying with a man. Even though Keia thought that the process was not gross, she did find the subject a bit embarrassing. Not that she thought the part of being with a man was embarrassing, it was just that as MiteraThrakena was explaining to her about the facts of life, and about the anatomy of women and men, Keia always had the image of Kord in her mind, and when she heard MiteraThrakena tell her about the overall process, she could not stop the images of her and Kord together. She was not sure exactly how that made her feel, and her discomfort did not go unnoticed by the dragon.

MiteraThrakena did not bring Keia to the river to give her another lesson on the birds and bees, but she did want to explain to the young woman just how important water is to all humans, especially about how they come from it.

"When a woman is with child, the child in her womb is protected by a fluid. This fluid is mainly made of water. This is to help the child grow and to protect it. That is why all humans come from water, and that is why they have a link to it. Also, the human body is made up of mostly water."

"Then how do we move around? Shouldn't we be more, I don't know, like water?"

Even though MiteraThrakena wanted to laugh, she did not. Keia's question was a good one, but it was not important for her to understand how to use the force of Water. "The human body is a complex thing. Creator made it so that it works the way it does. He alone knows the intricacies of what makes the human body the way it is. As for you, you need to remember that water is a part of life that a human needs, and comes from, which is why humans have a connection with it."

"Yes, My Lady," Keia replied, satisfied with the answer she was given.

MiteraThrakena was ready to move the conversation and the lesson forward. "Walk out into the river until the water comes up to your knees." Without hesitation, Keia did as she was instructed. When she was about ten paces from the shore, she turned around and looked at MiteraThrakena. "Now I want you to take up some water with your right hand and hold it in your palm. Once again, Keia did what the dragon had told her to do. "You feel it, do you not?"

Keia looked at the water she was holding and understood what the dragon had asked her. Yes, she could feel the water in her hand, but she felt something more. She felt the water itself. She felt the force of it, not just in her hand but in herself as well. She could feel the water in her hand resonating through her. This was due to the blessing Keia received from the dragon. It allowed her to be more aware of the forces of nature, to be able to sense the forces in a way that any other human would not be able to.

MiteraThrakena could tell by the expression on her face that Keia was sensing exactly what the dragon wanted her to feel. "The water you are holding is a link to the surrounding water. You feel it in your hand, now feel it all around you."

Keia was not sure what the dragon meant, then suddenly, she felt the water she was standing in. Not just the water that was touching her legs, but also the water that was in contact with that water. She felt the river itself.

"Water is connected. The water you hold in your hand is from the river that you are standing in. That water is connected to all the water around you."

Keia did not need any more explanation. She understood what MiteraThrakena had said because she could feel it.

"Now, walk to the shore, but do not drop the water in your hand."

Once again, Keia did as MiteraThrakena said. When she made her way back to the shore, she was still holding the water in her hand and could still sense the river that was behind her. She turned around and looked at it. She could feel the river, even though she was no longer standing in it.

"Are you ready to begin your next step in using the force of Water?" MiteraThrakena asked.

Keia turned her head to the left to look at the dragon and nodded.

"Very well. With the water in your hand, I want you to shape it into a sphere."

"How?" Keia asked because she did not know how to perform the task given to her.

"You feel the water in your hand, not just with your hand, but with yourself as well. Now that you can feel it, use your will to shape it into a sphere. Feel the water as it is in your hand and picture it as a sphere of water, while at the same time, feel it as a sphere of water that you are holding."

Keia nodded to let the dragon know that she understood what she was to do. She just was not sure if she could.

She looked at the water that she was holding in her right hand. It was not as much as she started with when she lifted the handful out of the river. She had spilled some as she was walking to the shore, but since she did have enough to work with, she did not try to collect more.

Keia sensed the water in her hand. She thought about the water as being formed into a sphere, but it did not take on that form. It stayed in the middle of her palm. She did not know how long she had tried, and she did not realize the amount of time that had passed. Even after two sun-marks, she did not stop trying, nor did MiteraThrakena offer her any assistance or additional training. In fact, the dragon had lowered herself to the ground and curled up to wait and see just what the young woman would do.

After the third sun-mark, Keia turned her palm over, and the water fell to the ground. "Giving up?" MiteraThrakena asked.

Keia looked over her left shoulder and saw that the dragon was watching her. She also saw that the dragon was smiling as if to say she knew that the young woman would not succeed.

She did not reply to the dragon's question. She was not going to give up, but she did know that what she had been trying was not working. She had to come up with another way to complete the task. She remembered how MiteraThrakena had taught her about Fire. The dragon gave her the beginnings of the method, but she left it up to Keia to finish the lesson on her own.

Keia looked at the river before her, and not to her surprise, she saw water. Of course, that is why she was brought to the river in the first place. She then remembered the first instruction MiteraThrakena had given to her, which was to walk out into the river. The dragon then told her to come back to the shore. Keia looked over at the dragon, who was still watching her and still smiling. Keia smiled back, turned, and faced the river, then walked back into the same spot in the river where she had been standing with the water up to her knees.

MiteraThrakena did not say anything to her. She wanted Keia to realize what she needed to do to be more familiar with Water. She had instructed her to enter the river, then brought her back to see if she would realize that in the river, she was more connected with Water because she was physically in contact with it.

When she was in place, Keia turned around and faced the shore and saw the dragon smiling at her. She was not going to let the dragon's amusement bother her, so she reached down and grabbed hold of another handful of water. Once again, she put her focus on trying to form the water she was holding into a sphere. This time, she felt the connection to the water she was holding as well as to the water she was standing in. She felt it throughout her body, and as she stared at the water she was holding, nothing happened. It did not change its form; in fact, it did not move at all, except when her own hand moved and caused a small ripple in the water.

Keia did not look at the dragon. She did not want to see the smirk that she thought MiteraThrakena would be showing her. Instead, she decided that she would do something that would make her even more connected to the water. She turned around so she was facing away from the shore and started walking.

"Where are you going?"

She heard MiteraThrakena call out to her, but she did not answer. When she walked out into the river, while her feet were still touching the bottom, and her head was just above the water, she immersed herself beneath the water so that her entire body was covered from head to toe by the river. She did remember to take a deep breath before she went under.

She did not try to form a sphere in her palm; she

just let herself feel the water. Not against her body, but the water itself. She could feel it all around her, and she could feel it stretched out on every side of her as well. She could feel it over her; she could feel it under her. She could feel it as a part of her. That is when she did not just feel the water, she was the water. It was a part of her as she was a part of it.

She opened her eyes and looked through the water. She felt as if she not only opened her eyes to see the water but saw a whole new world. She looked around and saw fish swimming, but she thought that they were not just swimming, they were living in the water. She knew that fish lived in water and even breathed in it, but now that her eyes were open, she realized that life existed in water just as life existed on land, and for some reason, she felt that it was Water that connected everything in it to everything else that called it home. She felt the connection that Water had, even to her.

She was human, and humans were not meant to breathe underwater, so when she felt that she needed to take another breath of air, she turned around and started walking back toward the shore. She did not rush. She was not afraid of the water, even though she knew that humans could die if they spent too long under it.

As soon as her head came above the water, she took a breath. She continued to walk forward, but as she did, she closed her eyes and remembered what she felt when she was completely underwater. She remembered the connection she had as she continued to walk to the shore.

When she had both feet on dry land, she took a moment and kept her eyes closed. When she was ready, she opened her eyes and looked down to her right and saw what she was holding in her right hand. It was an orb of water. She had formed it while she was walking back to the shore and still had her arm submerged. Now that she knew how to perform the task, especially now that she could feel the connection with Water, she let go of her thoughts, and the orb of water changed its shape and fell to the ground. She had done so on purpose because she wanted to try again from the beginning.

Keia turned around, bent down, and with her right hand grabbed a handful of water. She saw it lying in her palm, and felt the connection, and with a thought, the handful of water she was holding took on the shape of an orb.

"Impressive," MiteraThrakena said. She had watched the entire spectacle from the beginning. She had an idea of what Keia was planning to do, but did not stop her. There was one moment when the dragon thought that the young woman had stayed under the water for too long, and just as MiteraThrakena was about to jump into the river and rescue Keia, she saw her start moving toward the shore. The dragon quickly took up the position she was in when Keia started walking into the river, to make sure she did not show any worry over the young woman.

Keia turned to her right and looked at the dragon. Even though she took her eyes off the orb in her hand, it did not lose its shape. She still felt the connection between her and it. "That's not all," she said and smiled. She saw that MiteraThrakena did not know what she was referring to, and that made Keia happy.

She allowed the orb to fall back into her hand as a small pool of water. She then turned her palm over, and the water fell to the ground. She then turned around and faced the river. She took a breath, lifted her right hand with her palm facing upward, and willed an orb of water to appear in the palm of her hand. With her next motion, she twisted her palm over and then outward. When it was facing the river, Keia released the orb of water, and it flew out across the river, landing about halfway. With her next attempt, she repeated the same process and created an orb of water in her right palm, then released it. Before it was two paces away, she released a second orb of water. When those two had gone halfway over the river, they fell into the river, disappearing. She repeated the same steps as before, but she released three orbs of water. She continued and only stopped when she had performed the task of releasing five consecutive orbs of water outward over the river. She then turned and faced MiteraThrakena.

"Remarkable," MiteraThrakena not only said, but meant it. She did not think that Keia would have mastered the control of Water so quickly. She did so in less than half the time it took her to control Fire. "How were you able to learn to cast the orbs of water? You had not even practiced it, but you were able to cast it on your first attempt."

"From casting Fire." Keia saw the way MiteraThrakena looked at her, and she knew the dragon wanted her to explain it more. "Creating Water was different from creating Fire. You taught me that Fire and Water are opposites of each other, yet they are still forces of nature. You taught me to cast a ball of fire by creating it in my hand, but with water, you wanted me to form the orb of water by holding water itself. Once I felt the connection I had with water, I could feel that it was no different than fire. I believe you taught me this way because if you had told me to put my body directly into fire, I probably would not have wanted to."

"And why is that?" MiteraThrakena asked.

"Because fire burns. Even when I use it to cook, I have moved too close to it, and it has burned me, but when I cast the fireballs, they did not. When I went under the water and felt the connection I had with it, I realized that I have the same connection with Fire. Although I don't think I want to put my entire body in it, I do understand it better, now that I understand Water. With that understanding, I realized that forming an orb of Water is the same as forming a ball of Fire, so I had no difficulty in creating an orb and releasing it just as I did with Fire."

MiteraThrakena could not help but be impressed with what Keia had done. She had used her knowledge of Fire and Water to help her understand the two forces even more. She was becoming a true Dragon Kastera.

"There's one more thing," Keia said.

"And what is that?" MiteraThrakena asked.

Keia turned back to look out over the river. She did not say anything to MiteraThrakena; she just lifted her right hand with her arm extended outward with her fingers toward the sky and her palm facing away from her. She took a deep breath, and when she was ready, she began to breathe out. As she did, she released a spout of water that reached beyond the midpoint of the river. As she released the last of her breath, the spout ended in her palm and finally died out as it reached its limit.

Keia knew that she would be able to perform the task she had just completed. She knew it because she knew that with what she had learned with Fire, she would be able to perform the same act with Water.

MiteraThrakena could not help but smile at what she had just witnessed. Keia had learned to work with Fire and Water. Having learned the first two, it would help her to learn more about the others. The dragon had hoped that she would be able to do so, and that hope had not been for nothing.

Unfortunately, Keia had three more forces of nature to learn and also master them, and the dragon knew that she would have to master all five for her to become the Dragon Kastera. Something the dragon was not entirely sure would come to pass.

TWENTY-SIX

Two moon-cycles had passed since MiteraThrakena had instructed Keia on the force of Water. The dragon wanted the young woman to use the time to become more comfortable with both Fire and Water before she moved on to the more unfamiliar aspects of nature.

Keia would practice daily with the first two forces of nature that she had learned. MiteraThrakena had given her permission to use the two forces on her own while performing her normal daily routine. If Keia needed to start a fire for cooking, she would do so by calling forth Fire. She even started filling up the water jar behind the small hut she lived in. When Kord saw what she was able to do, he realized that MiteraThrakena had him work a lot harder at the chore than Keia had to. Something he thought was not very fair.

Keia also practiced on her own with the two forces. She would find an area where she could cast Fire and Water without setting anything on fire. Although she did set up some practice targets made out of wood and would throw fireballs at them, and when they caught on fire, she would cast orbs of water at the targets to put the fires out.

She also practiced casting streams of fire and spouts of water. Although she had to be quick, because by the time she stopped the stream of fire, the targets were already burning, so she had to douse the flames with a spout of water.

She only practiced with her right hand. MiteraThrakena had informed her that she was never to use her left hand when casting, and she never did.

After spending time mastering Fire and Water, when she was ready to continue with Keia's training, MiteraThrakena arrived at her hut just as she had finished eating her morning meal. The dragon had come to take her to where she would begin the next step in her training, and that was to learn the force of Wind.

MiteraThrakena had brought Keia to an area in the middle of the forest. She looked around and saw that there was not much to see except for a lot of trees. Keia knew that the dragon was going to train her to use the force of Wind, but she did not see anything that would allow her to be able to do so.

"You are wondering why I have brought you here, are you not?" MiteraThrakena asked, seeing the puzzled look Keia had on her face.

Keia looked up and to her right to see the dragon looking back at her. "I know you said that you would be training me on the force of Wind, but I don't see what we will be using to do so. With Fire, there were boulders that I practiced with. With Water, you took me to the river." Keia looked around and saw the only thing that was in the area. "Here I only see trees. So do you want me to learn to use Wind on the trees?"

MiteraThrakena held back her laugh. She did not want to embarrass the young woman, but at the same time, she had to show her that with Wind, there are different degrees of power. "I think that you should start with something a little more to your level. Look down at your feet and tell me what you see."

Keia did, and when she noticed what was on the ground, she looked back at the dragon. "Leaves," she said, because there was nothing else she could see. Keia looked around the area and saw that there were leaves covering the entire area. She realized that the leaves were older than the ones on the trees in the area. The leaves still attached to the trees were different shades of green. The colors of the leaves on the ground were a variety of yellows, browns, and reds.

MiteraThrakena began explaining about the weather within KhoraThraks. "Within our land, the seasons follow the same pattern as the rest of the world. We have different seasons for a reason. During the cold season, the trees shed their leaves so that when the warm season arrives, they can sprout new ones. They must shed their old leaves so that new life can be made."

At that moment, Keia realized something. "Since Kord and I have been here, there has never been a cold season. Why haven't we seen one?"

"Are you just realizing that now?" MiteraThrakena asked.

"Yes. I just thought that the weather here stayed the same."

MiteraThrakena had more wisdom to pass on to Keia. "My child, time stands still for no one, not even for us dragons. Yes, the seasons last longer in KhoraThraks than in the world outside, but not even a dragon can stop time. Time is always moving; only here it moves more slowly for us." The dragon took a few steps forward and moved to stand in the center of the area they were in. "The leaves that you see at your feet fell from the trees around you over fifty normal seasons ago. At this point, both you and Kord are in this land during the warm season, and it will be many seasons before the cold season is upon us. Do you understand?"

"Yes, My Lady." Keia took a moment because she realized something, and she was hesitant to ask, but she had to know. "Will Kord and I be alive when the cold season returns?"

MiteraThrakena could only give her the answer that was the truth. "There is no guarantee on when any one of us will see our last season arrive."

Keia did not know how she felt about the dragon's response. She knew that what MiteraThrakena had said was the truth, and in some way, Keia did not have any feelings one way or the other about it. That is, until she thought that one day, Kord would no longer be in her life.

MiteraThrakena saw how her answer had made the expression on the young woman's face take on a more somber appearance. She had not brought Keia to the area to discuss the aspects of life and death, and it was not the time for it, but it was time to move on. "Reach down and pick up a leaf at your feet."

With the instructions given, Keia brought her focus back to the present and did as the dragon said. She bent down and picked up a single leaf. It looked much like the other leaves on the ground with it. There was nothing special about why she selected the one she was holding. "Will this do?" she asked.

"Yes, that is fine. Now hold it in the palm of your hand."

Keia placed the leaf in the palm of her right hand and stretched out her arm. "Now what?"

It was now time for MiteraThrakena to show Keia that she was not always going to give her the answer. "I told you that you would be learning about Wind today, so use Wind to move the leaf."

Keia looked at the leaf in her palm, then at the dragon. "You're not going to tell me how, are you?"

"If you are intelligent enough to figure that out, then you should be able to figure out the way to make it happen." MiteraThrakena positioned herself so that she was resting on her underbelly with her tail curled at her side. She kept her eyes on Keia to see just how long it would take the young woman to come up with a way to start her training. The dragon was not trying to be cruel to her student. What she was doing was just another part of the young woman's training. Keia also had to learn that there would be times when she would have to figure out a way to face a challenge on her own. She had done so when she learned about Fire, when she realized that breathing was the answer. Now she had to do the same with Wind.

Keia was not upset with the dragon. She knew that MiteraThrakena was only doing what was best for her to learn the force of Wind. The only problem was that Keia did not know where to begin.

Learning Fire and Water was different. She had been around them for as long as she could remember. Her parents used fire to cook their food and to heat their home during the cold season. Water was also always a part of her life. She drank water, she used water to cook, she used it to bathe, and even used it to play in. Wind, on the other hand, was not something that she ever used.

Keia looked at the leaf she was holding, then she looked at the leaves on the ground. She did not see them moving, so she looked at the leaves still attached to the trees. Unfortunately, there was no wind in the area, so none of the leaves on the trees were moving either.

"No, there is no wind here," MiteraThrakena

said when she saw Keia looking around. "I would not want the natural wind to interfere with your training."

"When you taught me about Water, you took me to the river where there was water, so why couldn't you take me to where there is some wind?"

"Why do I not just take you back to your hut and we forget the whole thing?" MiteraThrakena replied, ending with a smile.

Keia smiled as well when she heard the dragon's remark. She had no animosity about the way MiteraThrakena wanted her to learn the force of Wind. Although that did not help her with figuring out what to do.

Keia put her focus back on the leaf she held in her palm. She knew that it would not take much wind to make the leaf move. It was very light, so light that there was no weight to the leaf in her hand at all.

She did not know how long she stood there looking at the leaf. She did know that she was getting tired of standing, and since MiteraThrakena was leaving it up to her to learn on her own, she decided that she could learn just as easily sitting down. So, she did, crossing her legs with her knees to her sides. To get more comfortable, she brought her right hand and the leaf closer to her by bending her elbow. With her left arm, she placed her elbow on her left leg and rested her head on her left hand.

She continued to keep her focus on the leaf in her palm, but no matter how long she stared at it, no matter how much she tried to force the leaf to move just the slightest bit by trying to make it move, it did not, and after some time, she became frustrated and sighed.

With that sigh, the leaf moved in her hand. It was not much, but with the small amount of air that she released when she sighed, it reached her palm and the leaf.

At first, she did not think much about what had just happened. She was sure that MiteraThrakena would not take the movement of the leaf in that manner as a step in the right direction. Then she remembered what she did with Fire. She realized that what she wanted to accomplish was all in her breathing, only this time it was something different.

Keia moved her head off her left hand and brought her right hand closer to her face. With the leaf still in her palm, she blew on it. It was not much, but there was enough air to move the leaf off her palm and land on her leg. She picked the leaf back up with her left hand and placed it once again in the palm of her right. She then blew on the leaf again, and just like before, it moved out of her palm and landed on her leg.

She repeated the process over and over until she was sure she found what she was looking for, a connection. A connection between her and the leaf. A connection that would allow her to feel the movement of the leaf in her hand. Not by touch, but by the force of Wind between her palm and the leaf. Every time she exhaled, the air she blew out touched her palm and the leaf. She felt the way the slight breeze moved the leaf out of her hand. She felt the force of Wind.

She stood up because she wanted to be fully alert for what she was about to try. She bent over and picked up a leaf off the ground, stood up, and placed the leaf in the palm of her right hand. It was not even the same leaf she had before, but that was not important. It was not about the leaf; it was about the slightest touch that allowed her to see the effects of the force of Wind.

When she was ready, she closed her eyes. She thought about how the air she blew felt between the palm of her hand and the leaf. She thought about it over and over, and when she was ready, she opened her eyes and thought about the air between her palm and the leaf, and suddenly the thought became reality. The leaf lifted into the air and floated to the ground.

Keia smiled. She now understood what it felt like to use the force of Wind to move the leaf. Now she did not need the leaf. She knew the force of Wind, the leaf was not important, and so with her arm stretched out, with her palm facing upward, Keia called forth the force of Wind in the middle of her palm.

It came to her in an instant, and even though she could not see it, she could feel Wind in the palm of her right hand. She knew that it was there, but just so she could feel it, not just in her right palm, she took her left hand and moved it back and forth over her right hand. When she did, she felt the wind that she was holding.

Keia was ready to move on to the next step. With the wind still in her right palm, she adjusted her hand so that her palm was toward the ground. As she moved it, there was enough force from the wind she was creating to move the leaves on the ground around her. When her hand was completely toward the ground, she moved her arm from side to side, and as she did, the leaves on the ground at her feet moved in different directions as the wind came into contact with them.

Now for the next step. Keia put more force into the wind in her palm. As she did, more of the leaves at a greater distance spread out over the ground were disturbed, causing them to move. There was no control in the way they moved. Keia did not control the leaves; she controlled the wind in her hand. She knew then that it would take practice not just to control the wind, but to control the effect it had on what she focused it on. For now, she was satisfied with what she had accomplished.

To continue with what she had learned, she put more force into the wind she controlled and slightly adjusted her palm so that it was facing outward. She bent it slightly toward the ground and moved her hand so that she could see the leaves on the ground, five paces from her move. She turned around in a circle, all the while keeping her palm out and allowing the wind to move the leaves. When she was satisfied with what she had achieved, she simply willed the wind in her hand to cease, and it did. She then turned and faced MiteraThrakena.

"Well done, my child," the dragon said, very pleased with what she saw the young woman accomplish. "You started with the slightest breeze, and that is how Wind announces its presence. As I told you before, Wind can be gentle, but it can also be fierce. It can force the mightiest of trees to bend or even break."

Keia looked around and then looked up. She saw the tall trees that were in the area. Taller than even the Queen of Dragons. She then remembered what she did with Fire and Water. She remembered how she cast them into a stream and a spout when she put more power into them, allowing her to control the forces in a different way. Now she would do so with Wind.

She lifted her right hand and looked at her palm. She started by bringing forth the slightest breeze. When she had it, she willed more power into it. She then stretched out her arm and angled it so that her palm was toward the upper part of the trees. Higher than even the head of MiteraThrakena.

Keia then put more force into the wind in her hand, and it was enough for her to see the effect it had on the tree her hand was toward. It only moved the leaves that were attached to the tree; however, that was not what she wanted, so she increased the force of Wind.

She saw that it was enough to move the branches that it came in contact with, but even that was not the desired result for which she was striving. She increased the force again, and she did not stop until she saw the entire tree begin to sway from the wind that she sent toward it. As it swayed, she moved her body along with her hand in a circle so that she could witness the wind moving the tops of every tree she put her focus on.

Now that she had achieved the desired results, she did not put any more force into the wind. She remembered what MiteraThrakena had said about Wind being fierce, so fierce that it could even break the trees. She did not want to destroy the trees, although she knew that if she were to add more force to the wind, the trees would bend and break if the force was strong enough. Since she had accomplished what she wanted to do, she ceased the wind in her hand, seeing the last of the wind move the trees until it was gone.

She brought her arm down to her side and faced MiteraThrakena; both of them were smiling.

The dragon was very pleased with what Keia had accomplished. Wind was the first of the forces of nature that she had to learn in a way different from Fire and Water. Keia, as with all humans, has a different relationship with the first two forces. Wind was new to Keia, and she only had two more forces to learn. The last would be the most difficult.

TWENTY-SEVEN

For Keia, Wind was easy to learn but difficult to master. It took her over three moon-cycles before she was finally able to cast Wind in a manner where she did not lose control. One of her more *successful failures* was when she was practicing and was concentrating so hard on trying to control the wind that she did not hear Kord come up behind her. When he reached her, he placed his hand on her left shoulder, which startled her, causing her to turn immediately to face him. Unfortunately, she forgot to stop the flow of the gust of wind coming from the palm of her right hand, so when she turned, the force of the wind struck him on the side of his body, tossing him far to Keia's left. If it were not for his body's instinct to alter his skin so he was protected with dragon scales, when he landed against a tree, he would have suffered serious injury.

Over the past few moon-cycles, Kord and Keia had not been spending much time together. They were both immersed in their own training, and by the end of the sun-cycle, they had very little time to be with each other as they did when they were younger.

On most nights, Kord would sleep in the area where he was training. He did settle into one of the numerous caves in KhoraThraks since he did not sleep in the hut with Keia any longer, but he was just as comfortable sleeping out in the open where he trained. The river next to it supplied him with water, and the forest around him had a variety of fruits, so he could eat from them when he needed to.

Now and then, when something came over him that made him feel that he just wanted to see Keia, he would finish with his training, then head over to the hut where she stayed. Making sure that he stopped by the small pond, which he used to take his baths, before he met her.

When he did go to her hut, she was mostly finishing up with her training, and since it was late into the evening, they would sit outside and talk about the things that they had learned. He would show her how he was able to have the dragon scales cover his body from the bottom of his feet all the way up to his neck. They would appear so quickly that it seemed as if he did not even have to think about them. His body reacted as soon as he needed them to. This saved him a great deal of pain when he struck the tree after Keia's Wind attack.

While sitting together, Keia would give him demonstrations of what she learned. She would show him how she could call upon Fire, Water, and Wind. After her little mishap with him and Wind, he told her that he did not need to see any more feats that had to do with Wind. The comment brought a laugh from them both.

Very seldom did Keia have time to fix a hot meal for herself or for Kord like she did before she began her training. She would wake up in the morning and perform her chores, which were basically the same as her training. Working in the garden behind the hut was the way she learned how to grow vegetables, along with certain herbs that MiteraThrakena taught her to use in making medicines and ointments for healing. She would also go into the forest and look for flowers and herbs that grew in the wild, which she could use for medicines as well. All of this was part of her training to be the Dragon Kastera.

The other part of her training, which took up the majority of her time, was when she practiced using Fire, Water, and Wind. MiteraThrakena told her that she had to be able to use each of the forces of nature as naturally as she would take a breath.

Keia had to not only learn to control the forces of nature but also learn how to use them in a way that would help her in any situation. Starting fires for cooking and filling water jars was not the purpose of the Dragon Kastera. The purpose was to help others. That is why Keia was being taught how to make medicines and ointments, along with mastering the forces of nature.

One part of helping others was to defend those who could not defend themselves. To protect those who could not protect themselves. Another was to stop those who would use evil to hurt others. This was a lesson that Keia understood but did not know if she would be able to do so.

Taking a life is not easy for someone to do, that is for most humans. Some, such as the Mountain Raiders, did not hesitate when it came to killing. Keia was not a Mountain Raider, and when MiteraThrakena explained to her that there may come a time when she might have to take the life of another, to save the life of someone else, Keia did not think she had it in her to do so.

MiteraThrakena was not surprised when Keia told her how she felt about killing someone. Part of the dragon was relieved that the young woman felt the way she did. Unfortunately, as the Dragon Kastera, taking a life is sometimes the only way to ensure that others will not have to face death themselves at the hands of another.

During their conversation, MiteraThrakena asked Keia a simple question, one that she knew the young woman would have to think about someone she loved. "With what you have learned about the forces of Fire, Water, and Wind, if you were able to go back and stop the Mountain Raiders from killing your parents, would you?"

Keia stood where she was, deep in thought. She was thinking about the day she lost her parents to the Mountain Raiders that had attacked the caravan that both she and Kord were traveling with. She could see the entire scene in her mind. She could see the panic on her mother's face. She could see the people lying on the ground not far from her and knew that they were dead. She could remember everything she saw that day, and as she recalled the memories and played them over and over in her thoughts, eventually she saw herself. Not as the frightened girl who did not know what to do. Not as the child who was waiting for her mother and father to save her. No, she saw herself as she was now. Someone who was not defenseless any longer.

She closed her eyes and replayed the attack in her mind. Every time she saw one of the Mountain Raiders, she changed the image. She changed it to what she would have done if she had the knowledge and the use of the forces of nature.

A Mountain Raider was about to bring his weapon, made from some animal bone, down onto a woman who was with the caravan. She did not know the woman, but it did not matter. She was about to lose her life, and Keia could not let that happen. Not this time, not now. It might have been only in her thoughts, but Keia forced out her arm, and with speed and accuracy, she let loose a ball of fire from her right hand. It made contact with the Mountain Raider, and he caught on fire. Surprised at what happened, he stopped his attack on the woman before him to deal with the fire that had caught onto his clothing.

Keia, still focused on the scene in her mind, launched another fireball at the Mountain Raider.

With the second strike, he stepped backward, trying to put the fire out. Keia did not even think about what to do next. Her reaction was to send out a spout of water from her right hand. This was not to put out the fire, but to force the Mountain Raider away from his attended victim. The force of the water attack was so powerful that when it struck its target, the man went flying all the way back to the forest and only stopped when his body struck a tree. He did not get back up.

Keia still had the vision of that day in her mind, and she continued to play it over and over. Every time she remembered how one of the Mountain Raiders attacked one of the people of the caravan, Keia altered the scene. She used one of the forces of nature that she had learned to deal with the attacker; she made sure that what she witnessed that day was not what happened as she relived the moment. For that to take place, even though it was only in her thoughts, Keia killed.

Every Mountain Raider that she remembered, she ended their life. They died in some way when she used either Fire, Water, or Wind. One Raider she used Wind on and forced his body straight up into the air. He went flying twice as high as the tallest tree in the area, and when Keia thought he was high enough, she ceased the flow of the wind, and the Raider came falling back to the ground, landing with a loud thump.

As the vision continued, Keia continued to

defend the caravan, and when all the Mountain Raiders were dead, Keia saw the look on all the people's faces whose lives she had just saved. She saw her mother and father run up to her and grab her in their arms. Happy that all of them were safe, but they were not.

Keia did not open her eyes. It was not that she did not want to, but she knew that when she did, she would see where she really was. What she did in her vision did not happen. That day, Keia was only a little girl. A scared little girl who did not have the power to save anyone. Not even her mother and father.

She could not stop the tears from flowing. It had been many seasons since she had suffered the greatest loss in her life, and she knew that it was never going to be the way she had altered it in her mind. While still crying, with her eyes still closed, she fell to the ground on her hands and knees. She felt pain in her heart. Was it for the loss of her mother and father? Yes, but also, because if she had the power she has now, the outcome would have been different, but it never would be.

"Open your eyes, child," MiteraThrakena said when she felt she had given her enough time to weep. Even though Keia heard the dragon, she did not open them. "Open your eyes and look around you," MiteraThrakena said to bring Keia back to the present and her surroundings.

Keia was afraid to open her eyes. In her thoughts, she had saved her mother and father, but the moment she brought herself back to reality, she knew they would not be with her. She also knew that she had to put the past behind her. Behind her, but not forgotten.

Keia stood up and opened her eyes. When she did, she saw that the area around her looked as if it had been through a natural disaster. "What happened?" she asked MiteraThrakena, but before she allowed the dragon to answer, she asked what she thought had taken place. "Did I do this?"

MiteraThrakena walked over to where Keia was standing. The dragon had to move away from where she had been, not because she was afraid Keia would hurt her, but to give Keia the room she needed to deal with the question at hand. The question of killing someone.

"I have no doubts about what you were seeing." Keia stopped looking around and looked up at the dragon. "You relived that day. The day your caravan was attacked. The day you lost your parents." Keia only nodded to reply. "You remembered the events that took place, only you were lost in your memories, and you did not want to live through that pain again. So, you altered what you experienced during that moment."

Both Keia and MiteraThrakena looked around the area they were in. As they focused on the ground, they saw the scorch marks where fire had burnt the grass. There were pools of water lying around as well. When they both looked to their left, they saw two trees that were broken off near their trunks, with the bulk of them lying on the ground next to each other. Destroyed when Keia used the wind attacks to defend the people in her memories.

"I'm sorry, I did not mean to cause so much destruction. I should not have lost control," Keia said as more tears started running down her face.

"It is ok, child. I was here with you and made sure that when something caught fire, I put it out immediately. The water will dry up within a couple of sun-cycles. As for the trees." They both turned their heads and looked at the two trees across the way. "We will have Kord chop them up for firewood."

They looked at each other, and Keia was even able to force a slight smile at the dragon's comment. "Why didn't you stop me?" Keia asked.

MiteraThrakena lowered her head so that she was directly in front of Keia. "When I realized what you were doing, I thought it was best for you to work through the memories and emotions. You thought you would not be able to take a life. However, in your memories, you learned that there is one thing worse than killing someone and that is standing by and watching someone being killed when you have the power to protect them."

Keia sniffled and used the back of her right hand to wipe her eyes. Not that it did much good, because more tears just replaced the ones she had just wiped away. "I couldn't save them," Keia said.

"No, you could not; but now do you understand

why it is sometimes necessary for the Dragon Kastera to take a life?"

Keia nodded and gave her answer, "Because that is the only way that someone else, someone whose life is in danger and cannot defend themselves, is able to live."

"That is correct. There is a difference between killing and murder. The difference is in the heart of the one who must take a life. Your heart is full of love, and yes, that love is what will allow you to be the Dragon Kastera and do what is necessary for others to live."

The tears continued to flow, but Keia understood what she might have to do. She did not like the thought of taking a life, but she would if she had no other choice in saving the life of someone else. As the Dragon Kastera, it was part of her responsibility.

TWENTY-EIGHT

MiteraThrakena gave Keia another moon-cycle to master the force of Wind. She knew that she was ready to move on with her lessons when she saw that Keia had created and controlled a tornado that was five times the height of the young woman. It was not so much the actual tornado that convinced the dragon it was time to continue with Keia's training, but more to the point that she was controlling the tornado to chase Kord around a large open field. Kord did not seem as if he was amused with what Keia was doing, and even though Kord was fast at running, especially with his legs in their dragon form, the tornado was moving so fast that he had to jump out of its way just before it swept him up and threw him, who knows how far away.

It was another way that they trained. They would use their skills that they had acquired against each other. Keia would use Fire, Water, and Wind against Kord. While Kord used his skills to evade the attacks from Keia. Before they had even begun to practice in this manner, they both asked permission from

MiteraThrakena and PateraThrakon. The two humans remembered what happened when they had just received the dragons' blessings and used them in a way that the two dragons were not pleased. However, now that both Keia and Kord had matured, the King and Queen of Dragons gave their permission to train together to help them develop their skills.

With what they had learned, Keia and Kord would sometimes test their abilities against each other. Each time, it may have started as a training session for the two, but it usually ended up with one of them getting the upper hand in some manner. Most of the time, it was Kord who was the one ending up surrendering before Keia forced him into submission.

Even though MiteraThrakena was amused at the sight, she knew that if Keia could control a tornado of such a size, she was ready to learn the next force of nature, Ice.

MiteraThrakena had brought Keia to the same area by the river where she learned about the force of Water. Ice was nothing more than water frozen, so the dragon was going to start her off with the basics.

"Ice is another form of water. So how do you suppose you will be able to call forth the force of Ice?" MiteraThrakena asked.

Keia thought for a moment, then gave her answer, "I should concentrate on forming Water and turn it into Ice," Keia said to answer the dragon's question.

The young woman's statement was exactly how the dragon thought Keia would reply. "No, that is incorrect." MiteraThrakena was not trying to trick Keia; she just wanted to show her how her line of thinking was not like that of a dragon's. "Even though Ice is a form of Water, it is its own force. Just as Fire is."

"I don't understand," Keia said, not seeing the path the dragon was trying to lead her down.

MiteraThrakena knew that Keia would have more difficulty with Ice than she did with the first three forces. Ice was not common to humans except during the cold season. Even more important was the fact that humans, nor any of the other sentient beings on Eirene, had much use for ice.

"What do you need to start a fire?" MiteraThrakena asked.

"I just focus on it, and it appears," Keia answered.

Even though Keia was correct, it was not the answer the dragon was trying to have her see. "Let me rephrase the question. What would Kord need to start a fire?" Just before Keia responded with her answer, MiteraThrakena thought it was best to let her know that what she was about to reply with was not correct either. "Do not say that he just has to ask you." They both smiled, and the female dragon asked her next question. "How would Kord start a fire by himself, without any assistance from you?"

Keia thought a moment, then gave her answer, "He would need some wood, some flint, and his dagger."

"That is correct, but when you cast Fire, you do not use wood or flint, do you?"

"No."

"Which means that the items humans need to start a fire are not required by you. The same goes for the force of Ice. You do not need Water to summon Ice."

It seemed to Keia that MiteraThrakena was taking a long while to even begin to teach her to use Ice. What the dragon was trying to do was to show Keia that she had to stop thinking like a human and start thinking like a dragon.

MiteraThrakena looked up to the sky, and while doing so, she looked back into the past. A past that she was very proud of, and one that would never be again. "There was a time when there were many dragons. There were different colors of them, and each color was part of its own Dragon Brood. The red dragons, the Cinnabar Brood, used the force of Fire. The blue dragons, the Azure Brood, used the force of Water. The green dragons, the Emerald Brood, used the force of Wind, and the white dragons, the Opal Brood, used the force of Ice." MiteraThrakena did not think it was wise to mention how the purple dragons, the Amethyst Brood, were the ones that used the force of Lightning. She did not want Keia to get distracted from the lesson at hand.

"Dragons use the forces of nature without the use of any items. It is part of their own natural abilities. Even though you are human, because you were given our blessing, you have those abilities as well, and you must learn to tap into them. Fire and Water were easier for you, and even though Wind was a little more difficult, you were able to bring it forth. Now you must learn to do the same with Ice." MiteraThrakena was also preparing Keia for the last force of nature, which was Lightning. She wanted the young woman to learn that dragons are born with a connection to the forces of nature, and even though she is human, to be the Dragon Kastera, Keia had to become attuned to them as well. She would need it even more when she began to learn Lightning. It was the force that was farthest away from the realm of humans.

"So why did you bring me to the river if I do not need to use Water to bring forth Ice?" Keia asked.

"So that you can leave your old thoughts behind and start thinking more like a dragon."

MiteraThrakena decided it was time to take Keia to where she would begin to learn the force of Ice. She turned to her right and opened a portal, "Follow me," she said, and since the dragon's body was almost the size of the portal's opening, Keia could not see what was on the other side.

When she was through the portal, it took her less than a blink of an eye to realize where the dragon had brought her. She looked around, and even though she did not know the exact location, she knew that she was somewhere she had never been before.

Keia turned around, ready to run back through the portal, but when she was facing the direction she had just come from, she did not see the portal, so she immediately turned to face the dragon.

MiteraThrakena had taken a few steps away from the young woman and made herself comfortable by resting her body on the snow-covered ground. It was apparent to Keia that the cold environment did not affect the dragon in any way. The same could not be said for the human.

Keia was freezing. She did not know that MiteraThrakena was going to bring her to the area where she was. If she had known, she would have dressed appropriately. "What are we doing here?" Keia shouted to the dragon because not only was it cold, but the wind was blowing so fiercely that Keia had trouble even hearing herself yell out.

"Why do you think we are here?" MiteraThrakena replied sarcastically. "You are here to learn to use the force of Ice. You did not think you were going to learn it standing next to a river where you would be able to bathe."

Keia looked around, while at the same time, she crossed her arms and began to rub them with the opposite hand. "I am going to freeze to death if I do not leave this place," she said as she looked at the dragon again.

"Then use that as your motivation. The sooner you learn the force of Ice, the sooner you will be able to leave," MiteraThrakena said. Even though she wanted Keia to learn Ice, high up in the mountains where the temperature is so cold that it snows continuously, MiteraThrakena would not let Keia freeze to death, though she did not tell her, wanting Keia to have an incentive to learn.

Keia looked at the dragon, and from the expression MiteraThrakena was giving her, she knew that the dragon was not going to open a portal for them to return to a more comfortable environment. Her hut with a nice warm fire was the first location that came to mind. Keia looked around again, only seeing snow on the ground and in the air. She decided that the quicker she started, the sooner she would be finished and out of the hostile environment.

As much as she did not want to, Keia needed her right hand to start to learn the force of Ice. She had been using it to rub the upper part of her left arm, but that had to come to an end, and to help her focus more on the lesson, she stopped rubbing her right upper arm with her left hand.

MiteraThrakena had told her that dragons had a natural ability to use the forces of nature. Keia understood what the dragon had said, and she even understood that she had also used the first three forces of nature: Fire, Water, and Wind. She now had to figure out how to use Ice.

She started by closing her eyes and picturing ice in her hand. The problem was that she could only remember images from when she was younger and had seen water in a bucket that had frozen over. She did not think that it was going to help her.

She then remembered something else MiteraThrakena had explained to her before she brought her to the ungodly area. She had said that Ice was like Fire. The dragon had also talked about Fire and how to start one when telling her about Ice. That gave Keia an idea, and even though she was not sure if it would work, it might help her current situation.

Keia, with her palm facing upward and just one handbreadth away from her chest, brought forth a flame of fire. Even though the fire did not burn her hand, Keia could feel the heat coming from it. Which was not much, but even the smallest amount of heat was a change for the better.

Keia only took a brief moment to enjoy the slight bit of warmth. She had made the flame of fire for another reason. MiteraThrakena had said that Ice was just like Fire, but Keia knew that it was not. Fire was hot, and even though she did not have much use or familiarity with Ice, as she did with Fire, Keia knew that Ice was cold. The moment that thought came to her, she knew that she was beginning to unravel the mystery of Ice.

She now had to do something she did not want to do, and that was to discard the flame she had in her hand. She did not need it any longer to get her thoughts together, but the small amount of heat was comforting, even if it was not much.

With the fire gone, there was nothing that gave

her any heat. Keia thought that it might be for the best, and she began to work through the problem. Fire is hot, and Ice is cold. She remembered the feeling of heat from the flame a moment ago, but she did not need the heat. MiteraThrakena had said that Ice is like Fire. Keia pushed the thought of heat out of her mind, which made it very easy for her to think about the cold. She herself was cold. Colder than she had ever been before. So cold that when she started thinking about how cold she was, she wanted to bring back the flame of fire, but knew that was not going to help her.

Keia closed her eyes and thought about how cold she was. Not in a way where she desired that she was warm, she wanted to feel the cold that was all around her as well as inside her. The environment was so cold that she could feel the coldness that was enveloping her. After a few deep breaths, not only could she feel the cold inside her, but she felt as if she could take hold of the cold and bring it out.

With her eyes still closed, she extended her right arm with her palm facing upward. She took in a deep breath, and with that breath she drew in a bit of the cold air that was surrounding her. When she felt the coldness enter, she smiled because she knew that she could add that to the coldness already inside her.

When she was ready, she simply allowed the coldness inside her to travel through her body, down her right arm, and into the palm of her hand. When she was sure that what she wanted was there, she opened her eyes and saw the sphere of ice sitting in the palm of her hand that was twice the size of her own fist.

Keia did not get overly excited. She wanted to concentrate. She had learned the forces of Fire, Water, and Wind, and with what she had learned by using them, she applied her knowledge to what she had just accomplished.

She turned her palm over, and the sphere of ice fell to the ground. She then positioned her palm upward again, and without hesitation, she called forth another sphere of ice, only this time she did not let it fall to the ground. Instead, she simply cast it outward the same way she would cast out a ball of fire. MiteraThrakena had explained that Ice is like Fire, and it was. One was hot, and one was cold, but for Keia, they both came from within her.

To continue to see what she could do, Keia cast one, then another, then another sphere of ice outward. She did it with the same ease and comfort as she did with Fire.

She then remembered how she could cast out a stream of Fire, a spout of Water, and a gust of Wind, so she tried the same with Ice by extending her arm and having her right palm face outward, away from her. A spiral of ice extended out and only stopped when she willed it to.

"Very good," MiteraThrakena said from where she was watching Keia the entire time. The dragon decided that the best way for the young woman to learn how to control the force of Ice would be to let her feel the effects of the coldness directly, and that is why the dragon had brought her to the highest mountain peak in KhoraThraks. "Let us return," MiteraThrakena said and opened a portal, and even though Keia was pleased with what she had accomplished, she was even more pleased when she stepped through the portal and was standing next to the river where they had first been.

"Now, see if you can perform the same task in a more comfortable environment," MiteraThrakena said.

Keia nodded and did the same as before. Even though she did not have the cold around her, she still remembered feeling the cold inside her. She closed her eyes, and she could sense the presence of the coldness within her. She thought that maybe it was always there, and it was only from being in the cold and feeling it all around her, and inside her, that allowed her to sense it now.

She opened her eyes and saw the sphere of ice in the palm of her hand. She quickly cast it outward and away from her, but before it was two paces from her, she cast out another and another. She then took a deep breath, and when she released it, a spiral of ice came forth out of the palm of her hand. When she decided that she had allowed it to extend far enough, she stopped it by closing her palm.

She then thought of something else that she

remembered from her childhood. Something that she always found amusing, and she decided that she wanted to try what she was thinking about.

She did not close her eyes; she kept them open because she wanted to see it appear, and it did. She had her palm facing upward, and her arm stretched out, and with a single thought, Keia formed an icicle in the center of her hand. It rose from her palm upward and was about four handbreadths tall. She used to see icicles form on the edges of her house where she lived as a child, and now, she was holding one right in front of her.

While still having it in her palm, she flicked her wrist, forcing her hand out away from her, and the icicle went flying off in the distance. With what she saw, she tried the next test and created another icicle, sent it flying away from her, and as soon as it left her palm, she released another one, then another one, and since she was enjoying herself, she released a fourth one just for fun.

"Impressive," MiteraThrakena said to praise Keia on what she had accomplished.

Keia looked at the dragon and was pleased with the compliment. She then turned around and saw something else. She walked over to where MiteraThrakena was standing about twenty paces away from a tree. When she was ready, Keia brought forth another icicle and released it outward. When it reached the tree, since the icicle had a very sharp point on the end of it and was very solid, it did not shatter when it struck the tree, but embedded itself in it about half the length of the icicle.

Keia turned around and saw the dragon looking at her, and thought that she was going to be scolded. Instead, MiteraThrakena's comment on the situation surprised her. "That could come in handy. Only do not use it against Kord. At least not until you are sure that he has brought forth his dragon scales. Just to be fair."

Keia and MiteraThrakena both started laughing. Maybe it was about what the dragon had said about Kord, or maybe they were both happy that Keia had learned the force of Ice.

Only one more force remained.

TWENTY-NINE

Kord walked to the opening of the cave he was using as his home. As he was standing there, the male bear that had also taken up residence in the cave walked past him and headed out to do its morning routine.

When Kord found the cave and decided to move in, he did not realize that the cave already had an owner. When the two confronted each other, the bear roared while Kord screamed at the top of his lungs. Since neither of them could decide which was making the most ruckus, they decided to share the cave, and that was how Kord and the bear began living together.

He watched the bear wander away, going about its daily business. Kord also had to begin his morning routine. He would stop by a tree and pick some fruit from the many trees in the forest, or he might decide that he preferred berries and pick some from one of the bushes. Either way, he would eat his morning meal as he made his way to the training area.

When he arrived, he did not see Vrom for his daily training, though he did see PateraThrakon lying in the area where he and the golem would train. As he approached, the dragon lifted his head and watched Kord make his way over to him. "Where is Vrom?" Kord asked.

PateraThrakon always thought that it was strange how Kord named the golem. To the dragon, it was only a lump of dirt that he had enchanted so it could teach the human male. Even though PateraThrakon hated to admit it, Kord, or the boy, as he preferred to call him, had made great advancement in his training toward becoming the Dragon Klau, and because of that, it was time to move on with his training.

PateraThrakon, being the dragon that he is, did not answer the boy's question. He simply stood and faced the river that was next to the training area. He then lifted his right front leg and made a motion to the water with his paw. When he finished, a spout of water rose upward, then moved onto the shore and stopped. It then started moving, swirling, and spinning, and in a moment, it took on a new shape. The shape of Kord. An exact replica of the young man.

"This is what you will be training with from this moment forward," PateraThrakon said and turned his head to look at Kord.

"What about Vrom?" Kord asked.

PateraThrakon did not answer Kord's question, at least not in the way the human wanted. "This golem will instruct you in how to use attack skills. The golem before taught you about defense. It is time for you to learn the second aspect of fighting."

"But where is Vrom?" Kord asked again with more determination in his voice to get an answer from the dragon.

"You do not need him. This golem will train you from now on."

Kord had asked repeatedly and did not receive a reply as to what happened to Vrom, so to him, it was time for more direct questions. He took two steps closer to the dragon. "It is not about me not needing him. What did you do? Did you send him away, or something worse?" Kord took a moment, then looked the dragon straight in his eyes and asked, "Did you kill him?"

PateraThrakon had no patience for what he thought was nothing more than a human child throwing a tantrum. The dragon did not react as a human adult would; he acted as a dragon would when a young dragon thought it knew better than its elders. From where he was standing, PateraThrakon flicked his tail, hitting Kord directly in his torso. The human went flying back twenty paces beyond the training area.

What Kord had learned saved his life. If he had been any other human, if the strike from the dragon's tail had not shattered his bones, when he landed on the ground, every bone in his body would have broken. Even before the dragon's tail struck him, Kord's reflexes instinctively responded, bringing forth the dragon scales, and that was the only thing that saved his life.

Even though he was a bit shaken, Kord did not stay on the ground long. Only enough to take hold of his anger. Not to control it, but to use it. Use it for what he believed was right. As soon as he stood, he started making his way back toward the dragon and immediately voiced his command, "Bring him back!" When Kord saw that the dragon did not make any move to do as he had spoken, he repeated his demand even louder. "I said, bring him back, now!"

PateraThrakon watched as the foolish boy continued to make his way to the center of the training area. The dragon was trying to decide on how to handle the situation. The first thought that came to him was that he should use his tail again, only this time, put enough force into the attack that the boy went flying ten times the distance he had previously traveled. His second thought, the one he was really considering, was that it was finally time to eat the boy and end his life once and for all. As much as he wanted to do just that, the male dragon knew that he would never hear the end of it from his mate, and that would be even worse than dealing with the human brat.

He decided to try to speak to the boy in a more compassionate manner, just as his mate would want him to do. "The golem is no longer needed to teach you. You have learned all you can from it, so it is time to move on with your training." It was a simple explanation, one that the dragon thought the boy would be able to understand. He was wrong. Not because he was wrong in his overall take on the situation, but only because he did not understand Kord.

Kord made his way over to where PateraThrakon was watching him. He stopped when he was standing close enough so he could look directly up at the dragon. "It is not about whether he is no longer needed or not, and that is only your opinion about him. To you, he is nothing more than some object that you created and a tool used to train me. Now that you don't think he is needed, you just toss him away. Is that what you are going to do with me? Are you going to have me train, and when you have no more need of me, are you going to get rid of me as well?" Kord put the anger he had into the words he spoke, and not once did he take his eyes off the dragon. He stared him down, even though PateraThrakon stood much, much taller than the human.

The dragon had little patience for the boy on a normal day, with the way the human was acting, PateraThrakon had run out of patience right before he struck Kord with his tail. "You will train with the golem that I have created, and that is the end of the discussion. As for getting rid of you, do not tempt me." PateraThrakon turned away from Kord, spread his wings, and was about to take to the air to be away from the annoying human. He only stopped when he heard Kord say the most outrageous thing the boy had ever said.

"Fight me!"

Dragons do not laugh often, but with what he

had just heard, PateraThrakon wanted to fall to the ground and laugh until he could hardly breathe. That would have been beneath the King of Dragons; however, he had to respond to what he thought was a fool's request. "Boy, you must have hit your head on the ground when you landed after I struck you," PateraThrakon said as he turned his head and neck to look at Kord standing behind him. Though what he saw was not the face of someone who had wanted to end his own life, the dragon saw the determination on Kord's face, even more so in his eyes.

Kord took another step toward the dragon. "I said, fight me. If I lose, I will forget about Vrom and train with the new golem; but if I win, you bring Vrom back."

Once again, PateraThrakon wanted to laugh but did not. "If I fight you, then you will lose. You might even end up dead. As for you winning, it would take an intervention of Creator for that to happen." The dragon then turned his head and was once again about to take to the air, that is, until he felt a slight impact on his right hind leg. He turned his head enough to see that Kord had run into his leg as if that was going to hurt the dragon. The human, not ready to concede, took two paces back, and when he was ready, he once again ran forward, throwing his body with as much force as possible into the dragon's leg.

PateraThrakon could have allowed the boy to continue with what he was doing until a full season had passed, but the dragon did not have the patience to do so, and he was ready to go back to his den and back to his nap. Unfortunately, he had to show the boy that the King of Dragons was the King.

Just as Kord was about to ram into the dragon's leg for the fifth time, PateraThrakon quickly turned his body, and with speed that seemed to Kord to be too fast for the dragon's size, he extended his left front paw out and pinned Kord to the ground. He had a claw on each side of the boy's head, which was the only thing that could be seen by the dragon, since Kord's body was covered by the dragon's paw.

PateraThrakon lowered his head so that his maw was only four handbreadths away from the human's face. Kord got a very close look at the fangs of the dragon, as well as the inside of the dragon's mouth, which was where he thought he was about to end up, but did not care. He was not going to back down. "Go ahead, eat me! But you'd better make sure that I don't survive when you swallow me, because if I do, I am going to cause you so much pain when I get inside that you are going to have to toss me back up, and when you do, we will continue our battle!"

The boy's suggestion about eating him was exactly what the dragon wanted to do, but he knew that he would have to deal with his queen, one of the two that he would bow to, and did not want to go through the never-ending lecture that he would hear for the rest of his life, which would be a very long time.

"I could crush your body with the least amount of

my strength, and you lie there still trying to threaten me." PateraThrakon looked directly into Kord's eyes. "Would you give up your life just to have your way?" PateraThrakon asked.

Kord looked directly into the dragon's eyes and gave his answer. "I would give up my life to save the life of someone else." Kord had never spoken more truthful words from his heart.

It was no use. PateraThrakon knew at that moment that he had lost. Not in a physical battle, but in sheer determination and commitment from the boy; no, the young man, who put someone else above his own life. The dragon knew that there was no need to continue; he had been defeated.

PateraThrakon moved back, removing his paw off Kord. As soon as he was free, he jumped up, and the dragon saw that the young man was about to take another run at him, so he decided to end the confrontation. "Enough," the dragon said, and saw Kord remain where he was but kept his stance with his arms and fists raised, prepared to attack. PateraThrakon had not expected to waste so much of his time with the human when the dragon woke early in the morning, and he was more than ready to leave and go back to his den, where he could take a nap and be away from Kord. "You want Vrom back, then so be it." PateraThrakon lifted his right front paw, and when he made a sweeping motion, a mound of dirt rose between where he was standing and Kord. The mound began to twist, swirl, and spin, and when it stopped, it looked exactly like Kord, only made from dirt.

"Vrom?" Kord asked the golem. Not only to see if it knew who it was, but also to see if it was the same golem as before.

The golem raised its hands and arms and looked at them, moving its head from side to side, inspecting itself. When it was done, it lifted his head and looked directly at Kord, and just before Kord was about to say something, believing that the golem standing before him was not the same as before, Vrom threw his arms up in the air, slightly angled in the same manner both he and Kord did when they decided who was the victor in their wrestling matches.

Kord ran over to Vrom, and they grabbed each other by the right forearm and shook, which was a normal greeting for them. Then Kord, seeing that his friend was back with him, smiled, and to mimic his friend, Vrom smiled as well.

With the reunion over, Kord let go of Vrom's arm and looked up at PateraThrakon and said, "Don't think I'm going to thank you." Which was his way of saying, *"Thank you,"* to the dragon.

"Do not think that I want you to," PateraThrakon said, which was his way of saying, *"You are welcome,"* to Kord. Nothing else needed to be said between the human and the dragon, so PateraThrakon spread his wings and took to the air, ready to return to his den for a nice, long nap.

Kord put his attention back on Vrom, "Come on," he said, and started walking toward the river, with Vrom walking next to him. When they reached where the new golem was standing, the one made of water, Kord immediately got down to the most important task. He looked at the water golem, then at Vrom, then back to the water golem, and asked everyone present, "What should we call you?"

PateraThrakon had flown away out of the sight of the human and the two golems. Dragons have very good eyesight, and even though the three on the ground could not see the dragon, PateraThrakon could see all of them when he turned his head and neck to look at them standing by the river. Dragons also have very good hearing, so when Kord decided on the name Morv, which is Vrom spelled backward, as the name for the water golem, PateraThrakon just turned and looked ahead as he flew through the sky.

Unfortunately, humans do not have the hearing of a dragon, or else Kord might have heard PateraThrakon say, "I am proud of you, Kord," as he was flying away. The dragon did not care whether Kord wanted both golems or not, but he was impressed by how the human boy, no, the young man, was ready to die for the sake of another, whether that individual was human or formed from a mound of dirt. To be willing to give their life to save the life of another is what the Dragon Klau is expected to do.

THIRTY

For the first three sun-cycles, since the arrival of Morv, Kord and the two golems did not partake in any training. At least not the training Kord was supposed to be doing. He thought that it would be best to teach Morv how to communicate. He had been able to teach Vrom, so he wanted Morv to be able to join in the conversations as well so that they could all converse with each other.

Kord started with the basics. Teaching Morv to nod his head to a question when the answer was *yes* and shake his head from side to side if the answer was *no*. It went reasonably well since it was the second time Kord was teaching a golem, so he knew what would work best.

After Morv understood the yes and no gestures, Kord moved on to the more challenging part, which was to teach the water golem how to write. Kord began his training the same way he started with Vrom, which was to write his name in the dirt. It was the same way Keia had taught Kord. After he learned how to write his name, Kord began to teach Morv the rest of the letters.

On the third sun-cycle, while Kord was trying to explain what the difference between a man and a woman was, Kord found out something about the two golems that he did not know. He was getting frustrated, so he turned away from Vrom and Morv for a moment to calm down, but when he turned around, he saw the two golems looking at each other while Vrom was moving his hands around. It was at that moment that Kord realized that the two golems could communicate with each other without talking. This made Kord even angrier because he had spent the last three sun-cycles trying to teach Morv, while all along, Vrom could have explained everything Kord wanted him to learn with a lot more ease. To show that he was not happy about not knowing the two could talk to each other, Kord decided that he needed to take a break from the two golems, which lasted another three sun-cycles.

When Kord finally decided to return to the training area, Vrom and Morv were waiting for him. When he was ten paces away, both golems lifted their right hand and waved to him. When Kord finally reached where the golems were standing, the two golems were smiling, looking directly at Kord. Once he saw his two friends, who looked exactly like himself, he could not be angry with the golems any longer. He just shook his head and smiled. “Let’s get down to training,” Kord said, and the two golems nodded their heads at the same time.

Morv taught Kord the same way that Vrom did.

The water golem would perform the motion that he wanted Kord to mimic. Just like the way Kord started teaching the golem how to write, Morv started with the basics.

The first move Kord learned was how to punch outward. Morv stood beside Kord, and with his left hand, he made a fist and punched outward. Kord, believing that he already knew how to punch, performed the move two times and was ready to move on to the next set of instructions. Morv would not let him. The water golem simply made the same motion over and over to let Kord know what he was supposed to do. When Kord saw that the golem was not going to show him the next part of his training, Kord went back to punching out with his left fist.

After about two sun-marks, Kord's left arm felt so heavy to him that he could not even keep it up in front of him. When he lowered it to his side, Morv went over to where he was standing and positioned himself so that once again he was standing next to Kord. The golem then lifted his right arm, with his right hand in a fist, and began to punch outward. Kord understood what the golem wanted, so he began to duplicate the golem's movement. He had just spent two sun-marks punching with his left arm and fist, so Kord was pretty sure he knew what he would be doing for the next two sun-marks, and he was correct.

When Kord was unable to keep his right arm up, Morv went over to him and motioned with his hands that he could stop. Kord immediately dropped his right arm, even though it was more as if it fell all on its own, with Kord having little control over not only his right arm but his left as well, since it still felt heavy even though he had stopped practicing with it over two sun-marks ago. He knew that after he had rested for the night, his arms would feel better when he woke up.

Seeing that his pupil was worn out, Morv motioned for Kord to sit down on one of the logs in the area. Kord thought that was a good idea, but he had a bit of difficulty sitting down since he could hardly use his arms for balance.

Each of the golems sat down next to him, Vrom on his left and Morv on his right. The dirt golem picked up a stick and began writing on the ground. When he was through, he tried to hand the stick to Kord so he could write as well, but Kord just gave Vrom a look to let him know that he did not have the strength to move his arms even to pick up and hold the stick, which hardly had any weight to it.

Kord looked at the ground and saw what Vrom had written and responded verbally. “No, I haven’t talked to Keia in about five sun-cycles.” Kord put his focus back on the ground in front of him. He thought about how he sees Keia less, the more the two of them go about their training. By the time he is done with his daily routine, he either sleeps at the training area or makes his way back to his cave. He also remembered that when they first arrived in

KhoraThraks, the two spent all their time together. Now that has changed.

Morv reached across in front of Kord, and Vrom handed him the stick that he was holding. He then wrote his own question on the ground. When he had finished, and Kord saw what he had written, Kord felt very uncomfortable and gave his response immediately.

"She is not my mate!"

Morv looked at Kord, then at Vrom. The dirt golem simply shrugged his shoulders.

Kord was not sure why Vrom had wanted to know why he had not gone and seen Keia, or his mate, as the water golem put it, but Kord felt that what they had when they were younger was not the same. He remembered MiteraThrakena explaining to him about the difference between men and women, but he knew that there was something more to it. He was not sure what it was, so to stop the confusion that he felt whenever he saw Keia, he decided to visit her less. Only when he felt as if he had to see her would he go back to the hut where they both used to live. They would sit and talk for a while, usually over an evening meal, but afterward, Kord would go back to his cave where he lived alone, that is, with the exception of the bear.

Now, having thought about Keia, Kord felt that he was not up for any more training for the day. His arms were so sore he could barely move them, and it was even difficult for him to stand up from the log since he had trouble using his arms.

"I think I've had enough training for the day. I'm heading back to the cave," Kord said as he turned away from the two golems and started walking.

Vrom and Morv were golems, and they could not understand how their friend was feeling. So as Kord walked away, the two golems just looked at each other and shrugged their shoulders, stating to each other that they had no idea what was bothering their human companion.

When he made his way back to his cave, Kord went inside and fell down on the pile of straw that he covered with a blanket and used for a bed. Even though he had not struck his bed with force, the slightest movement of his arms caused him pain. Because of the pain in his arms, he had trouble falling asleep, but it was the small pain in his heart that was bothering him the most.

When he woke up the next morning, Kord felt refreshed and ready to start another day of training. He always felt good when he woke up after having trained so hard the previous day. One night of rest, and his body felt like he was a new person. One of the advantages of training to be the Dragon Klau.

He reached the training area and saw that Vrom and Morv were waiting for him. "So, what is the training going to be today? More practicing with punches?" Kord asked when he had made his way over to the two golems, and to emphasize what he thought he would be doing, Kord thrust his right arm out with his hand in a fist twice, then did the same with his left.

The water golem shook his head to let Kord know that was not what he would be working on. Instead, Morv moved to the center of the training area and positioned himself so that he was facing Kord. When he was ready and saw that Kord was watching him, Morv lifted his right leg, bent at the knee, while slightly turning his body to simulate a person moving their leg with their knee leading the way to make contact with someone else. To further explain to Kord, Morv gestured for Vrom to join him in the center of the training area. Once there, Morv lifted his right leg again, bent at the knee, and slightly turned his body, so that when his leg was up and out in front of him, Morv's knee connected with Vrom's midsection.

Kord understood what the water golem wanted him to do, so he moved to the center of the training area. As he was about to begin to repeat the motion he saw Morv make, he stopped when he saw both Morv and Vrom walk away and take their positions near the log, then turned to watch him.

"Don't I get to practice with one of you?" Kord asked, thinking that practicing with someone else would be better than practicing alone. For his answer, Morv simply shook his head from side to side to let Kord know that he would not be training with an actual opponent. Kord, not happy with the golem's reply, made a grumbling noise, but went about making the same move Morv had shown him.

After about two sun-marks, Kord stopped. Not that he had much of a choice. He had been performing the same motion with his right leg for so long that it simply gave out. He could not lift it any longer. Not only that, when he lowered his right leg and his foot touched the ground, it gave out on him, and Kord fell to the ground with no way of stopping himself.

As he lay there, he looked up and saw the two golems looking at him. They had not made a single motion to go over and help their friend, which Kord was beginning to reconsider just how much of a friend they really were.

Since he was not getting any help from the golems, Kord positioned his hands at his sides and pressed against the ground to try to push himself up. He was able to do so up to the point where he had to use his right leg to support himself. It would not, and he fell back on the ground.

He tried a second time and changed to use his left leg to give him the support he needed to stand. He was successful, and even though he was on his feet, he could barely put any pressure on his right leg. That was even more obvious when he limped over to where the two golems were standing next to the log that the three used to sit on.

When he reached the log, Kord tried to sit down, but it was more as if he fell when his right leg gave out on him once again. While sitting down next to the log with his back to it, because he did not fall on it when he lowered his body, he looked up at the two golems that were looking at him. “Don’t even think about having me continue with my training using my left leg,” Kord said to let the golems know that he was done for the day, even though the sun was not even midway in the sky. He had only trained for two sun-marks, but it was enough time for his leg to give out on him.

Kord rested for another sun-mark, then let the golems know what his plan was, “I’m going back to my cave and rest until tomorrow. I’ll be ready to start again in the morning.” When he tried to stand, he positioned his left leg under him and rose, but the moment he put the slightest pressure on his right leg, he fell back on the ground. Seeing that he was not going anywhere, he came up with a new plan and passed it along to the two golems. “I’ve decided to sleep here for the night,” Kord said as he leaned back against the log, stretched out his legs, closed his eyes, and tried to get some sleep. With the way he felt, he was ready to fall asleep and let his right leg heal. At least he hoped it would be by the time he woke up.

Kord jumped up when he woke the next morning. Even though he knew that he would feel better after a good night’s sleep, he was happy that he felt no pain in his right leg when he stood and put pressure on it. Once again, glad that he healed with just one night of rest.

Since he was already in the training area, Morv and Vrom thought that he would start his daily training immediately, but Kord informed them that he was going to find something to eat before he did any training, since he had missed both his midday meal and evening meal yesterday.

Once he came back from picking some fruit, Kord made his way to the center of the training area. Before Morv could even make the slightest motion to show him what he would be working on, Kord held up his hand to stop the golem, then proceeded to do what he knew the golem was going to show him. He began performing the same training he had previously, but instead of using his right leg, he used his left. Since he was already performing the task, Morv and Vrom took up their positions by the log where they watched Kord.

As if on cue, after about two sun-marks, Kord's left leg gave out on him, and he fell to the ground. Since he had suffered the same pain and indignity just the day before, he did not even bother trying to stand; he simply crawled over to the log where the two golems were and positioned himself so that he had his back against it. He then stretched out his legs and stayed there. He knew that he would eventually fall asleep and wake up refreshed and healed.

The next morning, after fetching something to eat for his morning meal, Kord made his way back to the training area. Since he had previously worked on his leg attacks as well as his punches, he was not sure what Morv would have him do next. “So, what will it be today?” he asked when he was standing with the two golems.

Morv did not hesitate to show Kord what he would be doing. He punched out once with his right fist, then he punched out once with his left fist, then brought his right leg up, bent at his knee, brought it back down, and then did the same with his left leg.

Kord saw what the golem did and realized that he was to practice all four movements that he had performed the past three sun-cycles. It made sense to him, and when he moved to the center of the training area, he began to repeat the motions Morv demonstrated to him.

On this day, Kord was able to continue training for four sun-marks before his body gave out. Luckily for him, he had enough strength to walk back to his cave and get some sleep.

The next day, when he arrived at the training area, having already eaten his morning meal, Morv and Vrom were waiting for him. “What is it going to be today?” Kord asked, thinking that the water golem would be showing him something new. To his surprise, Morv performed the same actions that he had the previous day. Alternating between the four motions with his arms and legs.

Kord did not even complain that it was just a repeat of the day before; he just went about his training, and after about eight sun-marks, he finally started feeling the effects of the training on his body. He stopped with enough energy to make it back to his cave to get some sleep and heal.

It was the same routine for three moon-marks. He would practice the punches and the leg kicks. During the day, once he felt that his body could not go on any further, Kord would stop and head back to his cave. By the end of the third moon-mark, the sun had gone out of the sky before Kord ended his training for the day. Not even feeling a bit of discomfort. Because of the extensive training and repetitive motion, his body had adapted to the movements. They were a part of him just as his legs and arms were. He was ready to move on to the next stage of his training to become the Dragon Klau.

THIRTY-ONE

Kord arrived at the training area ready to begin. He thought that he would be practicing the same movements he had been performing for the past three moon-marks, but when he stepped into the middle of the area where he practiced, Morv and Vrom stood there as well.

"What's going on with the two of you? You're in my way of practicing." Morv shook his head from side to side, and that led Kord to realize that they had other plans for his training. "What do you want me to do?" Kord asked.

The two golems, who were facing Kord, turned and faced each other. Morv then looked at Kord while at the same time he extended both his arms out. Using his fingers, he pointed his right arm at Kord and pointed his left arm at Vrom.

"You want me to fight Vrom?" Kord asked, believing that he understood what the golem was trying to relay to him.

Morv shook his head from side to side to let Kord know that was not what he wanted. Even though both golems could write some words and phrases, when it came to a more complex conversation that required more than a yes or no answer, the golems always communicated with Kord by actions instead of words.

Morv lowered his left hand while he kept his right hand pointing toward Kord. He held it there for a moment, then moved both of his arms and hands, and using a finger on both of his hands, he pointed to his own eyes, then pointed at both himself and at Vrom. Kord picked up on what the golem wanted. "You want me to watch the two of you," Kord said to relay his interpretation of Morv's actions. To let him know that he was correct, Morv nodded his head.

Kord was more than happy to let the two golems do whatever they had planned. Actually, he was hoping that maybe they would take up a good portion of his day, which would give him some time to sit down and relax. Something he had not had a chance to do since he started training with the water golem.

To stay out of their way and to be more comfortable, Kord walked over to the log they used to sit on and sat down facing the middle of the training area and the two golems. "Ok, I'm watching," Kord said to let the two golems know that he was ready to watch whatever they were about to do.

Vrom and Morv took a step away from each other, then adjusted their stances to a fighting position. Each of them raised their arms, bent at their elbows, with their hands in a fist. Once ready, they began.

Vrom made the first move. He punched out with

his right fist toward Morv, aiming for his left shoulder. The water golem adjusted his body to his right to dodge the attack, while at the same time he extended his own right fist, making contact with the dirt golem's left shoulder.

Vrom accepted the punch and began his countermove. He slightly leaned down to his left and punched out with his left fist, connecting with the right side of the water golem's body. Morv then extended his left fist and punched Vrom directly in the dirt golem's face.

Kord sat there and watched the two golems fight each other. It was obvious that the punches the two were delivering had no effect on their opponent, but Kord was more than happy to relax while the two golems went about their mock fight.

When the two golems thought that they had shown Kord enough, they both stopped, turned, and faced him. "Is that it?" Kord asked when they were just standing in the middle of the training area looking at him.

For his reply, Morv raised his right arm and hand and pointed his finger at Kord, who now understood that he was not going to have an easy, relaxing day as he thought he would. The two golems put on their demonstration to show him what he would be doing. Knowing that he had no choice in the matter, Kord stood up and walked toward the center of the training area, while at the same time, Vrom walked toward him, passed him, and made his way over to the log. Once there, he turned and faced the two combatants, Morv and Kord, whose training for the day was about to begin.

Kord positioned himself so that he was facing Morv. When he saw that the water golem had his arms raised and standing in a fighting position, Kord adjusted his body to mimic his opponent, with his own arms and fists raised in front of him, and his right foot forward a step from his body, with his left foot positioned a step behind him. When Morv thought that Kord had enough time to prepare himself, he nodded his head to let Kord know to begin.

Kord, thinking that he would try to first punch the water golem with his right fist, took two steps forward to close the distance between him and his opponent. When he thought that he was in the best position, he quickly punched out with his right fist, aiming for the water golem's face. He did not make contact, at least not in the way he had planned.

Morv was faster than Kord, much faster, and before Kord's fist was even halfway to the water golem's face, Morv had already punched out with his right fist and made contact with Kord's midsection, causing him to stumble back five steps. As he did, either from the force of the hit or from the surprise of how fast the punch came at him, Kord fell to the ground on his rear. Once there, he looked up at his opponent, and the only gesture Morv made was to motion with his raised fists, bringing them back toward himself, letting Kord know that he should stand up and try again.

Kord, being the stubborn person that he is, was not going to let the water golem get the best of him. He stood up, shook his shoulders and arms as if to throw off the last attack, then made his way back to his opponent. When he was in striking distance, Kord punched out with his left arm and fist, aiming for Morv's face, but that was only a ruse, or at least that is what Kord believed. He was sure that the water golem would dodge the first attack, but he was confident that his second attack, which he had planned while standing up a moment ago, would reach his target. Just as he saw Morv dodge his left fist, Kord punched out with his right fist, aiming for the golem's left side.

The water golem did not see the second attack; he did not have to. He knew what Kord was going to do before Kord even knew himself, so when Kord reached out with his right fist, Morv, having already dodged the first punch, simply bent slightly down and to his right and punched out with his own right fist, striking Kord in his stomach. The punch was so hard that he went stumbling backward and once again landed on the ground and on his rear.

Kord thought back to the day when PateraThrakon had struck him with his tail during his training. The pain Kord was feeling when Morv had just struck him was not as bad, but it was very close. He even opened his shirt to look at his chest. When he saw that it was covered with dragon scales, he knew that his instincts were reacting to him being attacked; the scales just did not soften the force of his opponent's attack to the point where he felt no pain.

Not ready to give up, Kord stood, and since he already had his shirt open, he decided to remove it completely. Maybe he thought that it would help him, but he would find out that with or without his shirt on, his opponent would not go down easily.

He began walking back over to Morv, ready to attack his opponent again. Just before he was about to release what he thought would be the attack to end the bout, he got a surprise from the golem. Kord pulled back his right arm, ready to release the most powerful punch he could strike with, but before he even had a chance to move his arm forward, Morv quickly, with the speed of a rapidly moving river, knelt down while at the same time, spun his body around with his left leg extended outward. When he had made a complete circling motion, his left leg struck Kord's left leg, sweeping the human off his feet. The attack came so fast that Kord was lying on his back before he even had a chance to get halfway through his own attack.

Lying there, even with his eyes closed, he knew that his body and legs were covered with dragon scales. His legs, because that was where the attack came from, and his body brought forth the scales just before he landed on the ground, because the force of the attack from his opponent and the force with which he struck when he landed, knocked the wind out of him. If he did not have the scales to protect himself, Kord was sure that he probably would have felt a lot more pain than what he was feeling, and for that, he was thankful.

He did not get up as fast as he did from the previous attacks, but when he did, he had a lot more sense to not rush into his opponent's reach, and he could not help but think that if PateraThrakon was there, he would have said: *"At least you got some sense knocked into that head of yours, and it only took three times of you landing on your rear, which is probably where your brain is anyway."* Kord pushed the thought out of his mind and put his focus back on his opponent. Morv was still in his fighting stance with his arms and fists raised. Kord decided that maybe he should slow his attacks down a little because going at his opponent, fast and furious, was not working for him.

Kord made his way back over to his opponent. He had his arms and fists raised to match the water golem, and when he reached him, Kord punched out with his right fist, aiming for the golem's head. He had not expected to make contact; he just wanted to see the reaction of Morv, which was simply to move his head to his right to avoid the punch. Kord then punched out with his left fist, so Morv just moved his head to the left, once again avoiding the attack.

Kord lowered his right arm and punched out toward the left side of the water golem's midsection.

Morv simply moved his body to the right once again, avoiding the attack. Kord then punched out with his left fist, aiming for the golem's face, but Morv simply moved to his left to avoid the next attack.

Kord, having failed to make contact with any of his punches, was getting annoyed. Partly because his attacks had failed, but also because it appeared to him as if Morv was mocking him by not attacking at all. He was simply avoiding the punches. To see if what he thought was true, Kord released a steady onslaught of punches, alternating with his fists between rights and lefts, aiming for his opponent's face, who easily avoided every attack, and not once did Morv strike back with his own attacks.

Now Kord knew that the golem was mocking him. Since Morv fought back the first three times Kord attacked him, he knew that the water golem was more than capable of attacking. What he was doing now was allowing Kord to attempt to make contact with his opponent by simply avoiding every attack thrown at him. It frustrated Kord even more because he believed that the golem was making fun of him. For that, Kord increased the speed of his attacks, alternating his left and right punches, but with each attack, Morv simply moved his body out of the way before the attacks even came close to the water golem.

Kord was getting angry, but at the same time, he was not going to give up. He continued to throw punches at his opponent, and when he thought that he had thrown enough, he attempted the same move Morv had done earlier in their match. Kord bent down and spun his body with his left leg extended outward. It was a move that he had never attempted before, and to his credit, he executed it perfectly. Unfortunately, Morv, not only being able to perform the move himself, as well as being skilled at attacks, which is why he was created by PateraThrakon to train Kord, was able to easily jump up and over Kord's leg as he brought it around.

Even though he had not made contact with the attempt, Kord was not surprised, and even more importantly, he did not give up. He came out of the low attack, standing up, facing his opponent, and once again began to throw punches at the water golem, who was able to avoid every attack. All the while not attacking Kord. He simply allowed the human to do whatever he thought was best in trying to land just one hit, which did not happen by the time they ended their training for the day.

The same training went on for the next few sun-cycles. Every day, Kord and Morv would fight each other, which was more along the lines of Kord attempting to land an attack on the water golem, which Morv would avoid with ease.

It was on the third sun-cycle that Kord realized that Morv, being made from water, moved as water did. Whenever he avoided an attack, the golem's body would not so much as move like a human but would flow like water. This gave the golem the advantage because water moved much more easily than a human.

To Kord's credit, he did begin to attempt different kinds of strategies in his attacks. He would alternate between straight-forward punches and ones that came from different angles. He also came up with attacks where he used his legs. Some were low, and he swept outward. Some were mid-level with his opponent's body and came as a straight outward kick, and he even attempted high kicks that were aimed at the water golem's head. Unfortunately, not one of Kord's attacks made contact with any part of his opponent's body.

It was going on a full moon-cycle with his one-on-one training with the water golem. Kord was in his cave, lying on his bed, thinking about the match he had for the day. In all the time he had been facing Morv, he had not been able to land a single attack, and he thought that he never would. He realized that he was not fast enough. No matter how hard he tried, he could not match the speed of the water golem. The only thing that he had accomplished was that he had developed a lot of different fighting techniques. His punches and kicks had improved greatly, but his speed was still that of a normal human, and he was not sure if he would ever be able to land a single attack.

Having thought the same thought every night over the last few moon-marks, Kord decided that he would get some sleep and try again when he started his training in the morning. He had no choice but to keep trying. He fell asleep, but on this night, he dreamt of something that had happened not too long ago.

The next morning, he arrived at the training area, and as usual, the two golems were waiting for him. Vrom stood by the log that the three used to sit on when Kord took his breaks. Morv waited for Kord at the center of the area where they practiced. Kord made his way over to him and took up his fighting position, facing Morv with his arms and fists raised. The water golem nodded his head to let Kord know to proceed.

He moved forward and began his attacks. Throwing out a couple of punches, attacking his opponent with leg sweeps and kicks. Alternating between a few series of attacks he had come up with, but not once did any of Kord's attacks connect with his opponent. That is, until Kord decided to test his idea.

As he was about to punch out with his right fist, Kord closed his eyes. He felt the speed at which he launched his attack, and when he pulled back his arm, he did not follow through with another one. He stopped, opened his eyes, and looked at his fist. It had water on it. That was not the only surprise that he had, for when he saw that there was water on his fist, he looked at his opponent, and even though he was a golem made out of water, Morv had a surprised look on his face. The surprise came from Kord almost landing a punch on his opponent. The golem was able to dodge the full force of the attack, but it had come at him so fast that he was not able to get out of the way completely, and Kord's fist brushed against the left side of the golem's face.

Kord could have savored that moment, but he did not have time for it. He simply took up his starting fighting position with his arms and fists raised out in front of him, then he made a motion with his arms, bringing them slightly back toward himself, to let the golem know that it was his turn to bring the fight to Kord, which he did.

Morv moved forward but did not attack. He allowed Kord to continue to make his own attacks. The first two punches missed the golem, but the third attack was a straightforward kick from Kord's left leg and foot, which connected with the golem's midsection.

Even though Morv was made from water, his body took on a form that allowed Kord to land attacks instead of going directly into or through the golem. It was the way that PateraThrakon had created the golem to train Kord. To have an opponent that would be able to act as a target for his attacks.

Kord took a moment for himself when he landed the last attack. He now knew how he would be able to succeed in fighting the water golem. Even though it was made from water, and its movements flowed like water, and were faster than a human's attack, its speed could be matched with that of a dragon.

The previous night, Kord dreamt of the time when he had challenged PateraThrakon to a fight. The dragon had attacked him with such speed that Kord was on the ground before he knew it. When Kord woke up from the dream, he realized that he had to attack his opponent with the speed of a dragon and not of a human.

He had developed the ability to have dragon scales appear on his body by instinct for defense. He did not have to think about them for them to surface and cover the area that needed protection. He realized that he had to do the same when he made an attack as well. He had to rely on his instincts to overcome the obstacle. To do just that, when he made the punch with his eyes closed, his instincts took over, and the dragon scales appeared on his right arm and fist, then on his legs, which increased the speed of his attack, and that allowed him to make contact with not only the punch but also the kick. He was ready.

The two began again, and now that he knew what he had to do, he did not rely on what he saw. Kord calmed himself, and that allowed his instincts to take over, which allowed the dragon scales to cover his body while he attacked, which allowed his speed to increase, which allowed his attacks to be successful. So successful that after he landed five consecutive hits on Morv, upon the sixth attack, the water golem used his left arm to block the punch Kord made with his right fist. This caused Kord to stop and look at Morv, eye to eye. Kord smiled and saw the same exact smile on the water golem, who looked exactly like him.

The two positioned their arms out in front of them with their hands in a fist. They both nodded and then began their attacks, only this time, Morv had to block every attack that came at him, and to his surprise, Kord was able to block the golem's attacks as well.

Now and then, one of the opponents would succeed in their attack, but that did not stop them from continuing their bout. Now that Kord was able to match the speed of the water golem, his training would take on a new level. One that would bring him even closer to becoming the Dragon Klau.

THIRTY-TWO

Kord took to his training with a new vigor. Now that he was able to defend and attack, he felt more like a fighter than just a pupil. There were times when he would take on both golems at the same time, then there were other times he would have a match that was just one-on-one, either between Vrom or Morv. No matter who his opponent was, they never went easy on him. They did not hold back their attacks, and if one were to land on Kord, then he would remember that even though they were practicing, the pain he received was part of the lesson.

As Kord was walking into the training area to begin his daily practice, he saw not only Vrom and Morv, but PateraThrakon as well. As usual, the male dragon had already settled down in his spot, resting with his legs under him and his tail wrapped around at his side. Also, as usual, he had to wait for Kord to arrive, and from the mood the dragon was in, he had been waiting for quite some time.

"If you took any longer to arrive for today's training, I would say that you were late, or you were early for tomorrow's," PateraThrakon said to let Kord know that he did not like to be kept waiting, especially by Kord.

Kord did not let the dragon's comment bother him. He knew that he had progressed quite well, and he also knew that he always put his full effort into his training. "Ah, it is so good to see you, My Lord," Kord said when he walked up to stand with Vrom and Morv, with PateraThrakon a few paces away in front of them. Kord continued with his sarcastic greeting. "You honor us with your presence, Lord Sleepiness," Kord said and bowed. "How may I be of service to you?" Kord remained in his bowing position while he waited for PateraThrakon to respond. All the while, Kord kept his face toward the ground, so that the dragon would not see him smiling.

PateraThrakon was not in the mood to put up with Kord's false admiration and was about to strike the young man with his tail, while Kord was still leaning over. The dragon thought that he would be able to put enough force into the attack to send Kord flying all the way back to the hut where Keia was. PateraThrakon decided that it was not worth his time and knew that the sooner he spoke with Kord concerning the reason he was there, the quicker he would be away from the annoying little ant of a man.

"I have brought you something to train with," PateraThrakon said, and saw that with what he had said, Kord tilted his head up enough to see just what the dragon was referring to. When he saw that Kord was now interested in why the dragon was there, he had to restrain himself from changing his mind. PateraThrakon was there for a reason, a very important one. “Here,” PateraThrakon said and removed his right front leg from under him, opened his paw, and tossed what he was holding toward Kord and the two golems.

The golems saw the items just as Kord did, but only Kord was surprised at what was lying on the ground at his feet and stood back up to look at them. Since the dragon tossed the items to them, Kord knew that one of them was for him, so he bent over and picked up one of the three swords PateraThrakon had brought.

“You will begin your training with swords,” the dragon said, and saw that Kord was surprised at what he was holding in his hands. “The golems will show you how to wield one.” PateraThrakon then stood, turned around, and was about to fly away, but decided to make one last comment to Kord. “Try not to cut off a hand or a foot, but if you must remove something belonging to you, try to cut out your tongue. At least then I will not have to listen to you speak.” The dragon spread its wings and leaped into the air.

Kord looked at the sword he was holding in his hand and smiled as he had never smiled before. He had always wanted to learn how to use a sword, and now he was going to. He turned to look at the two golems and saw that they had also picked up the remaining weapons. "This is going to be fun," Kord said, ready to begin the day's training.

There were about two more sun-marks left before the sun was out of the sky when PateraThrakon returned to the training area and saw Kord and the two golems practicing. What the dragon was quick to notice, even before he reached the area where Kord and the golems were, was that the young man was not practicing with the sword the dragon had given him. Once again, Kord and the golems were attacking each other, but only in the manner that they had been since they started training together.

When PateraThrakon landed, he looked over and saw that the three swords were lying against the log where Kord and the golems would take their breaks from practicing. As soon as Kord saw the dragon land, he and the golems stopped what they were doing and turned to face the King of Dragons. Kord knew that PateraThrakon would want an explanation for why he was not practicing with the swords.

"I know what you said, but..." Kord stopped talking and looked behind him at the three swords lying against the log, then turned back to look at PateraThrakon and continued. "I don't think I can use a sword," Kord said, as if he believed the dragon would reprimand him for not following his instructions on training with the sword. He was surprised when PateraThrakon spoke.

"Explain," was all the dragon said, and waited for Kord to give his answer.

Kord looked at the dragon, and even though he thought he was going to be lectured for disobeying PateraThrakon, he told the dragon exactly how he felt.

"I tried using the sword. Believe me, I did, but..." Kord stopped speaking, wondering how the dragon would react.

"But what?" PateraThrakon asked and waited for Kord to continue.

"It's just that, when I tried to use the sword, it did not feel right. As if it were something that I shouldn't use." Kord waited for PateraThrakon's response.

The dragon did not take his eyes off Kord. "What do you mean, 'it did not feel right'?" PateraThrakon asked, wanting Kord to explain himself and his answer.

Kord had practiced with the sword for over four sun-marks and had come to a decision on his own. One he felt PateraThrakon was not going to be happy with, but he believed in what he had decided and was going to have to stick to what he thought was right for him. He looked directly at the dragon and spoke about how he felt about using a sword. "When I was using it, I kept feeling as if it was wrong." Kord stopped talking, looked down at the ground, and let out a small laugh, which was heard by the dragon.

"What do you find amusing, boy?" PateraThrakon asked, and even though he may have sounded as if he was angry, referring to Kord as *boy*, he was not. He just wanted Kord to continue with what he was going to say.

Kord looked up at PateraThrakon and once again began explaining his reason for not using the sword. "I remember when I saw my father practicing with his sword. Every time I did, I always dreamt of the day when I would be able to use one as well." Kord turned around and looked at the swords behind him, then back at the dragon. "Since I have been training to become the Dragon Klau, I think that I am different. With what I have learned, I think..." Kord stopped so that he could change what he was going to say, "...I believe that I should not use a sword. There is nothing wrong if someone chooses to do so. I always admired my father for being able to wield one, but for me, I choose not to. I will use what you have given me. That is enough, and that is who I am." When he was finished, Kord waited for the scolding he thought he was about to receive.

PateraThrakon looked at Kord and saw that the young man looked as if he were waiting for the dragon to strike him with his tail. The strike never came. "Very well," PateraThrakon said, raised his right paw, and willed the three swords over to him. They flew off the log and landed in the dragon's palm. He then closed his claws around the weapons.

"You mean that's it?" Kord asked, expecting more of a berating from the dragon. "You're not going to tell me that you are the Dragon King, and I must do what you say, or that I am just some foolish little boy, and I am probably not smart enough to use a sword, unless it was to pick my nose."

PateraThrakon looked at Kord and told him the truth. "I agree with what you just said. You are a foolish little boy and are not smart enough to use a sword. Though I doubt you could even use one to pick your nose." The dragon waited a moment, then told him what else he had to say to him. "You explained how you felt about using a sword and the reason behind your decision. If you choose not to use one, so be it." The dragon turned around and prepared to leave, but made one last comment to Kord. "I suggest you get back to your training. You still have a long way to go." PateraThrakon opened his wings and jumped into the air. Leaving Kord to continue with his training. The dragon smiled as he flew away.

When he arrived back at his den, MiteraThrakena was already resting on her own dais. PateraThrakon climbed up onto the one belonging to him. He sat down with his legs under him, then curled his tail, neck, and head at his side.

"How did it proceed with Kord?" MiteraThrakena asked, knowing what her mate had planned for the young man. All she received for an answer was a grunt from the male dragon. "Could you elaborate a bit more?" she asked, to get PateraThrakon to explain what had happened.

He knew that he would not be able to nap until he told his queen what had transpired with Kord and the sword. "He said that he did not feel right using the sword. I watched him from the time he started training with the golems. He spent over four sun-marks practicing with the weapon, but eventually he abandoned it. He said he would use what I had given him, and that was enough for him."

MiteraThrakena smiled. Her mate had tested Kord with the sword to see if he would use it or not. The Dragon Klau, being blessed by a dragon, would have no need to wield a weapon crafted by humans. They had their own weapons; they were a weapon. Kord had passed the test, and even though PateraThrakon might have seemed as if he was dis-appointed that Kord had chosen the correct path, he was proud of the young man for making the decision on his own.

"And what of Keia?" PateraThrakon asked, know-ing that MiteraThrakena had given a similar test to the young woman.

"It only took her a few breaths to decide not to use the books that I had presented to her," MiteraThrakena said to answer her mate's question.

The female dragon had provided three books for Keia to study. As soon as she saw that the books were about poisons and mixtures, ones that could harm others, Keia immediately informed the Queen of Dragons that she did not feel comfortable learn-ing such topics and handed the books back to

MiteraThrakena. The dragon took the books and smiled at Keia to let the young woman know that she had chosen wisely. The Dragon Kastera would never use anything that would intentionally harm others to make them suffer.

PateraThrakon let out one last groan to let MiteraThrakena know that he was not in a good mood. It took Kord over four sun-marks to decide that what he was presented with was not right for him, yet Keia had arrived at her own conclusion within a few breaths. Even though PateraThrakon was proud of Kord for making the right choice, the dragon thought that if the human were smarter, he could have made the decision much sooner, just like Keia had. His last thought was that the boy may have improved with his training, but he was still slow-witted, even for a human.

THIRTY-THREE

PateraThrakon sat on the side of the mountain, looking down at the area below where Kord and the two golems were training. It had been over two moon-cycles since the dragon had given the test with the sword to Kord. He had progressed so much that when he trained, the dragon watched as he sparred against the water golem while at the same time, he fought with the dirt golem as well. Yes, there were times when the two golems would have the advantage, but it always seemed that Kord was able to come up with a plan to stop the attacks of the water golem, as well as get through the defenses of the dirt golem. PateraThrakon believed that it was not so much that Kord was able to devise some method to win, but more along the lines of pure dumb luck.

Even though the male dragon did not say it to Kord directly, he was very pleased with the way the young man had advanced so far in such a short amount of time. PateraThrakon would never give praise to Kord or even let him know that the dragon had taken up the spot on the side of the mountain to watch the young man practice ever since the day he assigned the water golem to train Kord. The mountain was far away from the training area, and it would not be possible for Kord to be able to see the dragon watching him from such a great distance, but as for PateraThrakon, he had no problem seeing Kord's progress, and he was most pleased.

He could not say the same for the young human that was being trained by his mate. Keia had been trying to learn the force of Lightning, and as much as MiteraThrakena worked with her, Keia was not able to overcome her fear of the last force of nature.

As much as he hated to admit it, PateraThrakon saw Kord as the one able to achieve his goal of becoming the Dragon Klau, but if Keia could not become the Dragon Kastera, then no matter what Kord did, the hope the two dragons had for the two children would be in vain. They needed both the Dragon Kastera and Dragon Klau.

PateraThrakon decided that it was time for him to get involved; unfortunately, his solution to the situation relied on Kord. He might have made progress, but the male dragon still had doubts about putting his full trust in the stubborn human; but for what needed to be done, he had no choice.

He stood up and stretched out his wings. He then leaped into the air and over the edge of the cliff where he had been resting. As he dove downward, he allowed his fall to guide him, and just as he was about to crash into the ground, he quickly adjusted his body and wings to take him upward into the sky. When he was at the desired height, he straightened out his body and flew on a path that would take him to the training area where Kord was.

As he arrived, the shadow of the dragon covered the three combatants, and as soon as the sun was blocked overhead, all three looked up into the sky, knowing what they were going to see. There were only two beings whose forms could block out the sun, and since the female dragon had never come to check on the human male, it could only be the male dragon that was approaching from above.

As he reached the training area, PateraThrakon landed close to the river. He did not make his way over to where the three were training. He was the Dragon King, so the two golems and the human made their way over to where he was waiting for them.

"I haven't seen you in over two moon-cycles," Kord said when he was closer to the dragon. "I thought you probably went off somewhere and died." He did not make the statement to be mean to the dragon, but Kord was still stubborn, and he wanted to show as much disrespect to the dragon as he could. It was just his way.

"I had to stay away from you. Your stench still makes me sick to my stomach," PateraThrakon said to return Kord's disrespect. It was just their way of talking to each other. "I see that you are still training. Maybe one day, you will be able to actually take on a real opponent. If you want, I can catch a fish from the river and toss it on land for you to fight. It will not be able to breathe, so you may have a chance at winning against it, though I doubt it."

Kord was ready with a reply, "No, that's ok. I would challenge you to a fight, but I think that beating up someone as old as you would be too dishonorable. Why have you come to see me?" Kord asked, wondering why the dragon had arrived at the training area after not being present for quite a while.

PateraThrakon was ready to move on to the real reason he was there to see Kord, and since they had both exchanged their banter with one another, it was time to do so. "You have not been to see Keia in some time, have you?" the dragon asked.

Kord was surprised by the question. He did not see the reason for the dragon to ask it, and what surprised him even more was the fact that PateraThrakon had known that he had indeed stopped going to see Keia a while ago. It was not that he did not want to see her, but he had been training so much that by the time he was done for the day, he just went back to his cave and slept. He could not even remember the last time he had a meal cooked by his childhood friend.

PateraThrakon did not wait for Kord to reply to his question. "Today would be a good day for you to cut your training short and go see Keia."

"I still have a lot of training to do," Kord said, and it was the truth, but he also had another reason for staying away from Keia. When he saw her, it only brought confusion to his heart and mind. He did not know how to deal with his feelings, so he immersed himself in his training. It may not have been the best solution for the awkward way he felt, but it was all he could come up with.

PateraThrakon did not want to spend more time with the young man than he had to, and the dragon was in no mood to bicker with Kord concerning the topic of discussion. "You will stop your training for today and visit Keia," the dragon said, and added one more command to make sure that his instructions would be followed. "Vrom, Morv, begone."

With the command from their creator, the two golems disappeared. Vrom, being made of dirt, melded back into the ground as Morv's body swirled around, then went back into the river behind the dragon.

"Hey, bring them back," Kord commanded, but the dragon did not.

"They will be waiting for you when the sun rises again. As for now, you have somewhere else to be." PateraThrakon did not wait for a reply or rebuff from Kord. He spread his wings, jumped into the air, and flew away. He did not even look back to see if Kord would follow his instructions. He knew that the human male would, he could see it on his face when he spoke the young woman's name. Kord wanted to see Keia.

Kord did not immediately go back to the hut where Keia was. First, he stopped by the pond he used for bathing and cleaned up, then he made his way back to his cave to change his clothes. Not that he was trying to impress Keia, he just did not want to arrive at her hut smelling of his daily training. At least that is what he told himself.

He left his cave so that he would arrive just around the time Keia would have been eating her evening meal. Not that he was sure she would be, but he could at least hope for a nice hot meal. He had been eating fruit and berries for a couple of moon-cycles, and the change in food would be a great welcome to his stomach.

As he approached the hut, he saw Keia outside standing over the pot she used to cook their meals. Kord's hopes increased at the sight. That was until he stopped focusing on the cooking pot and focused on the one doing the cooking. It seemed as if all his nervousness made him feel as if he even tried to take a single bite of food, he would toss it back up because his stomach was in knots. He hated the feeling because he did not know how to deal with it.

Keia saw Kord approaching, and when she did, she stopped stirring the contents of the pot, stood up, and watched as he made his way to her. "It seems like forever since you have come to see me," Keia said, then decided to check on one other reason. "Or is it that you came to get a hot meal?"

Surprisingly, Kord did not know how to answer

the question. Yes, he wanted a hot meal, but seeing Keia was worth more than what was in the pot cooking. "I was just in the area and wanted to see how you were doing."

"You are just in time to eat. Sit, I will go and get your bowl," Keia said, smiled, and went inside her hut. It did not take long for her to return, and when she was next to the pot, she continued their conversation. "You are in luck; I fixed wild rice with carrots and potatoes."

Kord was happy to hear what he would be eating, but he was happier at seeing the one who was placing the food in his bowl, and when she handed it to him, he thought that it was just like when they were younger. Only it was not. Kord never felt confused as he did, sitting there watching his friend. Confused about how he felt, as well as confused about what he should do about those feelings.

"How is your training going?" Keia asked once she sat down, having scooped a couple of spoonfuls of the soup into her own bowl.

Kord realized that Keia had just asked him a question, and even though he was focusing on her, he was thankful that he had heard what she asked, so he could give a reply. "It is going well," he said, put his eyes on his food, and began to eat his meal. It was easier to focus on something else than to stare at Keia and feel the awkwardness that he had.

"MiteraThrakena said that you now take on the two golems at the same time. That's really impressive," Keia said.

Kord looked up from his bowl and across the fire to look at Keia before he asked his question, "You talk to MiteraThrakena about me?"

Keia, surprised by the question or by the answer to it, put her eyes back on her own food. "I just asked, that's all." She put two spoonfuls in her mouth and made sure she took a longer time to chew her food, all the while keeping her eyes on her meal and off Kord.

He did not know what to say. Kord was intrigued by her asking the female dragon about him, but that did not mean anything. Or did it? "How is your training going?" Kord asked to end the awkward silence between them.

After she swallowed her food, she answered the question but did not look up at Kord. Not because of the bit of awkwardness a moment ago, but because her training was not going as well as she would have liked it to be. "I still cannot learn the last force of nature." When she finished the statement, she looked up at Kord to continue. "No matter how hard I try, no matter how much I train, the fear I have stops me from bringing it forth."

Kord heard the desperation in her voice. He had come a long way with his training, and even though it was not easy, he continued to progress and was very pleased with the results that he had. He knew that Keia was just as eager to become the Dragon Kastera as he was to become the Dragon Klau, only she had arrived at an impasse.

"It just takes time," Kord said to encourage his friend. "You will learn how to control Lightning. You are the strongest woman I know."

Keia looked up from her food and explained to Kord her logic on what he had just said. "I'm the only woman you know."

They sat there looking at each other for a moment, and when neither of them knew what to say next, they both started laughing. They laughed the same way they did when they were younger and before they had started their training.

They continued to talk until the moon was high in the sky. On his way back to his cave, Kord thought about how much he enjoyed the time he had just spent with Keia. Although the one thought he had more than any was not just that Keia was the strongest woman he knew, but the fact that he saw her as that, a woman.

THIRTY-FOUR

Keia looked down into the glade below from the top of the hill where she was standing with MiteraThrakena. She knew the reason the female dragon had brought her there, and she knew that there was no other way. The problem Keia had was that she was not sure if she would be able to go through with what MiteraThrakena had planned.

It had been three moon-cycles since she began to try to learn the last force of nature, which was Lightning. The last of the forces she needed to learn to become the Dragon Kastera. It was on the previous night that she had sat with Kord and talked to him about what she was unable to do. Even his words of comfort when he told her, "You are the strongest woman I know," did not give her the confidence to believe in herself.

"This is the only way," MiteraThrakena said, standing behind Keia and looking at the young woman. Keia did not turn around to look at the dragon; she kept her eyes on the glade below. MiteraThrakena explained one last time about the last opportunity Keia had to learn the force of Lightning. "Your fear of lightning is the only thing that is stopping you. If you do not overcome it tonight, you will not become the Dragon Kastera."

Keia turned her head and looked over her left shoulder at the dragon. "I have mastered the other four. Must I master the last one?" Keia would not even say the word of the thing that frightened her the most.

MiteraThrakena replied to her question, and it was the truth. "You must master all five or else you will not be complete, and anything that is not complete will fail. You can build a house from the ground up, but if you do not put on the rooftop, eventually it will crumble."

Keia did not say it, but she understood. She turned and put her focus on the glade below. She could even feel the incompleteness within her, and as much as she wanted to become the Dragon Kastera, her doubts, along with her fear, were holding her back.

"It is time. Make your way down below and wait," MiteraThrakena said.

Once again, Keia did not look at the dragon behind her. She took a deep breath, released it, then waited for the time it took for her to take another deep breath, then released it, then began to make her descent to the place where she would either succeed or fail. It was all up to her.

MiteraThrakena moved to the edge of the rise where Keia had been standing. The female dragon watched as the young woman walked toward her final test. MiteraThrakena did not know which of the two was more worried about what had to take place. She had explained to Keia what she was going to do, and even though she agreed with the dragon, neither of them was looking forward to this evening's event. The fact that Keia could fail and not become the Dragon Kastera was not the worst outcome possible, and both dragon and human knew it to be so.

"You are going to proceed with what you have planned?" PateraThrakon asked as he landed in the area where his mate was and came up to stand to her right.

"There is no other way," MiteraThrakena said, and the uncertainty of the situation was noticeable in her words. "Three moon-cycles have passed, and Keia is still unable to overcome her fear of lightning. She cannot move forward until she does."

"With what you are about to attempt, could prevent her completely," PateraThrakon said with no judgment. He knew that for Keia to become the Dragon Kastera, she had to master the force of Lightning. He was responsible for Kord's training, and he had succeeded with very little supervision from the male dragon, something PateraThrakon was thankful for. Even though he would not say it to Kord directly, the young man had come a long way in just a few seasons. There was only one last test for him, before he could be the Dragon Klau.

MiteraThrakena watched as Keia made her way

to the middle of the glade, just as the female dragon had instructed her to do. When she saw that Keia had come to a halt and waited for what was to happen next, MiteraThrakena began her part in the young woman's training.

As a dragon, especially as the Dragon Queen, MiteraThrakena could call upon the force of Lightning with no more than a single thought and her will on how much of the force she would bring forth. On this night, she did not hold back, and in a single breath, the first lightning bolt crashed out of the sky and struck the ground not ten paces away from Keia, where she was standing in the glade below. After the first bolt of lightning, a second struck the ground on the opposite side of her, only it landed closer than the previous one. Then another, then another, then another. Lightning came out of the sky, striking the ground all around the young woman, causing dirt and grass to fly into the air. With every strike, the sound could easily be heard by the dragons overlooking the glade below.

MiteraThrakena knew that what was happening below had to be done. That does not mean she was pleased with seeing Keia crouched down on the ground with her hands covering her ears in fear of what was taking place around her. No, MiteraThrakena was not pleased, and seeing her young pupil in fear and anguish, she was about to put an end to everything she had set in motion.

"Do not," PateraThrakon said, knowing exactly

what his mate was thinking. "You said there is no other way, so you must not interfere with her training."

MiteraThrakena agreed with her mate, but she did not want to lose Keia. She could not take another loss, not again. "I have called forth the lightning storm, and it will only intensify. If I do not stop it, Keia could die."

"Then she was not meant to be the Dragon Kastera," PateraThrakon said, not to be cruel, only to speak the truth.

MiteraThrakena knew that her mate was trying to help her through what she was witnessing. In the time Keia had been with her, she had become more than just another pupil; she had become the dragon's hope. Her last hope. She did not want to hurt Keia, but there was no other way for her to overcome her fear of lightning. What she had started, she had to allow it to finish. She only hoped the young woman would live through the trial.

"What is happening?"

Both dragons turned their heads and looked behind them. They saw Kord making his way over to them. "This is Keia's final test. This is the only way for her to complete her training," MiteraThrakena said to explain to Kord the reason that the two dragons and Keia were there, and now he was as well.

Kord positioned himself between the dragons and looked at the glade below. He had seen the lightning storm appear suddenly in the sky, and since he had been thinking of Keia the entire day, he wanted to see if the storm had something to do with her. When he saw Keia crouched down on the ground, covering her ears with her hands, he did not hesitate to start running to her.

"You must not interfere!" MiteraThrakena yelled to him. He stopped and looked at the female dragon, who continued to explain the situation. "This is the only way for Keia to overcome her fear. If she does not, she will fail."

Kord gave his response, "She will not fail." He once again took a step to go to Keia, but stopped when PateraThrakon called out to him.

"Kord!" the dragon yelled and waited until the human was looking at him to continue. "If you go, you could die."

Kord did not hesitate to give his response, "If that is what it takes to save her." He put his focus back on rushing to Keia to help her. He just did not know how.

PateraThrakon watched as Kord ran down the hill. He never felt prouder of his pupil than he did at that very moment.

"Now both their lives are at risk, and if they die, then we have failed once again," MiteraThrakena said. She could stop the lightning and the test altogether, but even that would be a failure. Keia would not become the Dragon Kastera, and without her, the Dragon Klau would not be complete. The test had to proceed; there was no other way.

Kord ran over to where Keia was kneeling on the

ground. When he reached her, he knelt so that they were at the same level. He now saw that not only was she using her hands to cover her ears, but she also had her eyes closed as well, and the look of fear on her face was the worst thing that Kord had seen in a very long time.

"Keia, look at me!" Kord shouted as the lightning crashed around the two. She did not respond, so he called to her again, "Keia!" Still, she did not move, too caught up in her own fear to see or hear her friend who had arrived to help her.

Kord looked at her and knew that there was nothing he could do to help her with her fear. It was too great, and kneeling there watching her only brought pain to his heart. He looked around, and all he saw were flashes of lightning striking the ground around him, and to him it appeared that they were getting closer with every strike.

He put his focus back on Keia and made a decision. "It's not worth it. I'm getting you out of here." He stood up and reached out to grab Keia's hand, but before he could take hold of it, a bolt of lightning struck the ground a single step to his right, and he went flying away, ten paces from where he was with Keia. It was as if the lightning storm itself knew what he was about to attempt, and it would not let him. As if Creator himself was controlling the storm to see if Keia was worthy of becoming the Dragon Kastera.

Somehow Keia knew. She could not respond to

Kord when he called out her name. Her body would not move because she was paralyzed with fear, but deep down she heard him, and she knew that something had happened and Kord was not standing in front of her any longer.

With that thought, she opened her eyes and saw Kord lying on the ground ten paces away from her. She had an idea of what had happened, and when she looked down and saw the ground a step away to her left blackened from the last lightning strike, her belief was verified. She put her eyes back on Kord and noticed one thing. He was not moving. It was at that moment that her fear of lightning was overpowered by her fear that the one person who had been with her for almost her entire life was dead.

She lowered her arms, jumped up, and ran over to Kord. Just as she reached him, a bolt of lightning struck the ground just two paces away from them. She did not hear it; she did not see it. She could not. All she saw was Kord's body, and that he was not moving.

"Kord," Keia said in a whisper, with tears in her eyes. "Kord," she called to him again, only a little louder, then called out his name a third time, "Kord!" She screamed so loud that it overpowered the sound of the lightning that was striking the ground around her. Each strike was no more than two paces away from them both.

She reached out and put her hands on Kord, shaking him as if to wake him from a deep sleep.

He did not respond, and after shaking him a couple more times, she lowered her head and placed her ear on his chest. Even with the lightning around her striking the ground, she could hear his heart beating. When she lifted her head, she noticed that his shirt, or what was left of it, was open, and she could see the dragon scales covering his body. She looked up to his face and saw that it was also covered with scales, which was the only reason that he was still alive. She did not see him get struck by lightning, but it had come close enough to activate his body's defenses.

The next bolt of lightning struck not a pace away from the two, then another, then another. They were landing faster and faster, and Keia knew that she had to help Kord. He had come to help her, and now he was hurt, and she could not let him get struck by lightning. If he did, the next strike could kill him.

With that thought, Keia became angry. Angry at herself for being the reason Kord was there. Angry at herself for allowing him to be hurt. Angry at herself for being afraid. Then she realized something had changed. She was no longer afraid.

She looked around and saw that the number of lightning strikes had increased as well as their ferocity. Yet, she was not afraid. It still struck the ground about a pace away from the two humans, but she was not afraid, nor was she angry. Now, she was determined.

Keia stood and looked up at the sky. "Come to

me," she said. The lightning continued to strike the ground around her. "Come to me," she said again, more determined. The lightning continued to strike a pace away from both of them. "I command you! Come...to...me!" she yelled to the sky, determined and demanding of what the lightning should do.

Lightning is fast. So fast that it can come and go in the blink of an eye. This time, Keia saw it, and it was coming right for her. Just as the bolt of lightning reached her, Keia raised her right arm toward the sky with her hand and fingers extended upward. The bolt of lightning struck her fingers and did not stop.

She felt it. She felt it enter through her fingers, as it traveled down her arm, and through her body. She closed her eyes and said to whoever was watching, "I mastered Fire, I mastered Water, I mastered Wind, and I mastered Ice!" She opened her eyes and, while looking toward the sky, made her final mandate, "I will master Lightning as well!"

The lightning continued into her for only a breath more then stopped. Lightning still struck the ground around her and Kord, but no more lightning entered her, yet Keia was not finished. She could feel it in her. The lightning that had entered her was still within. It traveled throughout her entire body, then gathered around her heart. There it circulated and gained speed and power; all the while, Keia could feel it. The power grew and grew until she knew that she had control of it. She then lifted her left arm with her hand and fingers extended to the sky.

"Keia, no!" MiteraThrakena yelled, but she was too late. Keia had already begun to cast.

"What is she doing?" PateraThrakon asked, not knowing what his queen was so concerned about.

MiteraThrakena answered but did not take her eyes off the sight below. "She is going to cast the Dragon's Heart Force. She is not ready; it will kill her."

Now, PateraThrakon knew why his mate was so concerned. The Dragon's Heart Force was the most powerful spell the Dragon Kastera could cast, and it could only be done by casting magic with the wielder's left hand, the one closest to the heart. Even the male dragon knew that it took many, many seasons for a human to wield such powerful magic, and Keia had not had enough time to grow strong enough. A human casting magic with so much power would obliterate themselves and anyone else in the vicinity.

MiteraThrakena knew that she would not have time to stop Keia, and with the one act, both dragons believed that their hope was lost.

Keia did not know what she was about to do. She only knew what her instincts were telling her. MiteraThrakena had told her that lightning helped break up nutrients in the sky, which helped the world; there was a use for lightning, and at the moment, Keia needed to use it to stop the storm above.

With her left arm, hand, and fingers stretching toward the sky, she focused on the Lightning that was circling her heart, and when she was ready, she cast it from her heart, up her arm, through her hand, out her fingers, and into the sky. The force of the lightning bolt that went upward was ten times the intensity of any lightning bolt that had come down since the storm began. When all the lightning had left her body, Keia saw that the sky was clear. There was no sign that there had ever been a storm at all. Keia saw the night sky, and there was not a single cloud.

"It is not possible," MiteraThrakena said when she had finished witnessing what her pupil had accomplished. "She cast the Dragon's Heart Force and survived. It is not possible," she said again, trying to convince herself.

"I believe your pupil has overcome her fear of lightning," PateraThrakon said.

MiteraThrakena did not reply, but her mate was correct.

Keia had no concern about what had happened except for the one lying at her feet. "Kord, wake up!" she yelled when she fell to her knees to shake her friend. "Kord, you stubborn fool, if you don't wake up, I will kill you myself."

"Then I'd better wake up," Kord said, still stretched out on the ground. The lightning bolt had not struck him directly, but if his dragon scales had not activated on their own, he would not have survived. He raised his right hand to his forehead to rub away the fogginess that he was feeling. If not being struck by lightning made him feel as bad as he did, he thought he would hate to get hit by it directly.

Even though he was still a bit dizzy, he sat up to make sure Keia did not follow through with her plan to kill him. As soon as he was in a sitting position, Keia began laughing. "What is so funny?" he asked.

Once she got control of herself, she answered his question, "Your hair is sticking up, and you look funny."

Even though when he arrived to help Keia, his hair was plaited, the strength of the lighting striking the ground next to him caused his braid to become undone. He did not know how he looked, but he did think that she should not be laughing at the one who had risked his own life to try to save her, but he did not tell her that. He just took his hands and rubbed them over the top of his head to fix his hair and his dignity. He failed at both.

Keia stood up and reached down with her right hand, offering it to Kord to help him stand. He accepted it and was thankful for the assistance since he was still a little unsteady. Once he was standing as stable as he could, he wanted to know how she was after everything that had occurred. "Are you ok?"

"I'm better than ok," she said, and they both knew that she had overcome her fear of lightning.

The two dragons flew down and landed next to the two humans. "Boy, what were you thinking, allowing yourself to be struck by lightning?" PateraThrakon asked Kord. The male dragon, once again, wondered how Kord always seemed to do something to make the dragon question his decision about choosing the boy to train to become the Dragon Klau.

"I didn't allow it; I did not have a choice; and it wasn't like I was actually struck by it," Kord said to explain his take on what had occurred.

"Your hair would suggest a different view of the matter," PateraThrakon said, turned around, and leaped into the sky to go back to his den for a nap.

Kord used his hands to pat his hair down, or at least he tried to with no success.

"I am proud of you, Keia," MiteraThrakena said and saw the young woman smiling back at her. "You overcame your fear and have not only learned, but have mastered the force of Lightning." Keia's smile grew. "Although, I remember telling you that you were never to cast magic with your left hand, and yet you did." Keia stopped smiling, ready to receive more of a scolding from the female dragon. "I have no choice...but to proclaim you as the Dragon Kastera." Keia's smile returned.

"What about me?" Kord asked. "Am I now the Dragon Klau?"

"Only the King of Dragons can grant you that title," MiteraThrakena said.

Kord did not smile. He just tried patting down his hair, believing that the Dragon King was once again disappointed with him.

MiteraThrakena arrived back at her den and took up her place on her dais. She wrapped her tail around her body, then positioned her head and neck at her side to take a nap as well. It had been a long night, but she still had something to discuss with her mate. "You made sure that he arrived tonight, did you not?" she asked.

PateraThrakon grunted to give his reply.

"You knew that he would go to her and with his help she would overcome her fear," MiteraThrakena said to state what she knew her mate had done. "So, you trust him?" she asked.

PateraThrakon realized that he was not going to be able to take his nap until he had the conversation with his mate. "I had faith in him to follow his heart, even if it meant his life."

"Something the Dragon Klau would do, would you not say?" MiteraThrakena asked. PateraThrakon mumbled something; however, the Dragon Queen wanted him to acknowledge the truth aloud. "I did not hear that. Could you repeat what you said?"

Knowing that he was not going to win, PateraThrakon heaved a sigh, then repeated what he had just said, "Yes, something the Dragon Klau would do." He said it; he just did not want to admit it.

"Maybe you should inform him to make it official."

PateraThrakon thought about it. "Maybe tomorrow. Let him suffer for a few sun-cycles." They both knew that he was just pretending to be upset. Deep down, he was very proud of Kord, and MiteraThrakena knew it.

They had accomplished a great deal over the last eight seasons, and now both children had become what the dragons had been hoping for.

Suddenly, before they could close their eyes to rest, their feelings of hope were interrupted. Even though they had just witnessed their greatest achievements, the awakening of their greatest failures had also taken place; they could feel it in their souls. The two dragons lifted their heads and looked toward the lands beyond KhoraThraks. They did not have to see what had happened, but they both knew what had just occurred. They knew because the ringing they had constantly heard over the past eight seasons had ceased. They could hear it no longer.

THIRTY-FIVE

X'Jahan knelt with his right knee on the ground. All around him, everyone present did the same. Thousands and thousands of humans knelt in honor of the ones that they had worked so hard to free. So many had died just so the two who stood before them could live once again.

"We are your loyal servants, command us and we shall obey," X'Jahan said, speaking from his heart and soul, for himself and for all those around him.

The two looked at their subjects. Neither of them knew how long it had been since they were able to move again. To breathe again. To live again.

The two turned and looked at each other. They both stood there with nothing covering their bodies. Their clothes had not survived the passage of time, but for them, time did not matter, nor did their clothes. All that mattered was that once again, they could be with each other.

The woman was looking at the man, and the man at her. With the moment of their revival over, the two walked over to each other and embraced the one they had not seen in many, many seasons. They stood there holding one another.

"It is good to see you again, my sister," the man said to the woman.

"It is good to see you again, my brother," the woman said to the man.

The two had been set free, and once again, they were ready to rule the world.

Adoni sat at the campsite he had chosen for the night. Even though his eyes were on the small fire that he had used to cook his and Mule's evening meal, he was not seeing the flames dancing before him. His sight reached far beyond his immediate surroundings. He had watched two separate events take place far away from one another; yet he had no doubts that what had transpired was about to make the lives of certain individuals very intriguing.

www.ingramcontent.com/pod-product-compliance
Lightning Source LLC
LaVergne TN
LVHW090547110826
845146LV00001B/47